OUR LADY OF THE
CIRCUS

ALSO BY DAVID TOSCANA

Tula Station

OUR LADY OF THE
CIRCUS

DAVID TOSCANA

TRANSLATED FROM THE SPANISH
BY PATRICIA J. DUNCAN

Thomas Dunne Books
St. Martin's Press ❧ *New York*

THOMAS DUNNE BOOKS.
An imprint of St. Martin's Press.

www.stmartins.com

Library of Congress Cataloging-in-Publication Data
Toscana, David.
  [Santa María del circo. English]
  Our lady of the circus / David Toscana ; translated from the Spanish by Patricia J. Duncan.—1st U.S. ed.
    p. cm.
    ISBN 0-312-27116-6
    I. Title.
PQ7298.3.078 S2613 2001
863'.64—dc21

                                            2001031814

First published in Mexico under the title Santa María del Circo by Plaza & Janés Editores (1998)
First U.S. Edition: September 2001

10 9 8 7 6 5 4 3 2 1

OUR LADY OF THE
CIRCUS

Nathaniel *would have* preferred not to see the light of day, but the sun filtering through the holes in the big top was already splashing down on him. The roaring laughter of his fellow workers, especially that of Hercules, still resounded in his head, and he wondered if the morning would be a continuation of the night before. He rolled over a couple of times in his cot before getting up. He was glad to note he was alone. After what had happened the previous night, he didn't feel like seeing anyone.

For the first time, he had felt comfortable enough with the group to tell them something about his life—something personal. He told them that one of his ancestors had been the President of the Republic, and he also explained how he had lost the sight in his left eye. "My father got pissed off at me and he picked up the ladle for the beans so he could give me a thrashing. And I, idiot that I was, curious to see how he was beating me, left my eyes wide open until the ladle sank into my left eye, slicing it just like a hard-boiled egg. We looked everywhere for the piece of my eye and finally gave up. Then, at dinner, my father asked my mother if the beans had bacon in them. When she replied no, he went straight to the kitchen sink and spat out." And while no one had believed such a story, everyone laughed, and it didn't bother Nathaniel that they were making fun of him, for even he had laughed at his beating after enough time had passed, and their search for the piece of eye had really just been an attempt to clean up, since at no time did it cross their minds that they could put it back in its place and make the eye like new.

Nathaniel also felt like telling them about the time when another of his ancestors had set off several rounds of explosives in a mine shaft, burying a hundred and twenty-three mine workers. "A mine that could very well have been that one," he said, pointing to an opening in the hillside behind him. Then his colleagues became curious and asked him what that man's name was, and Nathaniel pretended to be irritated, complaining that no one had bothered to ask the President's name, yet they all wanted to know who the murderer was. His colleagues were adamant—tell us more, tell us his name and how the mine workers died, did your relative kill himself along with them or did he escape, or was he thrown in jail or hanged or did he face the firing squad—and Nathaniel smiled in happiness, feeling like the center of the world.

The problem came later, when Nathaniel, wanting to share something personal said, "If it weren't for my height, no one would know I'm a midget." From that point on, it was all laughs and wisecracks, and Hercules saying, "And if you weren't missing an eye, no one would know you were blind in one eye." How little they understand, Nathaniel thought. If they too were midgets, they would realize that my condition goes beyond not being able to reach an onion in the pantry or being able to walk between a horse's legs without crouching down. As if they were perfectly normal!

He got dressed, washed his face in the washbasin and headed

for the big top. There he found Don Alejo and Harrieta halfway through their breakfast. They were using the box as a table, with which Mandrake performed his trick of cutting the girl in two.

Don Alejo was saying, "Did I already tell you about the day I plowed the land with elephants instead of oxen?"

"Yes, sir," Harrieta said.

"Ah, but our new friend doesn't know the story," he said, pointing at Nathaniel.

"The midget says that if it weren't for his height—"

"Mr. Barnum's," Don Alejo interrupted. "Now that was a circus, not like this crummy outfit."

Nathaniel looked at Harrieta, furious. She continued eating an orange, taking great care so that the juice did not drip down onto her beard.

"You know what, Harrieta?" Don Alejo said. "We have to come up with a name for this midget. Nathaniel won't sell a single ticket, not even on Sunday."

"Let's see if you have more imagination than you did with me."

The three glanced at one another, each feeling a little pity for the other.

"There was a midget working over at Barnum's. His name was something like General Tom Thumb. What do you think?" He looked at Nathaniel. "Would you like that to be your name?"

"No."

Don Alejo was wearing a sleeveless undershirt that revealed a large part of his pale and almost hairless chest. He stretched out his quivering hand to take a pear, and Nathaniel saw, with disgust, the flesh hanging under the extended arm. He wondered how old the man was. Seventy? Seventy-five? This speculation was cut off when another thought popped into his head. He had never seen an old midget, and for the first time in his life, he wondered if midgets ever got old or if they were like horses and had much shorter lives.

"Well, if you don't want to be called that, you'd better come up with something good by today, because don't even think about keeping Nathaniel," Don Alejo said, and he sat staring at the pear for a while, looking for the softest part to take the first bite. "For God's sake, who gave you that silly name?"

"How long did General Tom Thumb live?"

"What difference does it make? He married another midget and danced for Queen Victoria," he said, with a look of fascination as if lost in his thoughts, reliving the memories that were not his.

"Listen, Don Alejo," Harrieta began. "Did you hear what the midget said? He said that if it weren't for his height—"

"I was going to tell him about the day I used elephants to plow the land," Don Alejo said as he put the pear back.

He raised his arms slightly in a signal that Harrieta knew. She moved behind him, grabbed him beneath the armpits, and with a great effort, put him on his feet. Don Alejo left quickly and unsteadily.

"Come up with a name you like," Harrieta said to Nathaniel, "or else the old man will name you however he pleases. Just look at me."

"Did you choose it?"

She folded her arms and clenched her teeth. Then she shrugged and responded, "Of course not. My name is Angélica, and I wanted to keep it, but the old man has no imagination. Just look at Hercules. You have to have bats in your belfry to give the strong man a name like that and think it's an original idea."

"Do you know how long a horse lives?"

"If it weren't for my beard, no one would know that I'm the bearded lady."

"A horse—how long does it live?"

"Midgetowski. How do you like that name?"

"I think I like General Tom better."

"Microman?"

"I don't need any help," Nathaniel muttered, annoyed.

"We had a horse," Harrieta said. "They would dress it up in a golden robe and it would stand on its two hind legs, and Narcissa, scantily clad, would ride it, and they would go around and around. I never understood what was so great about it. Any work-horse can do the same thing. Even so, they applauded it as if it were a great thing, or else they were applauding Narcissa's butt, I don't know. One day the animal got too close to the tigers' cage and one of the tigers bit it on the snout. They stayed locked that way for about half an hour, because the tiger couldn't manage to pull the piece off and there was no way to separate them. When the horse was finally able to get free, it was missing half its face, and it took off running like crazy and nobody could catch up to it, until it fell to the ground, dead, twenty blocks away. It was about five years old, but who knows how long it would have lived if it hadn't been eaten, for after it died, they used it as food for the tigers."

Nathaniel picked up the pear that Don Alejo had put down and inspected it to make sure it hadn't been bitten.

"But at what age do they die of old age?"

"All that struggling just to end up as an afternoon snack for the tigers."

Nathaniel took a bite of the pear and walked toward the sunshine. Through the opening in the big top he could see the reddish color of the ground and an advancing cloud of dust that crashed into the hillside. He wanted to ask Harrieta why they had set the big top up there, in the mouth of a canyon, where you couldn't see any sign of life, not even a farm. He decided to add that question to the one about horses. As he left, he was hit by another cloud of dust blown up by the wind.

"Where are you going?" Harrieta asked.

He took a second bite of the pear and turned around. The contrast of the bright light from outside had transformed the inside of the big top into a black hole.

"Come on," he said in the direction of the darkness, and in seconds, Harrieta was next to him.

"Are you annoyed about last night?"

Nathaniel nodded and threw the pear pit as far as he could. Harrieta said, "Maybe a tree will grow."

"One of my relatives was President," Nathaniel said, "and I have others who were also important."

"Yeah, you mentioned something like that yesterday," Harrieta said. "I had an uncle who wrote for *El País*."

"Here comes Don Alejo."

"Every morning he walks around the big top five times."

Don Alejo managed to hear this last comment and stammered, "You have to stay young."

Nathaniel whispered to Harrieta that at his age, he should say, "You have to stay alive."

Each step Don Alejo took kicked up the dirt, raising more dust than the wind did. Nathaniel thought that if the old man did too many laps, he would end up digging a trench, and Harrieta thought almost the same thing, except that in her mind, it wasn't a trench but a moat around a castle, and she imagined their big top to be made of stones, with towers and ramparts and a watchtower from where you could spit into the moat. But since both trench and moat were so far-fetched, neither one wanted to share his thoughts.

Harrieta only dared to say, "He is going to make a rut."

They waited quietly for Don Alejo to finish his laps. It didn't look like he had worked up a sweat, except for the dirt, now turned to mud, that stuck to his ankles.

"Where are," he paused to catch his breath, "the others?"

"They went to the mine." Harrieta pointed toward the hill. "They went to look for gold."

"Tell them they should prepare their things, because early tomorrow morning we have the circus parade."

Harrieta looked around her. "A parade for who?" she asked.

"I'm not stupid," Don Alejo defended himself, and he pointed north. "According to my map, behind that hill there is a town, Sierra Vieja I think it's called. We are going to catch them by surprise. We'll make an entrance like an invading army, with our elephants, giraffes, polar bears, Bengal tigers, and llamas from Machu Picchu. Before they can even say good morning, they'll be amazed to see their streets filled with these rare species, beautiful women, monstrous women, magicians, jugglers and clowns, and they'll be willing to pay any price just to see them under the big top. Ladies and gentlemen, boys and girls, the Mantecón Circus has arrived."

A few heavy, stifling seconds went by until Harrieta got the courage to ask, "Are you serious?"

"I need to rest," Don Alejo said, and he went inside the small tent.

He yelled from inside that he was going to take a nap and warned Nathaniel that he had better have a good name by the time he woke up. Harrieta sat down on the ground but stood back up immediately, bothered by the dust stuck to her dress.

"What animals?" Nathaniel asked. "He wasn't referring to us, was he?"

"Think of a name for yourself and forget about what that crazy old man says."

"Can I put a number after the name, like the kings do?"

"Do whatever you want; just don't contradict him."

"This isn't bad. The Mantecón Circus presents King Nathaniel the First, sovereign of all big tops, supreme judge and scourge of those who do not applaud."

"He gets crazy and only Narcissa can control him. His brother controlled him too, and look what happened."

Nathaniel marched with short steps and carried his body as straight as he could, chin raised high and with a look of indifference.

"I enter the ring with crown, cape, and that stick that kings use. And the entire audience will have to bow before his royal majesty."

"Any name is going to seem bad to Don Alejo, except the one he chooses."

"Then I would go with my father," his face turned melancholy and then quickly turned harsh, "and spit in his face."

"It's called a scepter, idiot."

"Why didn't anyone ask me last night who the President was?"

"Which one?"

"The one I told you about, my relative."

"Nobody believed you. I, on the other hand, did have an uncle who wrote for *El País*."

"That's not important!"

"We didn't believe that your father took your eye out and ate it with his beans, either."

"He didn't take my eye out, he just cut off a piece," he said, and he lifted his eyelid with his index finger. "I still have the eyeball, it just doesn't work."

"Look," Harrieta said, pointing toward the hill. "Here they come."

"It doesn't look like their pockets are full of gold."

Harrieta shook the dust off her dress and headed toward the group. Nathaniel had the feeling that the jokes from the night before were going to continue, and he chose to go inside the tent. Before he went in, he set up a folding sign that read:

THE AMAZING MANTECÓN
BROTHERS CIRCUS
Box seats $1.00
Stands 25¢
Children Free
Except Sundays

And he assumed that the word "brothers" would have to be erased before the next performance.

When Don Alejo and Don Ernesto founded the circus, they had called it Mantecón Brothers, since they wanted to be just as successful as the Ringling Brothers. However, after several years, they finally accepted the fact that their circus would not be an international one and that in this country, there were not many people who understood English. So, without changing the syntax, they translated the name that they had used for more than two decades to Mantecón Hermanos. At that time, there was a lion tamer working with them who said, "You shouldn't worry about the Brothers; what you should change is the Mantecón. It sounds like the name of a pig farm." Neither his apologies nor his explanation that it was just a joke was to any avail. He was put out on the street that same day, with his lions and everything, and being without the means to transport them to another circus or to feed them, he wound up taking them to the slaughterhouse and opening a *taquería* called The Rampant Lion. The Mantecóns' bad temper meant that performers who were not very obliging would not last long working for them, and the day finally came when not even the brothers themselves wanted to work together.

The night of the very day Nathaniel joined the circus, the caravan was headed for Zacatecas. They decided to spend the night in a spot where the road was difficult to travel and there was a puddle that, while dirty, was good enough for the animals to drink from. Nights in the circus were never quiet: the restlessness of the animals could be heard continuously, and the mules did not trust the bears and were always alert to the intentions of the tigers. The tigers, for their part, did not snore when they slept, but rather, roared, making it clear who was in charge. The elephant couldn't get to sleep and would drag its chain against the rock, and the dancing dog would bark at whatever moved. Only the pig slept peacefully, and only every now and then would make some guttural noise that could almost be confused with Hercules' snoring. That night, one of the many discussions between Don Alejo and Don Ernesto added to the concert. Nathaniel was not used to those noises, so while the rest of the group was already dead to the world, he couldn't sleep a wink. The words he managed to catch were not enough to give him a complete picture of what was going on between the Mantecón brothers, but the matter was clarified the next morning. As circus hands and performers were waiting to leave for Zacatecas, the Mantecón brothers ordered that the stands be set up and that all personnel take a seat.

"You three." Don Ernesto pointed toward the Cabriolé brothers.

"Wait, Ernesto," Don Alejo complained. "What am I going to do with a trapeze and no trapeze artist?"

"If you want, I'll buy it from you."

"No, thank you. I'll just keep Mágala."

"Mágala!" Don Ernesto laughed. "That girl doesn't know the difference between a trapeze and a swing."

"At least she has more balls than those three sissies," Don Alejo said, pointing disparagingly at the Cabriolé brothers and then turning toward Mágala. "Right?" he said.

She nodded just to please him.

"You . . . and you, and Computencio." Don Ernesto continued pointing. "Ping and Pong, too."

"Go ahead, take Computencio. After all, figuring out square roots doesn't amuse anybody," Don Alejo said. "Ping and Pong are mine; I was the one who brought them over from India."

"From India?" Don Ernesto smiled in disbelief. "So now you believe the lies you make up for the public? I found those Siamese twins in Ahualulco."

Don Ernesto continued to toss people onto the heap, and one by one he pointed to Balancín and Balanzón, the five musicians in the Festival Orchestra, Timmy the Temararious, Bengalo the Tamer, Teary, Tufty, and Stretch, the Mi Alegría sisters, Little Miss Bell, Papillon the Escapist; and in one sweeping gesture, he called for all the circus hands, meaning those who carried out the work of feeding and cleaning the animals, setting up and taking down the big top, installing the lights and keeping the generator going, selling the tickets, and all the other activities that paid very little and got no applause.

Harrieta regretted having sat in the front row, because Don Ernesto mentioned few names—for the most part, he said "You" with his index finger and she couldn't see who was being chosen.

She recognized Hercules clearing his voice behind her and turned around to ask him what was going on.

"Shh," he responded.

"What's going on?" she insisted.

Hercules avoided looking at Harrieta as he responded in as few words as possible.

"Don't you see?"

"I think so," Harrieta said.

"Then why the question?"

Their conversation was interrupted by the Mantecón brothers, who had now raised their voices.

"The elephant!" Don Ernesto said, laughing.

They had finished with the people and were beginning with the animals.

"No!" Don Alejo shouted. "Not the elephant! You already took the clowns. Leave me the elephant!"

Don Ernesto was not in the mood for a discussion, and he kept right on picking out more animals. Don Alejo gestured desperately and protested halfheartedly over what he considered to be unfair. Then he changed his approach and began to beg.

"Even if it's just a mule," Don Alejo appealed, and his brother, his arms crossed, shook his head no.

Harrieta turned around again to Hercules.

"Did he pick you?"

"Shh."

"Give me another animal," Don Alejo exclaimed. "All you left me was the damned pig."

"And the midget, too," Don Ernesto said.

"Hey, I heard that," Nathaniel complained from the back of the stands. Don Ernesto ordered those he had pointed at to follow him. Almost everyone stood up and went with him. The minority remaining made Harrieta realize that it was preferable to belong to the other group, but she was comforted to see Hercules still sprawled out in the same place. Don Alejo went over and started to count.

"One . . . two . . . three . . . four . . ."

"There are eight of us," Nathaniel said.

"Seven and a half," Hercules laughed.

"Do you know how many times I've heard that joke?"

Don Alejo kept counting with the slowness of someone counting to eighty, as if taking his time would increase the numbers.

". . . five . . . six . . . seven . . . eight."

"I'm not a trapeze artist," Mágala said.

"No one is born knowing anything," Don Alejo pronounced, "but you can learn," and the inquisitive looks of those who remained in the stands, disconsolate and nervous, forced him to add something. "We have the big top," he said. "They might be many and have all the animals, but without the big top, there is no circus."

"Oh, sure," Harrieta mumbled, making sure the old man didn't hear her. "And we also have Narcissa."

Don Alejo went over to the cart where the big top was and said that it was just as pretty as the day it had arrived from Italy, and he hugged it as if it were a giant muffin with red, white, and blue stripes, and the Magnani Fabrics label right on top.

It took slightly less than six hours to set up the big top, including the ritual of placing the Mantecón Brothers flag on the pole and applauding when the work was finished. Those who *went* with Don Ernesto felt like staying, and those who *remained* with Don Alejo wanted to leave with the others. But no one dared object, since at that moment, not even the Mantecón brothers themselves knew who had gotten the best deal. And so began the good-byes, the hugs and the well wishes, and only Nathaniel, who had not yet made any friends, sought out a solitary place next to the cages and let out his frustration by tugging at the tail of an absentminded tiger.

Ladies and gentlemen," Don Alejo, still drowsy from his nap, began to proclaim enthusiastically, "we cannot keep this a secret any longer. Can your hearts stand the shocking facts about the true story of this insignificant creature? We have discovered that Alexander the Great, Alexander of Macedonia, conquerer of all Asia, the Indies, and Europe, victor in the battle of Trafalgar, sailor of the seven seas, emperor of the Peloponnese and prince of Flanders, the very one who, with his own hands, strangled Achilles and tore the flesh from Fu Manchu, has been reincarnated in the small body of this man. We have discovered that, masked behind the name Nathaniel until today, he is really none other than the very same Macedonian specimen, since on his stomach is a mole in the shape of his native Crete, and on his right gluteus a scar from the love bite with which his beloved Penelope swore to him her eternal love."

"Shut up, Don Alejo. You've never seen my ass."

Mágala gestured to Nathaniel to calm down; Don Alejo's expression changed from one of enthusiasm to one of anger. His naked torso revealed a pair of nipples that were out of position, off to the sides, which reminded Mágala of a hammerhead.

"Nobody tells me to shut up," Don Alejo yelled at the top of his lungs, and as if he had suddenly forgotten something, he went back to the small tent to finish his nap.

Harrieta waited to see what would happen. She could not believe that Don Alejo would leave without making more of a fuss. Normally, he would have thrown Nathaniel out of the circus just as he had done with the lion tamer and all the others, but in the end, he had probably realized that there were too few performers left for him to keep throwing people out of the show.

"I've come up with a name for you," Harrieta said. "What do you think of Dwarfonio?"

"What an idiot. I don't have scars from anybody on my ass."

"What do you think?"

"What are you asking me for?" the midget said, annoyed. "My name is Nathaniel Bocanegra, and I don't care one bit what you say or what names you come up with or if you have hair on your back. If only someone had shown some interest when I spoke about my relative who was President; but no, nobody asked me anything then."

"I already told you. We didn't believe you. Anyway, I don't know any President with that lousy last name."

From the small tent, you could hear Don Alejo let out a hoarse cry.

"Narcissa!"

And from somewhere Harrieta couldn't determine came the cry of Narcissa.

"Not now!"

Nathaniel wandered through the stands until he found a spot without threatening splinters. "Then I would surely have a scar," he thought. He had been told that the Mantecón brothers deliberately chipped away at the wood so they could raise more money renting cushions. Liars, he thought, pleased. I too have the right not to believe their stories. He was still uneasy about the idea that a midget's life could be shorter than a horse's. For years, he had had constant pains in almost all his joints, and he had no idea if the discomfort was a result of premature aging in those of his kind or if it was an illness particular to him or if any man of any height and build felt the same way.

Harrieta and Mandrake approached him.

"We were saying," Mandrake spoke first, "that Don Alejo isn't going to put up with Narcissa's no on top of your insult."

"Why don't you go and apologize to him?" Harrieta added. "If you don't, he's going to order us to do something just so he'll feel like he's in charge; he'll make us practice new tricks, fix the tent, throw sawdust in the ring, put—"

"Speaking of new tricks," Nathaniel interrupted, "nobody has told me what my act is."

"It doesn't matter," Mandrake said. "You're a midget; you just need to do a couple of somersaults. It's the normal people like me who have to work hard for the applause."

"I'll think of something," Nathaniel said. "I want my act to be impressive."

Harrieta burst out laughing, and jokingly said, "You don't have the brains to make up a name for yourself and you think you'll come up with an act."

"You'd be better off going to Narcissa," Nathaniel retorted, irritated, "and ask her to go make nice with the old man."

"Hercules and Rocket already went to try and convince her," Mandrake said. "You have no idea of how the old man gets when something is bothering him."

"He doesn't seem so fierce to me," Nathaniel said, and with a few hops, he climbed to the top of the stands.

From there, he could see Mandrake insulting him under his breath and then walk away from the tent with Harrieta. He could also see Hercules and Rocket escorting Narcissa. She looked reluctant; however, she was walking toward the opening of the small tent without being forced. Nathaniel thought she looked like a radiant priestess about to fulfill the mission for which she was created. He pictured her as a little girl being fed royal jelly, bathed with goat's milk, and completely covered by a kind of orange peel that would have to be removed on the day she was mature. His hands began to sweat when he noticed Hercules and Rocket emerge without their offering. Then he heard screams coming from the small tent, and they were not screams of pleasure but of pain; but after all, pain in Nathaniel's imagination was more pleasing than pleasure. He began to sweat profusely. The moisture covered his forehead, back and armpits, and he felt a sharp twinge running from his chest to his lower stomach. He ran to look for a hiding place where he could release his yearning. He had just found the perfect spot under the stands, behind a wooden sign, when Don Alejo, bursting with energy, made his appearance in the center of the ring.

"Ladies and gentlemen, get ready because the parade is about to begin."

The pig squealed just then, as if it had understood what the boss had said.

"Not now, who in their right mind would think of such a thing, it's already getting dark," Mágala said softly, loud enough so only she could hear.

Nathaniel came back to reality and noticed himself in a grotesque position, with his fingers on his zipper and crouched down behind the wooden sign with the image of a balled-up trapeze artist on it: FROM FRANCE, THE CABRIOLÉ BROTHERS. The sensation was still running from his chest to his lower stomach, and in light of the total limpness between his legs, he thought about the horses again, and he concluded that the feeling was not because of Narcissa. Maybe it was the beginning of a heart attack.

"I'm going to die," he mumbled.

Don Alejo had given the order that Harrieta had predicted he would give "so he'll feel like he's in charge." There was a prolonged silence. Nobody wanted to be the first to obey; nevertheless, one by one they began to gather around the ring, waiting for an order to the contrary, or for someone to dare to protest.

"Why don't we wait until tomorrow?" Mágala asked timidly.

This emboldened Harrieta, who lent a hand with the first excuse that popped into her head.

"Yeah, the midget doesn't have an act yet."

"But I already have a name," Nathaniel said, satisfied.

"We are only going to parade into town," Don Alejo said sharply. "Right now, before they discover us and the surprise is lost."

Rocket had just finished polishing his cannon, and he agreed at once to start the parade, before the dusty wind got it dirty again.

"I made up an act for the midget," he said. "It's so good that it alone will fill the stands."

At first Don Alejo got excited just imagining the stands filled to capacity, but that feeling was soon buried beneath his skepticism. He had seen too many circuses over the course of many years, and except for General Tom Thumb, he had never seen a midget capable of stealing the show. Midgets only knew how to dress up like clowns and hit each other on the behind with wooden paddles or help the magicians or stand on a bench in the ticket window and sell tickets. Despite his doubts, he gave Rocket the chance to present his idea.

"Look, Don Alejo." Nathaniel went over toward him, ready to interrupt if he heard something he didn't like. "We'll tie the midget facedown to Harrieta's body. She'll have to wear a baggy dress to cover *up him up*. Then she'll begin to lift up her skirt little by little, like a curtain, and just when the people are starting to think it's an erotic act, the midget's head will pop out from between Harrieta's legs. And then the master of ceremonies will say, 'Ladies and gentlemen, the man who refused to be born.' "

"Up yours!" Nathaniel cried, even though after thinking about it for a while, the idea of sticking his head into Harrieta's downy bush was not altogether unpleasant.

Don Alejo became excited again.

"It's a great idea," he said. "We can work out the details later. Now let's go to Sierra Vieja!"

O*riginally, Porcayo was not* our surname. We considered ourselves so unfortunate, so overlooked by divine protection, that since the seventeenth century the family genealogy had been built up as if it were the lineage of kings. We did this just to prove to ourselves that our blood was of illustrious origins, and that despite the subsequent downfall and name changes, there would always exist the possibility of returning to the days when we would go out into the street with our heads held high, educated words, and our pockets overflowing. These chronicles begin in 1662 when, in following the orders of a king who was still picking his nose and wetting his bed, Don Fernando de Olaguíbel y Ruiz arrived in the port of Veracruz, never to return again to his native Valencia. Don Fernando came to be the magistrate of New Spain, and he held that position for a long time. His jurisdiction covered all or part of the governments of the viceroys: Melchor Portocarrero Lazo de la Vega, count of Monclova, known as the man with the silver arm because he lost the one of flesh and blood fighting in Dunkirk; Gaspar de Sandoval Silva y Mendoza, count of Galve, whose history was so vague that the Porcayo memoirs do not speak of him except to mention that he must have had fast feet to have fled from the Indians when they tried to burn him alive; Juan de Ortega Montañés, more remembered for his work as public prosecutor for the Holy Office than for his talents as viceroy; and José Sarmiento Valladares, count of Moctezuma y Tula, who married a granddaughter or great-great-granddaughter (or whoever) of the last Aztec emperor and posted sentries every night so he could bust drunk Indians willing to do wrong. As the magistrate, it was natural that some spoke well and others poorly of Don Fernando, since in making judgments on locking up crooks and exonerating the innocent, he must have made more than one mistake, shackling those who neither deserved nor feared it, or leaving the jail gate open for more than one criminal. However, a good or bad reputation is not something earned by people of all social strata, but rather, reserved for those at the top; and Don Fernando was a great man who, by climbing one more notch, would arrive at viceroyalty. 'A real gentleman,' it was said in my family for almost two hundred years. And up until my last days in my parents' house, there was still a painting of Don Fernando in the dining room, and his image was worshiped along with the crucifix that hung on the opposite wall. That painting was a rather poor replica of the original, which for a century belonged to the family, then to a series of individuals, and which today is part of the collection of the Academy of San Carlos, bearing the title *The Magistrate*. It is not known for certain who painted it, but it is believed that it could have been Cristóbal de Villalpando. In any event, as an art critic said, whoever painted it was, without a doubt, the greatest painter of the Mexican baroque period. 'That man in the portrait is a relative of yours, and it's a pity that you don't even come up to his heels,' my father pointed out to me. Don Fernando de Olaguíbel y Ruiz lived forty-two years and begat Fernando the Second, and Don Fernando lived after he begat Fernando the Second twenty-four years more. After he died, it was all downhill. 'He might just as well have been a son of a bitch,' it occurred to me to say one day, and this was when my father came after me with the ladle; he said that it was because of ideas like that that I hadn't been created in his image and likeness, and that's why people made fun of me and no woman would ever love me. Fernando the Second dedicated himself to squandering the magistrate's fortune and to cursing his bad luck for not having been born on the Iberian Peninsula but in this remote and primitive land, which, in his words, was neither new nor Spain. Only a terrible cowardice that today could be explained as seaphobia or boatphobia or something like that impeded him from traveling to Valencia, the birthplace of his father, grandfather, and of all the Olaguíbel y Ruiz's who had come before him. In the Olaguíbels' family book, he wrote, 'Something takes hold of me when the ship is about to set sail, and it happens to me every time. I will have to settle for drinking pulque, playing cards Friday nights, watching the despicable Indians in their canoes, and hoping that my life is not so long that I should end it myself.' It is not known how long he lived or what the name was of the Moorish girl he married; it is only known that his death was attributed to natural causes and that he fathered a son named Fernando the Third. Fernando the Third lived thirty-six years and begat Fernando the Fourth. Fernando the Third lived only ten seconds after Fernando the Fourth was begat. He died because the heir to the Olaguíbels' squandered fortune was supposedly conceived by rape, and Fernando the Third had not quite finished doing his business when the girl's father, with all his angry might, chopped off his head with two hacks of a machete. The sudden rigor mortis made it impossible to separate the girl from the body until another part of Fernando the Third was chopped off, after which the evil thing was removed with some pliers. The girl, whose name was Remedios, did not stop screaming for three days, and when she was finally quiet, she was to never speak again. Her mind took a journey with no return to the point that it seemed she did not even realize she had given birth. People came to say that it hadn't been a rape at all, that it had been voluntary, and they explained Remedios' madness by asking how the devil was the poor girl not going to be affected if a headless lover was screwing her. 'Just tales,' I said, and this time my father didn't hit me because he was frightened after what had happened with the ladle. Fernando the Fourth did not take the last name of Fernando the Third, which was Olaguíbel y Ruiz, but instead took the ordinary, made-up one of Rivera, with no ties to the past except for the memories and the painting, perhaps by the painter Villalpando. The maternal family took the boy to Valladolid, today known as Morelia, left him in an orphanage after giving him the name Hipólito Rivera, and tried to keep him hidden away, far from society, since as Remedios was Spanish and the presumed rapist a low-bred mestizo, they were not at all proud to have a grandson who would tarnish their name. 'And why, if the painting was ours, do we have to settle for this bad copy?' I insisted. As soon as he was old enough to make a decision, Hipólito left the orphanage, sold the painting, changed his name to that of Fernando the Fourth, though he kept Rivera, and he went far away to work in a silver mine around these parts. There he married Estelita Ramírez and fathered Fernando the Fifth. The rest of the story can be read in the April 17, 1767 edition of *El Español*. The article, entitled 'Horrifying Tragedy,' tells of a man named Fernando Rivera, 'perhaps possessed by the devil, who set off at least twenty rounds of explosives at the entrance of a mine, burying the unfortunate bodies of a hundred and twenty-three men.' Some said he had flown into a rage because he was not named foreman and others blamed it on the nightlife of his wife, but for Fernando the Fourth to kill a hundred and twenty-three men for something like that, Estelita must have been quite a whore. He, of course, also died in the explosion, and in the face of rumors that the eighty-nine widows were thinking of stoning the damned descendant of the murderer to death, Estelita Ramírez took Fernando the Fifth and, leaving all her possessions behind, fled to Guanajuato. There she worked in a mill and took the last name Porcayo. 'The last name doesn't matter,' my father would say. 'We are still the Olaguíbel y Ruiz family by blood.' And since he was a drunk, my mother would say, 'You have more alcohol than Olaguíbel in your veins.' Fernando the Fifth also worked in a mine, but his death was not as remarkable as his father's. It was not accompanied by thunder and explosions or hysteria or devastation or suffocation or the company of a hundred and some odd souls. He simply inhaled mercury vapors, and they say he turned stiff, and it must have run in the family, because the same thing happened to the headless lover. Fernando the Fifth died on his feet, and on his feet he remained until they dropped him off. In order to avoid responsibility, by orders of the foreman of the mine they leaned him up against a pillar in front of his house, knocked on the door, and took off running. His wife opened the door and said, 'Come in, what the hell are you standing there for with that idiotic look on your face?' Years later, Fernando the Fifth would become the second museum piece in the family, although not nearly as elegant as the painting of *The Magistrate*, since along with the other mummies of Guanajuato, he was depicted naked and stiff, like a piñata without the sweets inside. The guides would explain that the open mouth and the frightened look are unmistakable signs that he was buried alive. After saying come in, what the devil are you doing there with that idiotic look on your face, his wife went back inside the house to lie down again because being eight months pregnant, she couldn't bear to stand up for a long time. When she realized that her husband had not come in, she went back outside and got the shock of her life when she saw him in the same position and with the same idiotic look on his face. From the mere fright, Fernando the Sixth was born right then and there. It was 1809, and sixty-three years would pass before the next Porcayo, my father, would be born. Fernando the Sixth was many things in his lifetime: soldier, shoemaker, beggar, water carrier, and most importantly, prisoner. Around 1834, when Santa Anna was President for the first time and still had both legs, my grandfather stole the painting of *The Magistrate* from the house of a landowner, the son of the one who had bought it from Fernando the Fourth in Valladolid. Unfortunately, the landowner caught him red-handed; unluckier still, there was a fight in which the landowner lost his left ring finger. To make matters even worse, the landowner was a close friend of President Santa Anna. It is not known how costly the robbery attempt would have been for him, but the ring finger cost him thirty-seven years in prison, and it would have cost him his life if not for what happened in 1871, when a group of rebels backed by Porfirio Díaz took control of the Belén prison and freed him on the condition that he join the forces that were trying to overthrow Benito Juárez. However, as soon as he saw the jail gates open, Fernando the Sixth abandoned his recently embraced political ideals, for as long as he was beginning a new life, he didn't care if it was Benito, Porfirio, or Mamá Carlota in the National Palace. Fernando the Sixth lived only two years after getting out of prison, and he begat Fernando the Seventh, dying before he saw him born. 'Long live Fernando the Seventh,' my father used to say when he was drunk. 'Long live the Virgin of Guadalupe.' I don't have much to say about him, except that my mother and an uncle who gave him a job in his tailor shop considered him to be a real zero. And speaking of zeroes, I was born at zero hours, New Year's Eve. People were partying as if something really were being left behind and something better about to begin. Everyone was celebrating, except my mother, who was writhing on a bed, screaming her brains out with a little head peeking out between her legs. There was no doctor or midwife because they too were in the town square setting off fireworks and drinking mescal. When the church bells rang, my mother heard the crying of a baby whom, until that moment, she had intended to name Fernando the Eighth. But at that moment there were millions of drunks all around the country, and one of them peered in through the window and upon witnessing the birth, said, 'And you shall call his name Nathaniel, which means Happy New Year.' She thought it was an angel and didn't want to upset him, fearful of the punishment. And so she ended the family tradition of using kings' names in the hope that we might at least have a cut-rate lawyer among us. 'I warned your mother that she should name you Fernando the Eighth. Calling you Nathaniel could bring a curse upon us, and you see, I wasn't wrong,' my father said. The priest assured us that my condition was a result of so much sin in the world; my mother attributed it to my father being a drunkard, and a doctor said that it was pure luck: 'One in a hundred thousand come out like that, more or less.' Once, with the clarity brought on by alcohol, my father wrote, 'He's not only short; he is also ugly, especially since he had a piece of his eye cut out. He tries to be an ordinary, normal person. He speaks and makes plans as if someone were really going to give him a job, and at times he even brushes his hair and picks out his clothes carefully, with the hope of making some woman fall in love with him. It's easy for him because he can't see himself. On the other hand, those of us who look at him seated at a table or walking down the street as if he were just another animal among the dogs, cows, goats, and chickens, see only an aberration. That is why it's annoying to see him looking so sure of himself, as if nothing were wrong. He should assume his role of freak, beast, mistake of nature. He is and always will be the most unfortunate of the Porcayos.' When he wrote that, he had no idea that I would become more than a mere drunk in a tailor's shop or a prisoner in the Belén jail or a mummy in Guanajuato or a mine worker who would bury alive a hundred and twenty-three fellow workers or a lover without a head or a squanderer who wants to run off to Spain. I would come to be something even greater than a magistrate. Yes, because from today on, I am a king, King Nathaniel the First, sovereign ruler of all performers."

"Enough of that," Don Alejo said without the slightest irritation or enthusiasm, and he raised his finger to his mouth in a sign to be quiet when he noticed that Harrieta wanted to speak.

Don Alejo ordered everyone to stop. He looked at his people to make sure that everything was in order. Not one of the eight faces revealed the enthusiasm he had seen on so many other occasions. More than circus performers about to begin the parade, they looked like mourners at a funeral. He was particularly intrigued by Mágala, for although he well knew she was fourteen years old, he saw the face of a mature, almost elderly, woman. He closed his eyes instinctively and didn't open them until he had turned around, for he did not want to be infected by the group's despondency. A few meters ahead, the road flattened out and revealed the roofs of the first houses. Not a noise seemed to be coming from them, and Don Alejo was baffled by so much silence. On the outskirts of town he had expected to hear the clucking of chickens or the tolling of the bells from the six-o'clock mass or the flat sound of a cowbell. He had expected smells emanating from a kitchen or the stench of manure or of rotten food from a weekend market. At the very least, he had expected a crowd of bratty kids acting as ambassadors, shouting to everyone that the circus was coming. Otherwise, he preferred it that way; the fewer the people who noticed them, the greater the surprise their entrance would create.

"Like an invasion," he said, hoping to liven them up.

The idea did not excite Harrieta. "God willing, we won't be welcomed by bullets."

Mandrake looked at her mockingly, and he would have insulted her if he had thought of an appropriate comment. He straightened his top hat. He was dressed entirely in black, including a black cape dotted with yellow stars and some red scrawl that read: "Mandrake the Magnificent Magician."

"Bitch," he finally said softly.

They remained motionless for a while, and one by one they realized that the place was too quiet. Harrieta was frightened by the silence. Flexor the contortionist wanted to sing just to give them something to hear, but before he could start, he was distracted by the shadow of a cloud. With a signal from Don Alejo, they resumed their course, and the silence was wiped out first by the lash that struck Hercules' back, then by the squeaking of the cart that was carrying the cannon, and finally by the dragging of the pig's hooves. A cloud of dust formed with every step, and the tracks of each and every one of them were left behind on the road.

"Do you see that?" Nathaniel asked.

Harrieta tried to ignore him, but then curiosity got the best of her. She looked at him without saying a word.

"In front of us there are no tracks, there are only those that we are leaving behind us."

"And what did you expect?" Harrieta asked, annoyed. "That the tracks would be in front of us?"

"That's not what I mean."

"Shh," Don Alejo interrupted. "Shut up and go see if there is any grease for that squeaking."

Nathaniel went back toward the cart, without the slightest intention of looking for the grease. He knew too well that there was none, and at any rate, he wasn't about to grease the axles while they were in motion. I'll lose a hand to go with my eye, he thought.

"Did anyone bring anything to eat?" he asked. "I'm hungry."

"What for?" Hercules said. "It's obvious you know nothing about this life."

Hercules was pulling the cart. It was common practice to walk through the town streets as if he were a beast of burden, with someone urging him on with some harmless lashes. For the women who saw the parade go by, this was a scene bordering on the erotic, and even Hercules himself, sweaty, with his muscles tense and an expression of resigned fury, enjoyed believing himself a Jewish slave in Egypt dragging a stone block up to the top of the pyramid. At times, his strength bored him, and he enjoyed the lashes that gave him a feminine feeling of defenselessness.

"And what do I need to know?" the midget asked.

Harrieta slowed down so that Nathaniel could catch up. Mandrake placed his arms on the back of the cart, as if it needed his push to move on. Rocket called his attention to his recently polished cannon and warned him not to put his grubby hands on it. Mandrake picked up a rock and threw it at him, missing on purpose. Harrieta leaned over a bit and asked Nathaniel, "Why is everyone so nervous? We've done this so many times before."

"It's the first time for me," Nathaniel said. "But no one is nervous. Only you."

"Could it be because there are so few of us?"

"What did Hercules mean?"

"Isn't it because there are so few of us?" she asked again.

"It could be, but I'm not nervous."

"Everything is so easy for Hercules; don't pay any attention to him."

"What did he mean? Why did he say that I don't know anything about this life?"

"You know your story by heart, right? You told it like a speech, even though you forgot the part about your relative the President."

The pace slowed, as if the road had begun to slope uphill. Mágala said she was thirsty. A sudden gust of wind moved the trees, and Don Alejo gave his interpretation of the sound of the leaves. "They are applauding us," he said.

Nathaniel smiled and whispered to Harrieta, "Silly old fool."

"Leave him alone," she said. "He's just feebleminded."

"We're all fools," Nathaniel added, "pretending we don't realize what's going on."

"What happened with his brother affected him a lot," Harrieta continued.

"I don't give a hoot about the Mantecón brothers."

Don Alejo raised his arms and bowed, in acknowledgment of the applause. He still didn't feel like looking at the group, and he turned a deaf ear to what was being said. Nathaniel tugged on Harrieta's arm.

"Who are we kidding?" he asked. "At this point, it's clear we aren't going anywhere."

"Don't be ridiculous," Harrieta said, freeing her arm.

The cannon wobbled as the cart ran into a rock, and even though it wasn't serious, for a few seconds all eyes turned to Hercules, who continued to move ahead as if nothing had happened.

"Look," Flexor said.

They were coming to the end of a curve in the road, and behind some walnut trees, a small town came into view.

"Now," Don Alejo ordered, "let the music begin."

He waved his right hand as if he were holding a baton, and the others, halfheartedly, began to hum *Over the Waves*. The Festival Orchestra opened each performance with this waltz. Rocket lifted up his shirt in order to play percussion on his stomach, although he thought a waltz was too dull for what should be a triumphant entrance. What they needed was a march, a fanfare, thundering cannons. They also needed more people parading and a stampede of animals. Nathaniel looked at Harrieta with an expression that she interpreted as "I told you the old guy is mad." She shrugged and stopped humming. Flexor was humming the loudest, off beat, and forcing the others to follow his rhythm. The melody would last for only a short time, and the first verse would be hummed by only three voices, since the others went silent when Narcissa shouted, "My God, where are we?"

Flexor took off running, suddenly overcome by happiness. He flapped his arms as if he wanted to fly, flung the promotional flyers one by one, and by then, was the only one humming the waltz.

"Yes, my friends." He stopped the music and began to recite as an announcer would, "Fun for young and old at reasonable prices."

Mágala thought he was funny and burst out laughing. Don Alejo, however, could not bear to look at that skinny body squeezed into that yellow leotard, running about and flapping its arms.

"Stop that idiot. He's wasting the flyers."

Hercules was delighted to obey the order. He let go of the ropes and, once a freedman, he took slow, heavy strides that caused his chest to shake as he pursued Flexor.

"Look," Mandrake said to Harrieta. "He has bigger tits than you."

Nathaniel lost interest in the pursuit, even though he envied Flexor's gracefulness, running as if he were a ballet dancer.

"What did Hercules mean?"

"For him, it's so easy," Harrieta responded. "Wherever he goes, he finds some woman to look after him. But forget about it, for you and me, it's no different than being in an abandoned town."

Flexor had turned around and was running back, giving Hercules a chance to finally catch him. A second later, with a punch to the face, the boy fell to his knees, teary-eyed, his hands covering his bloody nose, and all traces of sudden happiness gone. The stack of flyers was lying on the ground, with no wind to scatter it. And while like that, on his knees, Flexor felt Hercules grabbing him by the wrists and dragging him toward Don Alejo. He clenched his teeth and did not let out a sound, except for that of his leotard tearing and his knees digging into the ground.

"Don't you see what is happening?" Don Alejo said to him softly, caressing his hair.

The few houses in the town were lined up along the road. Some had rotted doors, on others the faded whitewash revealed a leprous façade of exposed adobes. Enough dust had accumulated on the roof of one house for thistles to grow, and these came cascading down as if they were bougainvilleas. The town square was filled with dried weeds and had a statue in the center. The door to the church was barred and its bell tower showed evidence of a past abundance of pigeons.

"And I thought my town was a dump," Rocket said.

Four cobbled streets were all there were. The houses, side by side, were lined up on one street, as if despite all the open space, the inhabitants had missed the overcrowding of the city. The church stood on another street, facing west. On the third street, there were some stones piled up, materials that had one day been intended for a building. The fourth street seemed to lead nowhere and was of use only in completing the square.

"If we take off running," Narcissa mumbled, "would we be able to catch up to Don Ernesto?"

"This is all your fault," Harrieta looked at her resentfully, "and now you want to be the first to make a run for it."

The pig squealed again because Mandrake had tied it to a tree. Harrieta turned around and could just see the top of the sun behind the mountain.

"Let's go to the tent," she said, annoyed. "We have to get back before nightfall."

Don Alejo slowly walked over to the porch of one of the houses. There he sat down and took off his shoes.

"Better yet, come and rub my feet. They're killing me."

Hercules *pushed against* the door of one of the houses; the hinges creaked and it gave way, releasing a wave of humidity. Mágala, who was right behind him, held her breath, thinking that the stale air was probably full of germs.

"Come on, Mágala, let's see what's inside."

"No," she responded, suspicious of Hercules' intentions. "It's so dark."

Even though it was still light outside, the windows inside were boarded up, and you could barely make out the three rooms, which were completely empty, except for a wooden bed with no mattress. Hercules felt his way along the whitewashed walls, and noticed with disgust how his hands were covered with dust. He looked around closely. Surely in a corner there would be a trunk, some housewares, something. He was disappointed not to find anything valuable, and he reproached himself for not having the guts to pillage the place. Something about the house bothered him. He realized it was a sense of death. Wandering around that house gave him the same sadness as seeing old photographs of smiling people, the impossibility of immortality. He deduced that the owners of the house were dead; this allowed him to justify his lack of guts, because it was okay to rob the living but not the dead.

He continued to feel his way along the walls until he came to a door at the back. It no longer had a lock or hinges, and it fell down as he tried to open it. He discovered a neglected patio full of weeds and dried branches, and an oyamel tree standing irreverent with its greenness amidst such withered surroundings. A paved walkway led him to the backyard, where he found an out-house. He walked over to it and was amazed to find a porcelain toilet bowl, a luxury out of place in such mediocrity. He undressed completely and sat down on the bowl, which had been stained by rain, dirt, and sun. Even though it was small for his considerable size, it felt comfortable and desirable, and it made him detest his fate as a circus performer, which did not give him the chance to sit and do his business with dignity and in peace, while smoking a cigarette or reading a newspaper, but instead forced him to go looking for a hiding place off the path or far from the tent, where there was a breeze, and where he was unable to shake from his mind the story of the man who had been bitten on his genitalia by a viper.

Hercules ran his finger between his bottom and the porcelain. I didn't remember how this felt, he thought, and he closed his eyes so he could feel like a little boy again. He thought back to those winter days in his childhood house, when before sitting down on the toilet, he would rub the seat with his hands, over and over again, until it was warm. Maybe I'll steal this for myself, he thought. After all, a dead man has no use for it.

"Are you in there?" Mágala shouted from outside.

Hercules got dressed, and with the little light that remained, he began to investigate how to remove the toilet so he could take it with him, as booty. However, it was firmly attached with mortar that over the years had turned to rock. It was impossible to pull it up without breaking it. He took out of his pocket a photograph of himself wearing no shirt and black breeches that hugged his skin; the dark tones made it clear that his body, now puffy, had once been solid and well toned. In his arms he was holding an eighty-kilo weight with the inscription "500k," and he was bending his knees, in a pose that protruded his manliness. He always carried those photos with him, as well as a pen to autograph them. Sometimes it was his way of thanking a woman for spending the night with him, sometimes he would exchange them for a drink, and sometimes, less frequently, he would come across someone who would pay for them. His dedication was always the same: *To so and so, a strong hug*, and he signed Hercules R.L., in honor of his former name Rubén Lombardo, and thinking that using the word *strong* to describe a hug was evidence of his wit. This time he changed the dedication and wrote: *Property of Hercules. Do not touch.* He put the photograph face down, and placed a small rock on top of the toilet so it wouldn't blow away. He caressed the toilet like a loved one and quickly went back out to meet Mágala.

"Did you find anything?"

He was excited about his discovery and would have liked to confide in someone.

"An oyamel," he responded, "and a bed."

Mágala assumed that there was no such bed, and that Hercules' mention of it was just a clumsy invitation to go inside.

"Were you sleeping in it? Is that where you were all this time?"

He put his right hand on Mágala's shoulder and tried to make an affectionate gesture.

"I don't want to do my business like an animal anymore," he said, unable to keep quiet. "I want to sit on a toilet as one should."

Mágala drew back, surprised, imagining Hercules walking on all fours and dropping his excrement as he went, like a horse at full gallop.

"Pig," she said, and she left quickly to join Harrieta and Don Alejo.

On the way, she bumped into Flexor, who was still trying to stop the flow of blood from his nose and his knees while threatening Hercules, saying that he would slice open his belly as soon as he wasn't looking.

Harrieta continued rubbing Don Alejo's feet like they were dough ready to stick in the oven.

"That's enough." Don Alejo was irritated. "You're pulverizing them, not massaging them."

"I was being gentle," Harrieta said, wiping on her dress the sweat from her hands, half hers and half Don Alejo's.

He put on some worn-out socks and then put his shoes on without tying them. He scratched his belly and began to walk slowly, clearly having nowhere to go. Harrieta caught up to him.

"What do you think of Nathaniel the First?"

Don Alejo shrugged; he didn't feel like filling his head with names for midgets when there were so many important things to think about. She smiled and went on, "I think they're just stories."

On their walk they bumped into Mágala.

"I just found out how Hercules does his business," she whispered loudly, amused.

Harrieta looked up in disbelief.

"I'm not interested."

"He says he gets down on all fours . . ." Mágala went on, but Don Alejo stopped her dead.

"Shut up."

Mágala looked down, embarrassed and annoyed, searching for something to say to vindicate herself.

"Don Alejo, tell Hercules not to come near me."

"What can he possibly do to you?" Harrieta asked.

"She's talking to me," Don Alejo said, and Mágala smiled in return.

The three looked at each other warily; the old man's eyes revealing his lack of patience for nonsense, the two women trying to think of a way to capture their boss's attention.

"The magistrate." Harrieta brought the subject up again. "Who would believe it?"

"He wants to get fresh with me," Mágala explained. "Just now he broke into a house and wanted to sleep with me in a bed he found there."

"You should be so lucky," Harrieta said.

"She's talking to me," Don Alejo repeated emphatically.

"I want to be respected, I'm still just a girl."

"Ha!" Harrieta forced a laugh. "Girls don't smell like red snapper."

"I'm talking to him," Mágala said, her muscles tensed.

Don Alejo lost his patience. Why did they bother him with their childishness? Did they not notice the problem that was right under their noses?

"Get out of here," he ordered Harrieta, "and let us talk in peace."

Harrieta was enraged and wanted to ask the old man if the massage didn't merit just a bit of tolerance. She stumbled on the words, though, and could only manage to move her hands in a gesture that was intended to simulate the action of massaging, but which to Don Alejo and Mágala seemed to be a way of saying that she had claws and could use them whenever she wished. Harrieta turned around and bumped into Hercules, who had just come over to join the group.

"Idiot," she said, and tried to slap him.

"What's wrong with her?" Hercules asked.

Harrieta let out a cry of frustration and headed for the square.

"I don't know," Don Alejo said.

"I think she's jealous," Mágala said.

When night fell, everyone gathered around a bonfire that Rocket had lit in the middle of the street. Flexor had stopped bleeding. He was breathing heavily and whimpering occasionally, making sure everyone was aware that his knee still hurt, and thus trying to generate hostility toward Hercules. Harrieta was hungry. She decided that the best thing would be to put out the fire and go back to the tent, for there was still enough moonlight for them to find their way. She didn't say anything, however, because she imagined it wouldn't be long before Don Alejo would come to the same conclusion. Nathaniel closed his eye so he could listen to the crackling of the burning wood.

"What do you think?" Rocket asked. "Shall we practice the act of the man who refused to be born?"

"Get out of here," Harrieta retorted, and in order to divert attention from herself, she added, "By the way, the midget still has no name."

"We have to do something," Rocket said. "There's no way we can just stay here, staring at each other."

"I suggested Midgetowski."

From the other side of the fire, Nathaniel gave her the finger.

"I found a marvelous toilet bowl," Hercules said excitedly.

"It's all right by me to practice the act," Nathaniel said, "as long as Harrieta is not in those days of the month."

Mágala smiled slyly. "Her days ended a long time ago."

Don Alejo lowered his head. He had had plans to sell hundreds of tickets to the people in this town. He had also thought about recruiting workers to take down the tent when the season ended and, if he found capable people, even to hire a small orchestra. Now, with no public, he had to change his plans. He needed to travel to the nearest town, sell the pig, the wood from the stands, the small tent, whatever was necessary to pay for their move to a populated area. Don Alejo's face became so transparent that Mandrake had no problem reading his mind.

"We can look for a place where they'll let us perform without a big top," he said. "And we can come back for it later."

"And how would we hang the trapeze?" Mágala asked.

"Let's practice the act," Nathaniel said.

"You can hang it from a lightpole."

"With no big top, the people climb up trees and don't pay," Hercules said.

"You're crazy, I could be electrocuted."

"And what if it rains?" Harrieta asked.

A gust of wind stoked up the fire and hundreds of sparks went flying like frightened fireflies. Mandrake let out a whine when one of them landed in his right eye.

"No one decides to be a circus performer," Don Alejo said, becoming more serious, and he stood up and began to walk around the fire. "It's something that just happens."

Everyone stared at him in silence, waiting for him to elaborate and arrive at some conclusion. But the old man continued to circle the fire, without opening his mouth again.

"It was made of porcelain," Hercules said when the silence became too heavy. "It felt good, very smooth."

No one knew what he was talking about, and his comment seemed as absurd as Don Alejo's.

"The man who refused to be born," Rocket persisted.

"Help the midget come up with a name," Harrieta said, hoping to prevent Rocket's idea from catching on.

For a moment, there was silence, and everyone seemed lost in thought. Don Alejo did a couple more laps around the fire, his feet dragging and his hands behind his back. Then he stopped.

"It's time to go," he said. "This town is a box-office flop."

"The cyclops of Lilliput," Flexor said excitedly, looking for approval on their faces.

"Let's wait a bit," Mágala said. "Maybe the people will return soon. They may have gone hunting and tomorrow morning they'll be back."

Mandrake burst out laughing.

"Hunting?" he asked. "What century are you living in?"

"I've got a name," Nathaniel said resentfully.

Mágala shrugged, embarrassed.

"Let's go," Don Alejo said again, firmly.

Hercules was still thinking about the porcelain toilet and how much he wanted to have it. He likened the houses there to empty caves, waiting for the arrival of an animal or a man to occupy them and take possession of all that was inside.

"Sir," he said with all due respect to Don Alejo. "Why don't we stay here?"

"Because it's very late," Don Alejo said. "Tomorrow morning, early, we have to—"

"I don't mean tonight," Hercules interrupted. "I'm talking about forever."

The idea had already occurred to the others, but in a vague way that nobody took seriously; they were merely giving free reign to their imaginations. However, hearing it from Hercules' mouth gave it shape and substance, and a quick glance at the faces in the group was enough to confirm that the proposal had been accepted with eight votes in favor and one, that of Don Alejo, against.

"If I had my house," Harrieta said, forgetting that just a moment earlier she had been hungry and wanted to go back to the tent, "I could remove my hair and I wouldn't need to make a living off it anymore."

"My knee hurts," Flexor moaned.

"Shut up, crybaby."

"Remove one hair at a time," Mandrake said. "Don't skin yourself."

"I would put my cannon in the entrance hall," Rocket said, "and pity the poor soul who tries to come in without knocking."

"At my age and with my own house," Mágala said, overcome by emotion. "I can't believe it."

"The toilet," Hercules said.

"I've always dreamed of having my own place," Nathaniel said, "and of filling it with furniture that's my size."

Each one spoke of his plans, without the slightest interest in listening to the others; each tried to picture, through the shadows of the buildings, which one would be his future home.

Hercules addressed the boss in an *authoritative* voice. "Sir, it is good for us to stay here."

Smiling, Don Alejo looked at him, trying to hide his outrage at what he sensed was an impending mutiny.

"You don't know what you're talking about."

In an attempt to show his authority, he began to walk off into the darkness in the direction of the tent. He went a few meters, then turned around to see if anyone was following him. Nobody; they were all sitting there silently, mesmerized by the fire, as if it were a great show. He softly said Narcissa's name and asked her not to leave him alone. There's no reason to worry: What can a bunch of circus performers do after taking over a few abandoned houses? Die of hunger? Kill themselves out of boredom from doing the same tired acts for only themselves? No, I have nothing to be alarmed about. Anyway, in the worst-case scenario, I can attract an audience by myself, promising wondrous things, and then I would need only to light a bonfire in the middle of the ring to leave them stupefied for a few hours as they watch the flames. Then I'll put it out with water, and as the smoke rises, they will erupt into a thunderous applause.

Nobody got up to follow him, and he wondered if they could be a family only when the stands were full, or if it was his brother who really had the authority, or if, simple as it sounded, a bunch of empty houses was a greater temptation than a life filled with applause, moving from one place to another, seeing the world, and knowing you are superior to everyone in the audience. It bothered him that after so many years of running a circus, it fell to pieces on the very first day his brother abandoned him. To leave by himself was as inconceivable as it was to insist that someone follow him. He went over to the tree where the pig was tied and he took it with him.

"Come with me," he said sweetly. "We'll wait for the others back at the tent."

And the animal followed him with short, quick steps and its tail straight, as if it were a pedigreed dog.

Harrieta took Hercules by the hand and led him away from the group. The fire was reduced to embers that barely lit up when the wind blew. Hercules made a halfhearted attempt to free himself from Harrieta's grasp; then he just gave in, and she led him to a bench in the town square.

"Is what Mágala said true?"

Although he understood Harrieta's question perfectly, he preferred to steer the conversation in another direction. "About your days having ended a long time ago?"

"Mágala is a liar," Harrieta cried out. "I still have plenty of them."

"I'm not so sure."

"It's not because of me," she said, trying to look seductive, but her stance was wasted in the dark.

Hercules noticed that they were still holding hands and, sitting alone on the bench in the square, he wished with all his heart that Harrieta were a beautiful woman. He tried in vain to use the darkness to fool himself. He tossed the idea around in his head for a few seconds, and since the beauty of that woman was just that, an idea, he ended up jerking his arm away.

"I'm talking about what Mágala said to Don Alejo." Harrieta would have preferred not having to be so explicit. "Did you want to get her inside that house?"

He sat back on the bench, his legs stretched out and crossed at the ankles. He pressed down on his stomach, trying to make it smaller, and when he let go and the flesh sprang back to its original size, he was deeply saddened.

"You said it," he blurted. "She's a liar."

In the middle of the square stood a stone statue of a man on horseback. The animal, openmouthed, was standing on its rear legs, while the horseman, his sword pointing toward the church, seemed to be rallying an army behind him. The granite pedestal stood in the center of what seemed to be the basin of a fountain, which had not a drop of water in it and was full of dirt and dried leaves. On one side there was an inscription that read: MY LIFE FOR YOUR HONOR. Harrieta got up and went over to the statue, surprised that despite the layer of dirt, the words were still visible in the moonlight. After looking at it for a while and trying unsuccessfully to determine the identity of the man, she said, "There are no men like that anymore."

Hercules leaned back on the stone bench and untied his shoes before responding.

"Stop complaining. You had someone risk his life for you."

"Don Alejo didn't risk a thing."

"They almost burned the big top down."

"That wasn't heroic; it was foolish."

"Maybe, but he saved you just the same."

Harrieta dusted off the pedestal, looking for a name or a date or any piece of information that would help identify that horseman willing to give his life for honor. On one side she found a rectangular cutting and thought that at one time there might have been a plaque there with the horseman's name.

"Don't get carried away," Hercules said lethargically, about to fall asleep. "He refers to the honor of his country."

Harrieta knew that. Nevertheless, she preferred to think about heroes sacrificing themselves for a woman, especially because she thought that had just one man like that existed, one who would have stood up for her, she would not have ended up a freak in the circus.

"No one fights for his country," she said, "unless he is in love with a woman."

When the first hairs had begun to sprout on her body, she didn't pay much attention; maybe it was something other women also experienced. After all, all she had to do was get ahold of her brother's razor or pull off that mixture of resin and sugarloaf syrup that her aunt rubbed all over her body. As time went by, the fine down turned into a thick thatch like cactus thorns, too painful to pluck and too visible to hide by shaving. Her aunt gave her a piece of advice: it was best not to defy nature and to let the beard and mustache grow. Harrieta was still called Angélica, and she locked herself up inside for more than a month, watching in desperation the assault of hair taking possession of her skin like weeds in an abandoned lot.

One morning, on Good Friday, her aunt told her that it was time she fixed herself up a bit. Armed with soap, scissors, and a brush, she bathed her, trimmed the beard, and arranged her hair in such a way that it would look as much as possible like the figure in the crucifix that hung on the wall. "It's a miracle," her aunt said. "Our Father reincarnated as a woman," and she knelt down at her feet and began to recite a series of praises replete with hallelujahs and Hail Mary's. Angélica told her not to be stupid, that her hair was not connected to divine things, but to the devil, that she had not been born by the grace of the Holy Spirit but rather, by means of a deflowering that had been settled in the justice of the peace's office, that she had never turned water into wine, only urine, and that her longest fast had been three days and that was when her father was unemployed. And she would have continued with her string of arguments if her aunt had not stopped her to say, "All right, I wasn't trying to convince you, but since everyone in town is so ignorant, they would willingly swallow the lie, and just imagine the fortune we are going to get out of them." And what faith could not move in Angélica, greed did.

That very afternoon they went in search of the official play of the Passion of Christ. Angélica improvised a tunic, a crown of barbed wire, and a cross so small that no one would have ever thought to use it for the crucifixion. On the way, they discussed whether she should call herself Jesusa Christa. They came to Progreso Street, the Via Dolorosa for the procession, just as the other Jesus was falling to his knees. Then her aunt ordered Angélica to get rid of her stupid cross, since it was time for her to take the place of the second-rate Christ, and she announced, "Step aside ladies and gentlemen, Pharisees, Jews, scribes, and sinners all; make way for the real Savior, reincarnated as a woman, just as it was written, because in the original Holy Scriptures, son and daughter are written the same." It took a while for the words to sink in, and only the other Jesus protested because he did not want to miss his moment of stardom. "Fuck off," he said. "Just when the good part is coming."

Little by little, the people began to whisper and comment, and their indignation grew, along with the idea that perhaps the reincarnation of Christ was included in the Bible. But to give him the body of a woman implied an unforgivable heresy. The demands to throw Angélica out turned into insults, and the insults turned into stone throwing. In her defense, her aunt said, "It is written: 'They will not recognize her and with stones they will deny her.'" This pronouncement managed to calm their rage, but only until the Pontius Pilate of the occasion yelled, "Crucify her!"

They dragged her through the rest of the Stations of the Cross up to the hill representing Calvary. There the Roman guards took off her clothing and, terrified by Angélica's hairy body, but especially by the curls sprouting from her nipples, they forgot to cast lots for the tunic. They tied her arms to the crossbar but could not find a way to lift the cross because Angélica was playing the role of Christ with very little dignity, and she began kicking and shouting, and she spit at Mary Magdalene and said to Dismas and Gestas to stop standing there like idiots and to help her.

Just then a voice full of authority said, "Harrieta, Harrieta, why hast thou forsaken me?" and for a moment, the struggle came to a stop.

Making the most of the fact that on Good Friday the circus was closed, Don Alejo had gone out for a walk. He witnessed what was happening and his vision as a showman assured him that the worst time to exhibit a woman like that was precisely during a religious feast. In the circus, on the other hand, it would be a smashing success. He decided at once to call her Harrieta.

Don Alejo went over to untie her, and he asked the people to forgive her for she did not know what she was doing. He quickly made up a story about the bearded lady: "She works for my circus, and as she is not right in the head, sometimes she runs off and gets into trouble." Angélica played along, sensing it was the best way out of the predicament, and she put on the face of an idiot as Don Alejo took her by the hand, covered her with the tunic, and led her toward salvation.

"Wake up, you animal," Harrieta said.

Hercules opened his eyes halfway and tried to find a more comfortable position in which to sleep, but his body was too large for the bench. He turned toward the back of the bench and noticed an inscription: COURTESY OF THE BOCANEGRA FAMILY.

[46]

"Don't be . . ." Hercules mumbled, before he began to snore.

When Don Alejo presented Harrieta's act for the first time, he learned that not even in the circus could he play with people's beliefs. The act consisted of a crucifixion, with a bit of melodrama and a few theatrical elements; and although he took care not to use words like Christa or Jesusa or things like that, and instead of Roman soldiers, he used federal policemen, and the thieves on the crosses on either side were two of the Cabriolé brothers, playing Chucho el Roto and Emiliano Zapata, and instead of I.N.R.I. on the cross, he put an advertisement for Victoria Beer, the people regarded it as a parody that was in bad taste and, just like on that Good Friday, they began booing and throwing things, and someone ended up setting fire to the stands. The situation did not go beyond that for the fire didn't spread, and of the objects thrown, only a stone that hit one of the Cabriolés right in the genitalia was of any consequence, as it was months before his member recovered its erectile ability. The Mantecón brothers lamented the money wasted on the mechanism designed to simulate Harrieta's ascension into heaven, and on the show of thunder and lightning, after which Hercules would enter the ring and say, "Truly, this was the mother of the circus." Only the musicians of the Festival Orchestra remained steady like the captain of a sinking ship, and as the people rushed out of the big top, they sounded their apocalyptic trumpets.

"Come on, Hercules. Make a little room for me on your bench."

The only response was a whistling noise that came from his nose. Harrieta turned toward the statue, wanting to give it a name. She sat down on the pedestal and at once became aware of her exhaustion. She was having a hard time keeping her eyes open when the name Timoteo de Roncesvalles popped into her head, and she wondered why such a stupid thing would have occurred to her. It was impossible that someone with a name like that would give his life for the honor of a woman. She realized that it had not been a very lucky day for making up names, for she had had no success with the midget either. She resigned herself to snuggling up next to Hercules. That would be enough to forget about Timoteo de Roncesvalles, and the next morning she would have time to think of a better name.

W*hat's wrong?*" Narcissa was trying to sleep, but Flexor's whining was preventing her from doing so.

"Look at my knees."

She was about to tell him to stop being such a crybaby, to just deal with it and stop whimpering, but the yellow leotard, torn in both knees and stained with blood and dirt, which clung to such a thin and fragile body, filled her with tenderness.

"You're still a little boy."

Flexor looked up, wondering what was the point of such a comment. Narcissa shrugged and began to caress his hair, allowing herself the time and patience to arrange it with a well-defined part. Then she lowered her hands and took him by the shoulders, and she went to kiss him on the mouth. Flexor squeezed his lips together, but aside from that resistance, he let her continue touching him. After a few seconds, Narcissa noticed that the yellow leotard was still lying flat against his body, no protuberance anywhere.

"I thought so," she said.

Flexor replied hastily, "What did you expect? Don't think you're so irresistible."

"It doesn't matter," Narcissa said while trying to suppress her laughter. "I always wanted someone like you."

He tried to explain. She changed the subject and asked him if he had washed the wound. Flexor bent his leg and felt the pain of the dried blood cracking like dirt that has seen no rain.

"How am I supposed to wash it if there's no water?"

"That's why I'm here," Narcissa said, hugging him. "I'm going to take care of you as if you were my son."

Flexor blushed at the hug. Narcissa's chest was warm, much more so than the solitude of his cot in the tent, and he let himself be lulled by the heartbeat. He ignored the burning on his knees, and closed his eyes and began to lose consciousness.

"Not so fast," Narcissa said.

She uncovered the right leg up to the middle of the thigh and spit where she believed the most severe part of the wound to be. With her fingers she formed a mixture of blood and mud, and she spit again to rinse it off. She wanted to do the same to the left leg, but her mouth was dry, and despite her efforts, sucking and imagining tasty dishes, she worked up only enough saliva to moisten the wound a bit, softening the scab and making it bleed again.

"Look what you did."

Narcissa paid no attention to the trickle of blood dripping steadily down, for something else was beginning to bother her. Her tongue needed that recently spit saliva and it was crying out for a drink of water. She looked around, and even though it was too dark to see beyond a stone's throw, she believed she knew enough to say, "We are a bunch of fools."

Flexor looked up for a second, then started to blow on the blood, hoping to stop the bleeding. Someone had told him about a disease: whether the wound was big or small, blood would spurt out in gushes or trickle out in drops with no human or divine power able to stop it. It wasn't unpleasant to die that way, since you only felt a little thirsty, a little cold, and very tired, and inevitably the victim would fall asleep and would no longer feel thirsty or cold or anything at all.

"I'm tired," he said.

"I'm dying of thirst," Narcissa said.

"Now we just need someone who's cold."

And as Narcissa did not know what he was talking about, Flexor made a face of disgust and turned around.

"This town is deserted because there's no water," she said. "How the devil do we think—?"

She fell quiet. It was pointless to tell Flexor, if the next morning she could throw it in everyone's face and make them see they were a bunch of fools. They'll realize that in addition to my buttocks, I've got brains, she thought. She curled up next to Flexor, caressing him as she spoke affectionately, using words like my boy, my child, and little by little she fell asleep, trying not to think about her dry mouth and making plans to explain to Don Alejo when they returned that she had never really wanted to leave him.

T*hose traveling circuses,* with the encyclopedic chichi pooch and irrelevant elephants taught me about comic triviality and the grandeur of uproarious tragedy.' These are verses from a poem that we should all know by heart. That is, if we were like people back in the days when intelligence, discipline, and vocation existed. 'The earlier aerialist hanging by the tips of his nervy toes was a dashing if topsy-turvy cosmographer who, if he kept climbing until he found where the north, or south, pole was, would also have personal questions for Aeolus.' A few days ago I recited this verses to the Cabriolé brothers, and they were stupefied, not knowing what to say. Finally one of them asked, 'Who is Aeolus?'

Bunch of ignoramuses. There's a reason they could never do the triple jump or the double loop-de-loop, or the flight of the hummingbird; they entrusted themselves to the Virgin of Guadalupe instead of praying to Aeolus. I entrusted myself to Barnum, to Saint Barnum, to Phineas Taylor Barnum or, as he would call himself, the Prince of Humbugs. 'Here is your disciple'—I invoked him before every performance. 'In you I entrust the successful outcome of all the moves, jokes, magic, and dangerous acts that my boys attempt.' That was back when I was full of ideas. Later on, I no longer felt worthy of calling myself his disciple. I failed to live up to his legacy of three or more rings, gigantic elephants, mighty gorillas, entire tribes of cannibals or Zulus, stands for ten thousand spectators, an arena for a thousand performers and, believe me, the most beautiful women in the world. My brother and I thought that we could go back to Mexico and say that we were disciples of Barnum, stars in his circus, so that we could fill our big top night after night. But in this country of morons, the maestro's name means as much as Aeolus did to the Cabriolés. Barnum was right when he said, 'There's a sucker born every minute,' although he didn't make it clear that almost all are born here. At first that bothered me, when we were the Mantecón Brothers and we really strove to present the greatest show on earth—or at least the greatest in Mexico. Now I feel grateful for that. Even a moderately cultured audience wouldn't pay five cents to see the pathetic show in this big top, and even less so now, without my elephant and, it pains me to say it, without the clowns. 'The clown erupted in strident ambiguity, in one essence, madhouse, childhood, confusion, nightmare, and license.' These men with their tufts of hair and their bright red noses are the greatest proof of the existence of such stupidity. Damn the one who opened the doors of the circus to clowns. That degrading move meant that in the midst of deadly and nerve-racking acts, the audience had to relax and laugh. The clowns began as filler, functional people who would kill time while the cages were set up, the wires drawn taut, the pool filled, or whatever. And who would have thought? The people laughed and applauded and enjoyed themselves as much or more than with the other acts, especially the children, the damned kids. You can easily tell which kids will grow into imbeciles: those who roar with laughter the most, who cry out to warn Tufty that Teary is going to kick him in the rear, and who curl up into a ball because they think they are going to be soaked when Teary throws a bucket of confetti at them. That's why I never wanted a child. Just imagining him laughing halfway through the show. . . . 'The children loved him because he burst from a magic candy land. Only his face was tragic, saddened by two crimson tears. Beneath all the dust, he could have been filthy or spic and span, and a teetering but impudent dunce cap crowned his clownly cranium.' We attempted to present a circus without clowns. 'Yes, ladies and gentlemen, the Mantecón Brothers will amaze you and keep you on the edge of your seats, with your hearts about to burst.' That was our idea, a show designed around astonishing, dangerous acts; no nonsense or practical jokes. We soon ended up accepting the fact that people had already grown accustomed to other circuses; they wanted to see their miserable little clowns. The women were always the first ones—they can never stay quiet. They would begin to shout we want clowns, where are the clowns, this is a rip-off, and they weren't speaking for their children, but for themselves. After a while, the uproar would spread. They booed and threw their cushions at us or, even worse, the stands were left empty, the parents no longer brought their little brats to see us. The circus couldn't sink any lower. Why send an expedition to deep Africa to catch lions? Why go to the trouble and expense of bringing a white elephant from Burma? Why spend our lives mastering juggling and balancing acts, stunts and fear, if now the star of the show is a nincompoop with a hat? There are clowns in every cheap circus. There are clowns in every family. Every cocky brother-in-law is a clown. Any unemployed drunk can be a clown; so can people who don't even take care of their appearance because they want to earn sympathy with their shabby clothes, unkempt hair, and their own shitty smell. I'm telling you, one clown kicks another in the ass, and that has greater merit than sticking your head in a tiger's mouth. A laugh-while-crying face draws more applause than juggling six balls while blindfolded. In the flyers, the names of Bengalo the tiger tamer and all the others appear in small black letters; only Teary, Tufty, and Stretch's names appear in big red letters like their noses, and their names are preceded by the caption, MANTECÓN BROTHERS CIRCUS PRESENTS ITS EXCLUSIVE PERFORMERS. Pay attention. Exclusive! I agree that the circus is repetitive; there's nothing new under the big top. But at the same time, nothing is as nonexclusive as the silly clown acts, which have been repeated since the beginning of man, inside and outside of the big top. And do you think I had the energy to fight such stupidity? I wound up accepting the rules of the game. Going to the circus is like going to a museum. 'Look, ladies and gentlemen, that's how people had fun in the old days, when the brain was a nut.' Once again, the thing I fought became a strength. Habit can kill a show that takes pride in being original; on the other hand, the circus, by being repetitive, became a tradition, and people don't question traditions, they simply accept them and live with the idea that they are good if they are religious, tasty if they have to do with food, interesting if they come from Indians, and fun if they

are part of a show. Does tradition dictate that the circus be entertaining and exciting? So let it be, although you and I know that it
is just as boring as other stupid traditions: the flying Papantlas,
the tambora brass band, the Dance of the Viejitos, the crown-
shaped *rosca* for Epiphany, the Guelaguetza. Thank heavens for
the traditions that provide a means of support to the most
anachronistic and repetitive souls in this shitty country. No sir,
people don't want poems, but ditties."

"Ggnt," the pig inhaled, dropping its ears like a sad donkey,
looking at the old man attentively, as if it were really paying
attention.

Rocket *woke up* in the middle of the road with a nagging pain
that felt like a sharp rock in his back. His clothes and hair were
caked with dirt, and he was more tired than when he had gone
to sleep. He could see the others, still sleeping; they were
stretched out on benches, lying on the sidewalk, muddled under
an overhang, and some resting their heads on the bellies of others. He shook his head, disappointed, and went over to Mandrake.

"We're a bunch of losers," he said as he tapped him lightly on
his side. "Worse than animals."

Mandrake opened his eyes and it took a while for him to figure
out where he was and what was poking at his ribs. He stretched
lazily and looked up. Dirt, dust, more dirt, heat, something green
in the background, heat, dirt. It wasn't how he had imagined paradise, but what the hell, it was free.

"Even a dog," Rocket continued, "would have gone inside one
of these houses," and although he wasn't speaking very loudly, in
the middle of so much silence his voice was like a bell tolling.

He saw someone rubbing the sleep from his eyes, someone else looking for a place to urinate. The hot sun was beating down, and it wasn't until Mágala asked what time it was that they realized no one had a watch. There was a clock in the church tower, but it had stopped and had only one hand, which was pointing to eight o'clock, if it was the hour hand, or forty minutes, if it was the minute hand.

"That's right," Mandrake said. "We aren't dogs. That's why we do things in an orderly way."

"That's a lie," Nathaniel refuted. "We're waiting for Don Alejo. We don't dare move an inch without his order."

Hercules raised his fist instinctively, but he was too lazy to speak.

Narcissa smiled. It was almost time to reveal her discovery to everyone. "You fools." She tried to straighten her hair, and she folded her arms in order to take on an air of authority. "Do you know why this town is deserted?"

Mandrake went over to her. How messy she appeared, so unlike that attractive woman on performance nights when she was smiling and looked properly groomed, made up, and had that small silver star on each thigh. Nevertheless, with her short, sequined dress, she was by far the most beautiful woman there.

"We already know," Rocket said. "Yesterday we explored the mine and didn't find anything; you can't keep a town alive like that."

"Then how are we going to make a living?" Harrieta hastened to ask. Narcissa didn't want to mention the lack of water until she had everyone's attention.

"What difference does it make?" Mandrake said. "Do we look like mine workers?"

Nathaniel thought it would be easier to make a living as a

miner without a mine than as a circus performer without an audience.

"Isn't anyone thirsty?" Narcissa asked impatiently, her arms still crossed.

Mágala at once felt the dryness in her mouth. She looked from one side to the other and saw only withered vegetation, especially huisaches as bare as in winter, trees that she imagined to be the giant hand of a half-buried body.

"I'm dying of thirst," she said.

"My knee hurts," Flexor whimpered.

The place seemed to respond to these words as a gust of wind blew up a dust storm, showing the dryness of the earth.

"Those walnut trees have a little green." Harrieta pointed toward the trees on the outskirts of town.

"And that dope, when does he plan to take off his hat and cape?" Nathaniel said, pointing at Mandrake.

"I saw an oyamel in the courtyard of a house," Hercules said. "It's green, too."

Narcissa became impatient. "Green isn't enough to drink and bathe and wash clothes and live properly."

Mandrake feigned a thoughtful pose until he had their attention. Then he ordered everyone to pick a direction and to go and look for water; otherwise, before night fell, they would be on their knees asking Don Alejo for forgiveness, and asking for oranges, and saying please take us to where they'll give us something in exchange for tricks and stunts. Mandrake was surprised that they listened to him, and at once he felt like the leader. The eight headed for the equestrian statue, and from there Mandrake pointed out to each one the direction he should take.

"I've seen that branches are used to find water," Harrieta said.

"If any branch around here knew how to find water," Rocket said, practically to himself, "the trees wouldn't be so dry."

One by one, they set out on their indicated courses, except for Nathaniel, who took only a few steps before sitting down on a bench. That two-bit magician, he thought, is assuming a lot of authority. Don't think I didn't notice his carefully chosen words when he said that we would be on our knees asking Don Alejo for forgiveness. And the idiots were taken in by that rhetoric. "On our knees," he repeated to himself, and without wanting to, he burst out laughing.

He watched them set off, so focused in their task that nobody noticed his small body lying on the bench.

Flexor was limping, not so much because of the pain, but rather, in search of compassion. Rocket was running, eager to be the one who found water first. Nathaniel had slept poorly, leaning against a huisache tree, and that bench felt so comfortable, cooled off by a newly arrived cloud, that it wasn't long before sleep overcame him again. The last thing he saw was a thrush pecking at a patch of moss on the mane of the horse, the only green visible from his position on the bench, aside from the rust on the bronze of the church bell.

Being a circus performer is wonderful. I can't think of a better life. As for remaining in a miserable little town to vegetate as if we were already a bunch of old folks . . . Instead of moving from here to there, traveling all around the country, we choose the passiveness of a place where nothing more exciting than walking around the town square awaits us. Adiós applause, adiós journeys, adiós life. Ah, but how happy everyone will be because now the walls are made of stone and not canvas; homes of our own, big deal, and that idiot Hercules, so happy with his toilet. I imagined life to be much more than sitting down and defecating. Nevertheless, it will do me good to spend a few days here. I have to organize my many ideas and plans. Don Alejo was lying when he said that nobody decides to be a circus performer. What does he think? That twisting your body into a knot is something spontaneous? That one day I woke up with my ankles wrapped around my neck just by chance? The poor guy spends his time thinking about what could have been and wasn't, and so everything looks grim. I always look ahead, and I can see myself as the greatest contortionist in history. I see myself in a Russian or Chinese or English circus, not in the Mantecón pigsty. Naturally, I don't see myself in this town for the rest of my life, wasting away. I'm young, I'm just beginning my career, and I have to envision my future with optimism. I can assure you of one thing: in a hundred or two hundred years, people will still be talking about me. Why? I don't know, I haven't thought it through yet. People don't always go down in history for the vigor with which they perform their jobs. We remember Louis the Fifteenth, once the most powerful man in the world, for his furniture; we remember Pierre Léotard, despite his being the greatest trapeze artist ever, for his leotard. The idea is to give your name to something, like the zeppelin, the newton, Morse code, the *chicuelina*. Edison was very stupid to name his invention the electric lightbulb, incandescent lamp, or whatever it's called. You see, I don't even remember. I can assure you that in a few years, nobody will be talking about him. If I were in his shoes, I'd have named it the 'edisonia,' or something like that. I'm not naïve. I'm aware that no one will remember me for my contortions. That's why I need something else, my own furniture, my own clothes, my own lightbulb, a special dish, or a special way to die, something. I'm not impatient. I still have many years left to think about that something that will make me memorable; and it doesn't matter if it's as Flexor or as Encarnación Ruiz, my name before I met Don Alejo. I am going to invent the flexoro, I'm certain of that, but I still don't know what it is, what it does, or what a flexoro tastes like. I've already thought it over; I'll never use the name Encarnación. Flexor is better, it has a better ring to it and is more memorable. Encarnación is a dumb name. Poor Nathaniel is always talking about his relatives because he knows that nobody is going to remember him. He has been in the circus for only three days, and I bet you even his family has already forgotten about him. Anyway, he is here as a freak and I as an artist. So I don't have the same view as the midget or Harrieta because for me, being a circus performer isn't bad. People come to see me and applaud for me and they surely don't do so only out of compassion, like with those other two. Clearly something draws them and excites them. My father, an accountant, used to laugh at me when I practiced my contortions. 'That's for girls,' he said. 'Not even for faggots, but for girls, plain and simple.' As for his job, when he squares the figures or finds a way to evade taxes, his boss gives him a pat on the back and sometimes promises him a raise. That's all. I can't imagine the day when hundreds of people gather to see how he does his income statements and balance sheets, how he tallies figures and erases mistakes. 'Ladies and gentlemen, boys and girls, from the north of the Republic, a graduate of Civil College, with a degree in public and private accounting, Otiliano Ruiz de la Vega. Let this fearless man amaze you as he spreads out his accounting sheets and writes a number six followed by an eight, followed by a four and then a two; watch as he takes a sip of his coffee that is gradually going cold, and then notice the care with which he puffs on his cigar, adds and subtracts, subtracts and adds. They are well-trained numbers that do exactly what he asks of them, magical numbers. Income disappears and expenses appear, they turn red or black according to the magician's whim; strong, valiant numbers that resist all tax authority.' What a bore. If my work is for girls, his is for idiots, no doubt about it. I chose to do something out of the ordinary, and nothing beats contortions, the complete control of the body by the body itself. You don't need equipment or animals or whips or nets or pins or top hats, nothing. I don't buy that this is for girls, although I do admit that it works better for them. Their movements are more erotic, and when the show ends, there are more contortions in bed than in the circus. On the other hand, we male contortionists are not so attractive, not to women or faggots, I don't know why. Our only advantage is that we can perform all thirty days of the month without risk. As the clothing is worn so tight and it would look bad to see a rag down there, the women have to douche themselves very conscientiously before going out into the ring. Then, at once you realize what is going on, because they appear in black leotards and there are two or three twists that they prefer not to do. Once I saw a pregnant contortionist perform. You have no idea of how disgusting it was. But I don't want to talk about that; I want to talk about my plans."

"Later, my son." Narcissa hugged him and caressed his hair. "Now we have to find water."

Nathaniel *awoke when he* felt a shove that made him fall off the bench. As he had rolled onto his blind side, he didn't understand what was happening, nor did he have the reflexes to put his hands down to break his fall.

"Why are you sleeping, good-for-nothing?" Hercules asked with his hands, as usual, closed into fists.

No doubt about it, Nathaniel thought, not even now, when I am about to get a beating, would I get down on my knees and ask for forgiveness.

"I already went and came back," he lied. "I went all the way beyond that hill and I didn't find a drop of water."

As Hercules was approaching him with his right arm drawn back and his fist threatening, Nathaniel remembered the rust on the church bell and the horse's mane and he was proud that his brain was working so well.

"Some people can't tell the difference between a midget and a mental retard," he said.

"Me either."

"Do you want to become the star of this place?"

Hercules did not respond with words; his eyes said yes, and the tension in his arm relaxed, at least while he ascertained if the midget was thinking of negotiating with gold or beads.

The other six circus performers could now be seen, some closer and some farther away, returning to the square, looking defeated.

"Pick up a rock," Nathaniel said. "A big rock, and beat the horse's head."

Neither Mágala nor Rocket returned empty-handed; she brought a large pile of nuts wrapped in her skirt, and he was carrying several joints and fruits from a prickly pear plant.

"Dinner is ready!" Mágala called out, like a housewife.

When Hercules picked up the rock, it made Nathaniel think of an orangutan picking up a coconut, and when he saw him go over to the statue, he cursed his lack of imagination because now he thought only of an orangutan going over to a horse. Hercules had just begun to hit the statue when Harrieta came running out of nowhere, shrieking:

"You scoundrel! Leave Timoteo alone."

Hercules did not clearly understand what Harrieta was saying, but he understood enough to put more vehemence in his beating. He didn't knock the head off, as he wanted to, because as soon as he had cracked the snout open, the horse began to vomit a thick, earth-colored liquid. With each retch, the liquid became clearer, and everyone looked on anxiously, waiting to see if it would become clear enough that they could stand underneath with an open mouth. The water pressure let up little by little, and by the time the first one of them dared to take a drink, a steady flow, the intensity of which reminded Nathaniel of a donkey urinating, was streaming out.

"It's a miracle," Mágala said.

"It's a damned spring," Mandrake said.

Harrieta insisted that it was neither a miracle nor a spring, but Timoteo de Roncesvalles performing another one of his heroic acts.

Amidst joyful shoving, each one sought his moment to drink and get wet, and afterward to eat nuts and prickly pears. The presence of water drove Flexor to say that now was a good time to hum the waltz *Over the Waves*, and the others turned to stare at him, with looks ranging from harsh to furious. It was a moment in which all happiness came to a halt; but it lasted only a second, because at once they resumed their splashing and joking, and Rocket took advantage of the crowding to paw Narcissa. Nathaniel was the last to join the party. No sooner had he approached than Hercules blocked his way and grabbed him by the hair.

"The horse idea was mine."

The midget nodded as best he could, given the pulling on his hair, and so as to leave no room for doubt, he mumbled, "Of course it was."

Hercules took off all his clothes except for his black tights. He stood directly under the stream so the water would splash him on the top of the head, and there he crossed his arms, making it known that he didn't intend to move from that spot for a long while. Rocket recognized Hercules' need for attention just then, and for lack of a performance that night, and of old maids sitting in the stands rubbing between their legs as the strong man juggled cannonballs, he would try to impress Harrieta, Mágala, Narcissa, and whoever else would let him.

"Look," Rocket said, making fun of Hercules. "He has nipples like an Aztec calendar."

The strong man's body was not athletic but bulky, with an enormous stomach, arms like cellulite-covered legs, a neck that was half neck and half double chin, and an ample, jiggling rear end. At rest, his chest looked soft and droopy, but it rose and became solid as soon as he picked up some weights. He kept his head shaved and had a long, curled mustache. For every show, he dressed in short, tight-fitting garments, especially below the waist, to show one more of his virtues to the women in the stands. That's why Hercules almost never slept in the small tent.

Nathaniel laughed at the joke about the Aztec calendar, even though deep down, seeing that body that was so different from his, he envied and resented Hercules.

The wind stopped blowing, and Don Alejo's mind was put at ease, for he had noticed that the big top was not secure and he had neither the energy nor the desire to tighten the moorings. He climbed up to the top of the stands and sat down. A series of poles, ropes, and nets, not to mention the distance, hindered the view of the ring. I don't know why those who sit here applaud, he thought, if they can't see anything. From way up here, the magician's work becomes very easy and the freak's very difficult. He clapped his hands a couple of times, barely enough to simulate a lukewarm applause. When he got no response, he climbed down to one of the box seats. He made himself comfortable with the arrogance of those who pay to sit there and shouted, "Come on, bastard!"

He clapped a few times again and waited. Everything was just as quiet and still as it was since the wind had stopped blowing. Then he remembered the whistle that he kept in his pocket and blew into it with his old man's breath. Now, at last, the diving pig came out of its hiding place in the wings. First it peered out timidly, then came forward with the firm step of a hog in its sty.

"Turn around," Don Alejo ordered. "Jump."

Nothing. The pig just started sniffing around.

Don Alejo considered the pig the most forgetful of all the circus performers. When they missed practice, the juggler dropped the pins; Mandrake revealed the secret behind his tricks; Flexor needed help untangling his legs from around his neck; and one of the Cabriolé brothers missed on the double deadly jump, only to show the audience that in fact there was nothing deadly about their act. Even though the pig's act did not require any skill, after a few days the animal would forget all about it. It wasn't like the other circus animals that had their tamer or personal trainer; any inexperienced employee could handle leading it to the trampoline. First, a leather harness with a metal hook was fastened around the pig's back. Then it was dressed in a light-blue velveteen robe and led to the base of the main flagpole, where it was hitched to a rope and, with a system of pulleys, hoisted onto the trampoline. The drums sounded, and the announcer spoke of the dangers of the act, the speed at which the pig would hit the water, the small diameter of the pool, about how the slightest breeze or error in calculation would throw it off course, about the many pigs that had met their fate while attempting such a dreadful act, and about the first few rows in the audience that would get wet from the splashing water, if all went well, or from the pig's blood, if something went wrong.

After the drums, the Festival Orchestra would sound its trumpets and then the drums again. The rope was tightened and loosened until the hook was freed, and once at the mercy of gravity, a mechanism controlled from the ground would click into motion, pushing the pig toward the front of the trampoline until it was a free falling object. The animal would kick its legs desperately, as if it wanted to fly, and before it knew what was happening, it was already in the water. That was it. There wasn't much to memorize, since willingly or not, it was dressed up, lifted, put into place and pushed. But if more than three days went by without being hooked up, the pig seemed to forget the pleasant ending of the dive, and once on the trampoline, it would let out horrifying squeals of terror and would fight furiously against the mechanism that was pushing it toward the precipice. The pig's terror would spread to the audience, which would side with the defenseless animal, and people would begin to hurl insults at the closest circus performer. Occasionally the act had to be suspended, at least until the announcer could calm the audience down.

"Jump, sing, do something, animal."

That morning, Don Alejo tried to teach the pig some new tricks. He would say "Turn around" and push the pig around in a circle, or "Stand up," and he would lift it so the creature was standing on its two back legs. These were simple efforts to avoid the reality that his circus could not survive with only a pig, not even if the pig learned to speak. What's more, the experience had shown him that animals don't understand words, only whips, pitchforks, and hot irons. He tried to put the harness and the velveteen outfit on it. He gave up when he realized that he would never be able to lift the pig up onto the diving platform.

Don Alejo felt so disappointed that he didn't even get angry at the animal. He came out of his box seat, and out of mere inertia ordered the pig to jump once more. But the pig just sniffed the ground around it until it found an apple core. It grunted with a happy-looking expression and swallowed the tidbit, dirt, sawdust, and all.

"Eat, my darling."

He didn't know why he had spoken affectionately, but since he already had, he hugged the pig, without objecting to its odor, and he unbuttoned his shirt.

"Come on, boy," he said. "Enjoy me."

The animal's enjoyment consisted of sniffing Don Alejo's armpits, but only for a moment. It soon got bored and moved its exploration to the stands.

"Jackass," Don Alejo reproached it. "I treat you like a superior being and you behave like you want to end up in a slaughter-house."

He showed the pig another apple, this time a shiny, whole one, in order to lure it toward its pen. The pig followed him gracelessly and didn't even complain when Don Alejo locked it up without giving it the fruit. The animal was immediately covered with flies but did not make the slightest effort to scare them off. The old man stood reading the sign: PLEASE KEEP PIG LOCKED UP. His brother had taken that measure because once the animal bit a lady who was walking around looking for Hercules. "We have lions, tigers, and bears," his brother said, annoyed, "and it turns out that none is as ferocious as this shitty little pig."

Don Alejo smiled ironically. There is no way I can call myself a pig tamer. He spit in the direction of the pen, thought about Narcissa for a moment and wondered what time his group would return, because he was sure it would.

Look at this picture. It's me a few years ago. See what a nice build I had. If you compare that face with mine, it's quite apparent that I

[66]

am getting old. With me, it's easy to notice that time has passed. Because I live off my body, I am aware of every wrinkle, of every bulge, of every millimeter that my chest falls, of those veins that no longer pop out on my skin, and of the damned flabbiness that is overtaking me at full speed. That's right. If I had to choose one word to describe myself, it would be 'flabby.' And that is just the word we strong men most fear. Weakness? No. We can always hide that, take weight off the weights, challenge someone from the audience who doesn't look very strong. Strength is the least of it. It's the body that matters. And not the trunk or the arms or the legs or anything is free. Just look at Narcissa. What did she do to get those buttocks? Who did she pray to? Nothing and nobody. She has and will continue to have them for a long time, just because. I have to work out every day, and even so, I can't stay in shape. The fat and the skin are like the sand and the ocean water in those holes on the beach: the more you dig, the less progress you make. You can't maintain your enthusiasm that way, and I'm tired of fighting, I want a life without so much uncertainty, waiting for the boy who will say to me, 'step aside, it's my turn.' I want a normal life, with a house and a toilet where I can forget about everything. I want to become a walrus, a spongy, gelatinous, sprawling being who doesn't have to explain anything to anyone. Maybe you don't understand me because you don't know what it's like to decline. Think about the day when Don Alejo took you down off the cross. Are you different now? Of course not. You are still a horrendous, bearded, hairy woman, and nobody cares any more or any less about you. You provoke the same reaction that you will for the rest of your life. It's not your age that matters, it's your hair. That's your measure. Now I am going to show you another photo so you can compare. It's of Eugene Sandow, the best-built man of all time. Sorry the photo is so faded. I've carried it with me for years. Look at that flat abdomen with its perfect veins. You could play a game of chess on it. And those pectorals of stone; they don't look human, do they? He's a statue in the park for the finest of Sundays, white skin made of white marble, hairless for you to envy, and look closely at that fig leaf that seems to want to rise like a curtain on opening night. I would bet that everything on Sandow was hefty. Do you know how many women since the last century have masturbated looking at this photograph? You have no idea, although if you want, I'll lend it to you one night to see if you can relieve yourself of some of that energy. I wanted to have a photo of myself like this taken, with a fig leaf, but Don Alejo wouldn't allow it. 'This is a circus,' he said, 'not a cabaret,' and I ended up with these black tights. I don't really like to talk about this. Remembering how your body used to be is always a sad process, like counting a fortune that is squandered and inevitably leads to bankruptcy. Are there no means still remaining to me to achieve the rejuvenation that these reminiscences being divulged to a younger companion render the more desirable? The indoor exercises, formerly intermittently practiced, subsequently abandoned, prescribed in Eugene Sandow's *Physical Strength and How to Obtain It* which, designed particularly for commercial men engaged in sedentary occupations, were to be made with mental concentration in front of a mirror so as to bring into play the various families of muscles and produce successively a pleasant relaxation and the most pleasant repristination of juvenile agility. Here there are no mirrors, and I don't have that red-cloth book anymore. Nonetheless, I remember all of the exercises and I think I would do them day after day, a thousand and one times, if I truly believed it would turn back time, if I could recover the excitement of earning applause again, if my vanity had not resigned itself. I was always taller than average, and as a child, I had a build that was muscularly superior, a quality that is not deserving of much praise in this country of puny Indians. That's why I couldn't accept that my assets came only from birth or from nourishment, and I signed up for a correspondence course at Sandow's school; or I should say, I signed up for two, because you know how the mail is, and sometimes I never got the lessons. In fact, I never received lesson number seven, on the thighs and calves, not even with the two chances. From the course, I obtained my bible, the *Sandow System of Physical Training*, with pages packed with photos, although none as good as the one I just showed you. This book gave advice on how to bulk up the muscles. The other promised physical conditioning, a mediocre substitute for youth, something I would say now seems more desirable and imperative to me. Don't you lose hope. Time is on your side. Right now, even with all my flab, there is still a big difference between us. I am still desirable, as you know, but less and less so, and the day will come, I don't know when, that the deterioration will make us equal. Maybe as an old man, I will end up turning into that sprawling, gelatinous walrus, into a monster like you, like the midget, like Don Alejo, and the distance between us will be so small that you and I will be able to share our lives, though it may be only for a short time."

"For the time being, just give me the photo of Sandow," Harrieta said, hiding her eyes.

The fountain continued to fill up until it overflowed. Hidden under the abandoned ground lay a ditch that in other times may have supplied the irrigation channel in the area, distributing water to the houses and gardens. The small stream of mud and floating leaves spilled out into the square. Hercules got tired of showing himself off and left the stream of water, giving someone else the chance to move in. Flexor finally saw his opportunity to wash off his knees.

"Roncesvallesville," Harrieta said. "That would be a good name for our town."

"Don Alejo told us this place is called Sierra Vieja," Nathaniel said.

"Accepting that name," Rocket complained, "would be like admitting that this land isn't ours."

Mandrake agreed and stated that the only way to legitimately take possession of a place was to refound it, renaming the town, its streets, the spring, and reinitiating its history. Harrieta suggested naming it San Timoteo. None of the others agreed, and they began to throw out names, most resorting to their native cities to come up with things like New Mazapil or New Acaponeta. Narcissa wanted to achieve immortality with her proposal of Narcissaland, and the midget was thinking of his relatives when he suggested Bocanegra City or Porcayo City or Olaguíbel City. Finally, among all the names called out simultaneously, one sent them all into a silent meditation that signified an approval: Santa María of the Circus.

Rocket stood up and said, "I hereby found the town of Santa María of the Circus."

Mandrake complained about the absence of historical pretension, saying that there was no moment more important or worthy of remembering than a founding, and that Rocket was wasting it with such a dull pronouncement. He went over to the equestrian statue and, with the water up to his ankles, said:

"By mandate of destiny, which brought us to this spot, and by the seduction of idleness and greed, which held us here, I declare that six men and three women, one of whom deserted and may have died, arrived here from a southern route to colonize these lands and to exploit them to yield benefits of vegetables, metals, stones, art, and ideas. And I chose this place and no other at which to stop our pilgrimage because here we found, just as the legend of our forefathers dictated, the horse that spouts water. Therefore, for lack of a saber, I point to the ground with my finger and say, 'Here,' and declare the Metropolitan City of Santa María of the Circus to be founded."

Still pointing to the ground, he knelt down on the water and bowed his head. Hercules also bowed his head, but in a sign of defeat; it was perfectly clear to him that Mandrake, as founder, had taken command, and his own strength would not be enough to oppose him. That's why he changed his usual boastful attitude and sounded almost shy when he said:

"Well, I liked the one over there." And he pointed to the house with the porcelain toilet. "If you don't mind, I'm going to take it."

Mandrake raised his hand in a signal to stop, and Hercules did not even have the energy to clench his fists.

"Wait," Mandrake said. "There are still things that need to be resolved."

"Like what?"

"We have responsibilities. We just founded a city and at once you think of disappearing inside a house."

"What's wrong with that?" Nathaniel objected. "I'm going to take over a house right now."

"We're all going to do that," Mandrake said, "after we know who we are."

Harrieta yawned. She had grown bored with the matter of founding the town, for which she had lost all interest when she knew it would not be called San Timoteo. Nor was she in the mood for Mandrake's philosophizing on questions of identity after ten years of wandering around from place to place, with an announcer always ready to remind her at every performance that she was no longer Angélica, but Harrieta, the bearded lady.

"I know perfectly well who I am," she said, stroking her beard.

"Me too," Mágala added, just to say something.

"We know who we are in the big top," Mandrake said, "but not in Santa María of the Circus."

No one said a word, and only the sound of the running water could be heard. The puddle had gotten a little bigger and now reached the street, where the dry dirt sucked up more than the horse could spit out.

"I know how to knit," Narcissa said, "but that's all. I don't even know how to cook."

"I used to paint houses," Rocket said, "and all these houses could use a coat of paint."

"Come off it," Hercules cried out in one last attempt to under-mine Mandrake's authority. "Why are you paying attention to this crap?"

There was no one to second him, and for the first time, he thought about the possibility of not getting his porcelain toilet.

"We need to determine what kind of people we are going to be, what the most important jobs are for the survival of our commu-nity."

"That's right," Rocket said. "Everyone should chose the job they want. If there's a conflict, we can resolve it with a vote."

Mandrake was now feeling very sure of himself. He put his hands behind him and walked around the pedestal, his feet splashing with every step.

"There will be no election or vote," he said as he scanned their faces.

Mágala went over to Hercules and whispered, "Now that's a man."

"Chance," Mandrake went on, "is the most powerful force in the world. We all know that. In all democracies, the minority rebels against the will of the majority. On the other hand, where chance is involved, everyone, whether he belongs to the minority or the majority, to the strong or to the weak, accepts whatever he is dealt without a word. If a lottery issues a thousand tickets and there is only one winner, the other nine hundred and ninety-nine will obediently respect the results. In matters of making decisions, chance is God."

There was silence, but Hercules figured it wouldn't last. It wouldn't be long before someone came up with an argument against such nonsense. Chance is God. How nice. Come on, Rocket, say something, think of something. Chance can determine that the toilet won't be mine. He felt a knot in his stomach just imaging Nathaniel on it, his feet dangling in the air. Someone say something. Not only did the silence go on, but little by little all the faces took on expressions of acceptance. Hercules then burst out, "You're wrong," he said, his finger pointing in the air. "In my opinion . . ."

He couldn't think of how to finish his idea. He needed Don Alejo to order him to beat up these troublemakers.

"Mandrake is right," Mágala said. "Nothing is left more to chance than birth, and every mother accepts what she gets." She turned around to point at Nathaniel and continued: "His mother could have given birth to Mozart and instead, she settled for the lizard that came out."

Nathaniel did not object. He was used to comments like that.

"What do you suggest?" Narcissa asked Mandrake.

"That we have a drawing," he responded. "Everyone will write down what they think are the three most important jobs on three slips of paper."

"And then?"

"We'll mix them up, and everyone will pick one."

"And why do we want—" She stopped for a few seconds as she did the mental calculations without coming up with an answer.

"Twenty-four," Mágala interrupted.

"Yes," Narcissa went on. "Why do we need twenty-four slips of paper if we are only going to pick eight?"

"It's a rule of chance," Mandrake replied. "The majority remains out of the game."

"There will be jobs that are lost forever and ever," Harrieta said, wanting to sound poetic, but she got only unfriendly scowls from the others.

Rocket took the promotional flyers out of the mouth of the cannon. If the wind had been favorable and the town inhabited, they would have activated the spring mechanism to fling the flyers into the street, papers that since the Mantecón brothers' separation had promised lies galore, like "the incendiary act of the fire-eater from Palestine," "friendly Ping and Pong will delight young and old," as well as "the perilous acrobatics of the Cabriolé brothers," and the "ferocious animals from distant jungles." They did not lie, however, about the prices. Those would have remained unchanged despite how pathetic the show had become: one peso for box seats, twenty-five cents for the stands, children free except Sundays, since they took in money from them on candy and souvenirs.

Mandrake noticed Hercules' impatience and said, "Some will have very important responsibilities and others will have more modest jobs. These responsibilities will determine whether a person receives a fine house or a modest one."

Quietly and secretly, each one filled out his slips of paper, taking turns with Hercules' autograph pen and solemnly tossing them into Mandrake's top hat.

"What if some jobs are repeated?" Flexor asked.

"In my town, there are a lot of shoe-shine boys and nobody complains."

"With chance, it doesn't matter in what order we pick our papers. We can do it alphabetically, by age, by height, or ladies first," Rocket suggested.

"By seniority," Nathaniel said. "And since I am the newest member of the circus . . ."

He walked over to the hat. He pulled up his sleeve and with a fixed, exaggerated smile, he reached into the hat several times and pulled his hand out without a paper. If this were a performance, he thought, people would laugh. However, at that moment no one was in the mood for humor. He reached in again and pulled out a slip of paper, opened it, and read it to himself.

"Say something, you idiot," Hercules said.

The midget made a sour face.

"Excuse me, my son, that is no way to talk to a priest."

"You, a priest? You, piece of shit?"

"Apologize, Hercules," Mandrake said.

"Yeah, ask for forgiveness," Mágala said.

Hercules laughed nervously, in disbelief. Nevertheless, everyone seemed to be taking the matter very seriously. They looked at him sharply, amid a silence that surpassed the authority of a mandate from Don Alejo himself.

"Forgive me, midget."

"Father."

"Forgive me, Father," he said, bowing his head in shame for letting a priest see him almost naked, in his tights.

There was no need to discuss who was next, for everyone knew it was Mágala's turn. She quickly reached in and pulled out the first paper she touched.

"Journalist," she said.

"A relative of mine used to write for *El País*. I should have gotten that one," Harrieta said.

"You're next, Flexor."

Flexor made the most of his turn by complaining in earnest about the pain in his right knee as he hobbled over to the hat. His trembling hand tossed the papers around until it felt what he would later describe as a hapless hunch. His thumb and index finger chose his fate.

"Negro."

"How is that?" Mágala asked.

"It's healthy for every society to have Negroes," Rocket pointed out. "If not, who is going to be responsible for cleaning the latrines and doing all the things nobody else wants to do?"

"Of course," Mandrake agreed. "It's impossible to live in a place where everyone is equal."

"I'll clean my own toilet," Hercules cried out. "I don't need a black man laying his hands on it."

"We can even blame him for a death," Nathaniel added.

"My God," Narcissa said. "I have a black son."

No one commented further, even though underneath that torn yellow leotard was the whitest skin in all Santa María of the Circus.

When Rocket read his slip of paper, his eyes lit up with excitement and he ran to his cannon and hugged it.

"I'm a soldier," he exclaimed.

"And what good does that do us?"

"None," Narcissa said, "but just look at how happy the poor fool is."

Harrieta swayed her hips as she went over to the hat. Her hand in the hat, she glanced at the others. She stroked her beard as she read the paper.

"Doctor," she said, satisfied. "The town surgeon."

"I need some ointment for my leg," Flexor said.

"Do I have to treat Negroes?"

Nathaniel remembered the pain in his chest from the previous day and was happy to have a doctor nearby.

"How long do horses live?" he asked.

Narcissa pulled out a paper and, without looking, handed it to Mandrake.

"I don't care," she said. "After all, I don't know how to do anything."

"Knife-grinder," Mandrake read and then added, "How stupid. What do we need a knife-grinder for?"

"On the street where I used to live," Flexor said, "a knife-grinder, a secondhand clothing dealer, and a sweet-potato seller would all come by."

"You had to be a Negro," Mandrake said. "I only hope that neither Hercules nor I pick one of your other two jobs, because we'll give you a good beating."

"Those three jobs lend the most charm to a town, because the knife-grinder plays a panpipe, the secondhand dealer plays bells, and the sweet-potato seller blows a steam whistle, almost like a train."

"What's a panpipe?" Narcissa asked.

Mandrake had reached his hand into the hat countless times to pull out rabbits, cards, unending handkerchiefs, and flowers. In a fit of conscientiousness, he let the slip of paper that he had hidden in his sleeve fall to the bottom of the hat. Now he would pull out his own life from the top hat just like any mortal. He wished with all his might to be able to pick that paper, betray all that he had said about chance, but the clips were all folded and looked alike in the darkness of the black hat, and he couldn't distinguish the one on which he had written "Mayor," and he gave himself up to fate with his eyes closed.

"What does it say?" someone asked.

He unfolded the paper clumsily. "Peasant," he said, furious, and then added, "Don't we already have the Negro for that?"

"Of course," Rocket said. "Just take over some land and you'll go from peasant to tenant farmer or landowner. I," he added, "have already promoted myself to general."

"Then I can become a bishop?" Nathaniel asked.

"I suppose we all have the right to move up," Rocket said. "Except him," and he pointed at Flexor.

Hercules was the last one, and there were still seventeen jobs waiting in the hat. He stuck his thick, clumsy hand in the hat and fiddled with the papers, missing the suspense-filled music of the Festival Orchestra. When he finally pulled his hand out, he was holding two slips of paper.

"Put them back and pick another one," Mágala said.

Mandrake, overexcited, cried out, "No!" He could tell that neither slip was the one containing "Mayor," and he didn't want to risk giving him a second chance. He calmed down and went on: "Choose one of the two."

Hercules looked at the two slips of paper in the palm of his hand. One was bigger, more wrinkled, and dirtier. Neither had any physical trait that could suggest the content or the correct decision. He finally chose the large, dirty, wrinkled one, characteristics, he thought indicated that a man had written it, and since he also thought that women were imbeciles, only God knew what jobs they would come up with.

"This one." He triumphantly held up one of the slips of paper and threw the other one on the ground. He read it, his eyes bulging. His hands were trembling, and his heart sank. "This is a joke, right?"

"What does it say?" Mandrake insisted.

"It's a joke."

"No, it's not."

"Tell us what the paper says," Narcissa shrieked.

"Yes, it has to be a joke."

Everyone drew closer to Hercules, curious to see a man always so proud now hesitant and trembling. The midget stretched out his hand.

"In the name of God, I order you to hand me that paper."

Hercules handed it to the priest who, in all his smallness, announced, "He's a whore."

My uncle used to tell me that the only news worth reading were news of crimes and blood. Pay attention; I know something about this. He would say there's no difference between political news and wash-house gossip, because in politics no reporter refers to the facts but rather to so and so said, and Mr. X mentioned. On the other hand, talking about a murdered woman is a visible, tangible, odorous thing; the blood, the dressed or naked body, the calm or horrified expression, the dagger or the blows or the bullet or the machete, the bashed-in head, the stomach slit open, the badly bruised face, or that feeling that nothing happened here, of a corpse sleeping. I don't know what kind of news there might be in Santa María of the Circus; let's hope just wash-house bantering. But don't discount the possibility of a crime being covered up or an accidental death. The latter is better still because you don't need to speculate on motives or who's to blame. As for that kind of story, my uncle told me that sometimes they made them up. Cut in half by trains, crushed in a landslide, buried in mines, like the lying midget talked about, drowned in rivers, you name it. So if when closing an edition of the newspaper, there was still blank space, the editor might say, 'I need a four-hundred-word accident.' And since they used ordinary, run-of-the-mill names, no reader would bother to check the facts. Once they even tried it with a murder: a guy was killed by blows from a machete on a local road. The incident ended badly, however, and two suspected murderers were executed. You don't know about that. Those were the days of Don Porfirio, when executions were carried out first and questions asked later. They were a couple of troublemakers, they said, whom they were going to kill anyway. Regardless, the newspaper then prohibited the making up of crime stories. My favorite news stories have to do with trains, from the bridge that collapses or the head-on collisions where more than a hundred die, to the poor guy split in two or more pieces. Can you imagine anything more horrifying? That's why I don't understand executions by firing squad or hangings. If you've already made the decision to execute someone, to punish him, put him on the train tracks. He won't be able to behave honorably, like standing erect to take the shots or preparing some last words before the neck snaps, not even by smoking a cigarette with a steady hand. There is no sense of dignity when lying across the train tracks with feet and hands tied. You would watch him struggle, gasp, yell, shriek like a cat as he hears the screeching of the wheels coming closer and closer. Of course I am telling you all this as if I agreed with executions, but I was taught that that is something for divine justice and that He is always fair, even though I may not understand why He gives so much to someone like Narcissa and to me . . . oh well, what can you do. A priest once told me that my mission on earth was to make others grateful for not being like me. If that is true, I should be compensated—one hair less for every grateful soul. It follows then that the midget would have the same mission as me. He is burdened with a thousand complexes because of his height, and he makes up magnificent stories about his nonexistent ancestors. He thinks he can compensate for the smallness of his body with the bigness of his spirit. That's why he pretends not to be bothered by his blind eye and even showed me the useless eyeball under his eyelid. But nevertheless, he overlooks his worst defect, for it is not his body or his eye or his lies or his pretentiousness. Did you see his hands? It disgusts me to imagine them touching me; tiny, pitiable, dark, weak, childlike, thin, mousy, with stumpy palms, like a fat lady's, and stubby, miniscule nails. At least he doesn't wear rings. That would be like putting silk on a sow. He'd be better off putting them on the train tracks. A stump is less disgusting. You're a woman, surely you feel the same repugnance I do. Again, I can't think of a better method of amputation than the wheels of a train, sharp like a carpenter's saw. For if I spoke of the train as a form of carrying out justice, now, as a doctor, I believe that medicine can also benefit from this. I remember well an article my uncle wrote: 'The México-Querértaro train cut down a life in its way; and *cut* is not a metaphor but the exact word, since this morning four chunks of what had once been her husband were delivered to Mrs. Esperanza Salgado, like pieces of a macabre jigsaw puzzle.' Do you see? A political article could never be so beautiful, or an article about any other type of accident, for that matter. However, my uncle assured me that in the future, photographers would take on greater importance in newspapers by filling them with images that are going to be much more important than the text. That is why he stopped writing about blood and switched to political gossip. 'Text will survive there,' he explained to me. 'You have to write every word of what Mister so and so said and Mister somebody-or-other mentioned.' On the other hand, a crime will be covered purely with photographs, and the text will most likely be limited to the headline or to the captions of the photos, like, 'Notice the cut on the neck.' I am telling you this as a warning, even though here in Santa María of the Circus, there is no way to take a photograph. I am also telling you this to make you see that the responsibility may be too much for you. Maybe we could make a switch—I give you my title of doctor, and you let me write the newspaper. What do you think? It would be called *El País*. What do you say?"

"I think your uncle is very stupid," Mágala said, "if he thinks that four pieces are enough to assemble a jigsaw puzzle."

Despite its pretentious name, the Metropolitan City of Santa María of the Circus was barely more than a "makeshift town with about twenty houses," in the words of Harrieta, built about a hundred years ago. But nobody was interested in how old the houses were, just how long they had been abandoned. All eight of the troupe had accepted the explanation that the exhaustion of the mine had prompted the exodus, and no longer did anyone believe that along the route toward the big top there could exist a mineral vein that would make them all rich. What's more, no one had chosen a slip of paper with the job of miner on it. Except for Nathaniel, the others wound up agreeing that the statue was of Timoteo de Roncesvalles, just as Harrieta had insisted, and that his words, "My life for your honor," had been directed to a lady and not to a piece of land. Mandrake realized that they would need to spend one or two years isolated from the rest of the world so that no one would question the way in which they had taken possession of the town, and after that time, the laws would recognize them as the owners of all that was there.

"And how do you know that?" Mágala asked.

The houses were more or less of the same size and design. The only evidence of individual taste lay in a few details on the façades, like moldings, splays, or batters, which on some houses were rounded and on others straight, sometimes simple and sometimes ornate. There were no arguments as to which had belonged to someone important or which one might have served as the government building. They were all built with an access in the center that was blocked by thick doors with latches and bars. At each extreme of the façade there was a window that rose from the ground, stopping one meter below the roof. The windows, without glass, had shutters of carved, rotted wood and were surely all made by the same cabinetmaker; they were protected by crude iron bars, a blacksmith's work barely good enough for a prison. The only façade with marked differences belonged to the second house facing west. This one was more damaged than the others, as if it had been shot at or stoned. On the upper part of the door and window frames there were marks from soot, and everything of wood was now charred. Likewise, with crude strokes in a red color that had faded over time, the numbers 1, 2, and 3 were written above the entrance.

The church escaped this symmetry and uniformity. It stood, modestly, on the other side of the square, toward where Timoteo's sword pointed. It reflected the simplicity and poverty of a sixteenth-century mission. Its walls and tower looked like they were made of melting mud. Only the stopped clock with Arabic numerals on the face testified to some modernity, and therefore looked like an intruder. Nathaniel pulled hard on the latch on the front door. He couldn't budge it, and he signaled to Harrieta to come and help him.

"If it weren't for the bell tower," she said, "no one would know this is a church."

"You're right, my child," Nathaniel said, not realizing that Harrieta was playing on the joke of *If it weren't for my height* . . .

By pulling and pushing, the door gave little by little until something began to creak. With a bit more effort, the bolt gave way. The nave was almost empty, except for four benches, a confessional that looked like an armoire, a couple of kneelers, and a limestone altar with no greater pretense than to serve as a table during the religious service. Not even a crucifix or a statue of a saint or a stained-glass window of the Virgin.

"You must have very little faith to build a church like this."

"More than I have left," Harrieta added before she went off.

Nathaniel noticed that in the best tradition of cathedrals, the four walls magnified the echo of his steps. According to him, this was the signal to wake up the priest in the confessional; the resounding quality of these buildings was meant to inform the entire congregation of who sneezed, coughed, or was whispering. That, Nathaniel thought, and nothing else, because I have never set foot in a cathedral where the organ works or where a chorus sings. He knelt down on one of the kneelers and tried to say a prayer.

"*Homo homini,*" he began, and he stopped at once. "To hell with it."

Although he was satisfied with his slip of paper, and even considered himself to be the luckiest one in town, he wasn't born to pray, and even less to clean that dirt-covered church. He stood up and wondered if, as a priest, he had the right to demand that the faithful come to sweep, mop, and clean. He went over to the door and leaned against it, waiting for the first Christian. He saw Narcissa in the distance, whistling, pretending to play a panpipe and asking at the top of her lungs if anyone had knives to sharpen.

Mandrake *searched the outskirts* of Santa María of the Circus. He found no fruit trees or anything edible to prevent them from starving to death except for the walnut trees, the prickly pears, and a straight line of magueys that marked the boundary of God knows what. He did not accept his position as peasant and had immediately promoted himself to landowner, and in that capacity, he called Rocket.

"If we keep eating prickly pears," he explained, "and we cook them with nut oil, in less than ten days we'll grow intestines that bypass the stomach and go directly from our mouths to our asses."

Rocket turned to one side and then to the other, as if he were keeping an eye on something. He became aware of his behavior and at once adopted a more formal demeanor. Sometimes he betrayed himself by behaving like a corporal. Other times he would lie down on a bench thinking only of having a pair of black boots and a lot of soldiers to give orders to. He would spend the rest of his time with his cannon, polishing it and making sure no one touched it. Deep down, he thought: my real vocation is to be an artilleryman.

"And what do you suggest we do?" he asked.

"You should go back to the big top and steal all the fruit, good, bad, rotten, or bitten. I need the seeds, and we have to eat something while they grow."

"Why me?" Rocket asked. Since the answer was so obvious, Mandrake said nothing. "All right," Rocket said. "But I don't want to go alone."

"Take Flexor with you," Mandrake suggested.

"Blacks are deserters," Rocket said. "That's why they are not even recruited as cannon fodder."

"Well, pick whoever you want. I suppose you have the right to levy troops."

Mágala was the chosen one. At first she was excited, but then they explained to her that she wasn't going as a war correspondent, but as a recruit under Rocket's command. Even so, she decided to take her paper and the pen for signing autographs with her.

"They're always handy," she said, "even if it's to write a military dispatch."

They left well after nightfall. They had agreed on this because Don Alejo would surely be asleep and the difficulty of the mission would lie only in making as little noise as possible and in groping their way in the dark. They said good-bye to those who had gathered in the square, and they were heading off, certain that they would return in a couple of hours, if everything went as planned and, in Rocket's words, "If we don't have to eliminate the enemy," when they heard Hercules' voice: "Don't forget the pig."

Those left behind saw them disappear into the darkness, although they could still hear the footsteps and the whisper of their voices. Harrieta waved a useless good-bye. Flexor was the only one who had not come to the square. He had spent the afternoon sweeping the doorways of the houses, using some dried branches for a broom. Being a Negro was extremely tiring, especially because his leg wasn't working as it should. So early that night he had gone inside the house he shared with Narcissa and had begun to snore in less than a minute, without even noticing the smell and sickly color of his knee.

"Good," Mandrake said. "Now go and mind your own business," and he clapped a few times and waved his hands, breaking up the meeting.

"Just a minute," Narcissa said. "I need to ask the midget something."

Nathaniel was moved, knowing that Narcissa needed him. He took on a judicious air, frowning and tilting his head to the right.

"Yes, my child."

"Father, I don't know if it's because of the way I was raised, but the truth is that it's very hard for me to live next to one of those," and she pointed at Hercules.

"What's wrong with that idiot?" Hercules burst out.

"And how were you raised, my child?" Nathaniel smiled to himself.

"My father's sister was like that. That's why they never invited her to the house. They said that you could catch it, like a disease."

"I see," Nathaniel said.

Hercules told himself that it was the darkness. If they were able to look me in the eye, no one would dare treat me with such contempt. Harrieta saw, with pleasure, the chance to get revenge for past rebuffs.

"Over there, on the outskirts of town," she pointed toward the west, parodying Timoteo and his sword, "you can build a shack. It's good for businesses like Hercules' to operate far from the city."

Nathaniel, taking on a fraternal air, went over to Hercules to put his hand on his shoulder, but his hand reached only to the top of his belly.

"Look, Herculina—" He stopped right there because his survival instincts warned him that a fist was coming his way at full speed. He managed to duck and felt only the gust of wind. Bastard, he thought, a priest deserves more respect. He chose to stay

quiet, promising himself not to mention the shack on the outskirts of town and never dare to call him by that name.

Hercules blurted out a series of muddled and incoherent comments that made perfectly clear how angry he was. He left, grunt-
ing like a bull, resigning himself to seek comfort in his porcelain
bowl.

Nathaniel went over to Mandrake and whispered:

"I wrote that slip of paper. I was hoping Narcissa would pick it."

"Don't let Hercules find out or he'll kill you."

The midget nodded in agreement, sorry for having spoken. He
should be the one receiving confessions, but instead, he ran off at
the mouth the first chance he got.

"And don't let Narcissa find out," he said, "because she'll kill
me, too."

The midget's stories about his ancestors don't seem like nonsense
to me. True or not, it's important to have stories—they are what
give us the right to walk the earth and have a name. According to
Mandrake, if we live in Santa María of the Circus for a year or
two, everything will become ours. I don't know where he got that
idea. Whether we reveal how we took possession of these houses
tomorrow or in ten years, not only will we be kicked out of town,
but we'll be thrown in jail for being thieves, too. Maybe there was
a time when a bunch of Indians could find an eagle devouring a
snake and say, "Here, we'll stay here to grow and multiply." But
today every piece of land has an owner; even this piece of desert
is registered in a judge's office with signatures, seals, and stamps.
Today people would welcome those Indians from Aztlán with
bullets, with no respect for their gods' prophecies. We need to
establish the right to be the legitimate owners of Santa María of

the Circus, and for that we need a history, with illustrious people and heroic deeds. The job thing was okay. You have to work in a town, even if it's in lowly things like sharpening knives, but we also have to take charge of our past. If Harrieta wants to call the man in the statue Timoteo de Roncesvalles, she needs to tell us who that person was, where he fought, what position he held, why he is important for our people, and all those personal details that give substance to a man, like if his dog accompanied him into battle, if he crossed himself before each shot, if he had lost his left thumb and, you know, silly things like if he had one or one hundred women, and if his horse ever saved his life. As a journalist, I can cover the daily news, and at the same time, I can document our history. I can ask Mandrake to repeat the words he spoke at the town's founding, say that it happened three hundred years ago, and attribute the founding to a fine Spanish soldier who later died at the stake for practicing Judaism. I would talk about the great catastrophes, because all towns have hurricanes, earthquakes, fires, or plagues, stories worth passing on from generation to generation, and I would create our legends, like the one about the traveling circus that every August eighth, the day on which the beasts devoured the beautiful Penelope, makes a nocturnal parade of lost souls. Everything will be in writing, since only the written word has the weight of truth. What do you think? If a foreigner were to arrive right now, it would take him less than half a minute to realize that we are a bunch of phonies. When is the patron saint's day? What road leads to Mazapil? How far is it? What is the traditional dish? Where can I have a drink? Who's in charge here? What street is this? What time is mass? What do you do on Sundays? Why is there no bandstand in the town square? The most common questions asked by a traveler will make us look like idiots and mutter I don't know, I don't know, and we will end up killing him to make sure he doesn't give us away. It is our obligation to know this place as if our families have lived here for generations. Yes sir, my grandparents arrrived when the mine was spitting out silver. Yes ma'am, this used to be an orchard. The men were men. And to have a great history, it doesn't matter that Santa María of the Circus is a miserable little hamlet, since in a similar fashion, Nathaniel, despite his insignificance, boasts of a magnificent past. It must be a formidable task to carry in your blood the death of a hundred and twenty-three Christians. Tell me who in our day can pride himself on that. If no one helps me, I am going to entrust most of our past to the midget, since it seems only he has one. We also need to work on the town's heraldry. We need a coat of arms, maybe with the Virgin of Guadalupe wearing a clown hat on the tightrope, Our Lady of the Circus bestowing her blessing upon elephants, lions, and horses, and with Latin words that say *panem et circences.* You don't look very enthusiastic about my idea. Come up with something else or I'm going to design and distribute the coat of arms, and that will be enough to make it official. If it will make you happy, I can put your cannon in the background. What do you think? Just like you promoted yourself from corporal to general, and Mandrake promoted himself from peasant to landowner, I can make myself an historian, without, of course, neglecting my job as journalist. In that way, I can write for the present and for posterity. It sounds good, doesn't it? Many years after I die, people will be able to read my *Brief History of Santa María of the Circus, From Its Foundation to Our Time.* I am open to other ideas, but I will publish only what I think is suitable and what I like. Now I understand why Harrieta wanted my job and why she insisted on bragging to the midget about her uncle who wrote for *El País.* I am beginning to sense how important I am. I can accuse

Nathaniel of being a promiscuous priest, Hercules of having syphilis, Narcissa of carrying Don Alejo's child, Mandrake of speculating on the crops—I don't know, whatever skulduggery that pops into my head. I have in my hands the most powerful weapon with which to attack . . . although the most useless for defending myself."

"You might be right about everything," Rocket said, "except for putting a clown hat on the Virgin."

Luckily for Don Alejo, our mission is only to steal fruit and kidnap a pig—a very small task for the army of Santa María of the Circus. Had we been ordered to completely destroy the enemy, we would have positioned my cannon on this hill, and with a single discharge, our mission would be completed. That is the ultimate proof of an artilleryman: a target, a shot, all or nothing. Most people shoot willy-nilly, and a stroke of luck is enough to shower oneself with glory. That is possible only when the enemy is numerous and dispersed. Then, no matter where you shoot, you can be sure of taking down more than one opponent, military or civilian, it doesn't matter. By wiping out those who are armed, you diminish the opponent's strength; by targeting women and children, you crush your foe's morale. That is why bombardments from boats are so effective. The Yankees and the French proved this to us. They needed only a few little boats in the port of Veracruz to subdue the entire country. We never sank one, but they, in return, demolished the city. In the old days, when generals put more trust in valor than in marksmanship, they would have sent an aquatic Pípila to sink, one by one, all the boats anchored opposite our ports. With today's strategies, what use is the strongest, bravest, and best-prepared soldier if he is crouched down behind a parapet waiting for some coward to blow his brains out? Now the art of war is developed on a desk, with scientists who have never even set foot on a battlefield, mathematicians talking about action, reaction, the force of gravity, parabolas, distance, and coordinates. And that is how they are putting an end to the virility of war. The way things are going, don't be surprised if the recruits are all queers. What could be more attractive than a long trip with a bunch of guys who get their jollies by being close together in a trench? Or worse still, in a few years, instead of facing off against the enemy, each army will commission its intellectuals to meet with those of the opposing side. They will do some calculations, take stock of the situation, apply some theories of probability, and determine, without a single death, who is the victor and who the defeated, leaving no room for bluffing, which even in a game of poker is a valuable recourse. I call the bluff, and the secrets are out. Look at the proliferation of military academies. How ridiculous. What we really need are academies for those with no balls. Adiós to the days when to kill the enemy, you had to look him in the eye. We live in an age of artillery. Now the one with the biggest cannon and the deepest trench wins. We exchanged strength and bravado for the ability to aim and crouch down, like the boy who throws a stone and then hides. Do I like this? No, but I can make the most of it. You are so sure that as a journalist, you possess a powerful weapon, and the truth is quite different. In Santa María of the Circus, there are only three weapons: stones, fists, and my cannon. It goes without saying who rules the roost. We can curse the German priest who invented the cannon, because he wound up screwing countries like ours: a world power when it comes to balls, a calamity when it comes to warfare gadgets. You need only see the huge epic battles we mount when Mexicans fight against

Mexicans, and the ease with which we give in when a foreign enemy desecrates us. And these guys are no geniuses. In fact, there is nothing quite as crass as seeing Yankees against Yankees. War strategy never fell so low as in their Civil War. It was all about marching like in a parade and firing every time the commanding officer lowered his sword and, without fail, on each side, the stupid, defenseless guy with the flag raised high, making himself the easiest target. The rules were clear: the first to break ranks would lose, because then the conflict would turn into a shameless rabbit hunt. The Chinese, on the other hand, were very smart. Although they had gunpowder thousands of years ago, they used it only to shoot off fireworks. That's why it's stupid to include the Niño Artillero among our national heroes in books, streets, monuments, and homages. What did the little angel do? Light a fuse like one who lights a firecracker? Kill a guy? He didn't even load or aim a weapon. I light a fuse at every performance, and I load and aim and prepare my own gunpowder with the exact amounts of coal, sulfur, and saltpeter, and I don't turn my back or cover my ears like some good-for-nothing artilleryman at the moment of detonation. No sir, I stick myself in that cylinder at the risk of death by explosion or burning or smashing flat into a pole. I truly risk my life, and even so, Don Alejo has the nerve to say that my act needs a dose of danger, like flying over men and horses, hoops and garters, and lastly through a hogshead of real fire. Nice. The world has to understand that I am no cowardly artilleryman. I am the human cannonball, the object of destruction, the one who looks into the eyes of the enemy before exterminating him. I have more than enough guts, and when I decide to aim this cannon at all of you, I will be the master of Santa María of the Circus. I don't like to admit it, but I would prefer to conquer you all with the sword. I didn't make up the rules. After all, I have a

powerful cannon that is eighteen inches in diameter and classi-
fied as heavy artillery, superheavy I would say. Do you know how
much an iron cannonball that size weighs? Almost four hundred
kilos. Not even Hercules can pick it up. I can use the entire city
as my bowling alley. The world should be thankful that I am a
peaceful man, with no ambition for power."

"Stop exaggerating," Mágala said. "Your cannon is a toy," and
Rocket lowered his head, angry and hurt.

In *the darkness* of the waning moon, without the sounds of conversation or the snorts of animals and, of course, without music or
applause or that stupid cry from the audience when a dangerous
act was being performed, the big top was now just a great big bubble about to burst. At least that is what Mágala thought, and she
was so satisfied with her idea that she decided to write about it as
soon as she had time and the light of day.

As for Rocket, he was beginning to regret having Mágala as his
companion for this adventure. When he chose her, the mission
had consisted only of stealing some fruit, but now, in addition,
they had to kidnap the pig.

"Are you ready?" he asked, out of obligation.

She nodded.

They were able to walk stealthily without having to take any
special precautions, as the ground was completely dry and cleared
of branches that could crack at the slightest slip of the foot.
According to Rocket's plan, they would begin by locating Don
Alejo to make sure he was asleep. Then they would go to the big
top to look for the fruit. Afterward they would rummage through
the garbage to find more seeds and, lastly, they would steal the
pig, and this way, if it began to squeal, it would be too late for
Don Alejo to do anything about it.

As they were heading for the small tent, Rocket stopped and whispered, "Kiss me."

Mágala, surprised, yet pleased, responded with a smile.

"What for?"

Haltingly, Rocket explained that it was a sign of camaraderie, a military tradition to ensure the good outcome of their under-taking. Now Mágala's smile was of pleasure only, and Rocket was the surprised one when she hugged him and searched for his mouth patiently, waiting for him to bend his knees a little so their mouths would be even. Then she applied an intense suction and shot her tongue into his mouth two or three times with the quickness and range of a chameleon. It all happened so fast that Rocket's excitement was caused not by the kiss, but by the mem-ory of it.

"Done," Mágala said. "I guess now everything will turn out all right?"

Rocket nodded, convinced that Mágala had always lied about her age.

There was no one in the small tent. The white, dirty, empty, canvas cots lent the place the feel of a hospital after an epidemic that had wiped out all the patients. As they were not prepared to deviate from the original plan, they blamed their poor night vision and gently felt their way from cot to cot, with touches incapable of waking up the old man, fearful of contact with his flaccid, naked body. Mágala recognized her own cot and com-pared its softness to the bed of rocks on which she had slept the night before.

"I want to take it with me," she said.

Rocket's only response was to raise a finger to his lips for her to be quiet. She drew the curtain that separated the men's area from the women's and laid down on her cot, satisfied, with a strong urge to rest for a few minutes. The smell of the place filled her with sadness. Even though she was happy not to have to sleep there anymore, she pledged never to forget that aroma, a mixture of sawdust, urine, stuffiness, makeup, and sweat.

"Let's go," Rocket whispered as he tugged on her arm.

"I don't want to follow your orders," Mágala complained. "Especially after listening to your stupid ideas on war."

From there, they went over to the big top, trying to be much more careful now, because at this point they assumed that Don Alejo was awake.

They stuck their heads inside to take a look. Their eyes were at once caught by a couple of lit candles in the center of the ring. Don Alejo, shirtless, shoeless, and inert, was sprawled between the two candles, which, judging from the dripping wax, had been burning for several hours. The pig, with its velveteen robe, was doing laps around the ring, as if it were one of those horses with plaited manes on which Narcissa would stand to show off her well-formed ass. A minute later, the pig walked over to the inert, pale body of Don Alejo. It sniffed at him for a moment and then began to lick Don Alejo's chest with relish.

"How awful," Mágala said when she had had enough of the scene. "It's going to eat him." And when Rocket ordered her to be quiet, she responded, "He can't hear us anymore. You can see he's dead from a mile away."

Rocket slowly walked over to the body, dragging his feet and without turning his back to the exit to facilitate his escape should Don Alejo move. He wanted to throw in the towel and go back to Santa María of the Circus, but the idea of being obligated to justify his cowardice made him keep going. Mágala urged him on from the entrance, and he gave in to her. When he had reached the edge of the ring, he kicked his leg into the air to scare away the pig, who was still delighting in Don Alejo's chest. The animal stepped aside and stood waiting. Rocket walked over to Don

Alejo and looked at him close up. The expression on the old man's face disgusted him, an expression that could have been either of fear or of pleasure. Rocket looked down to begin his examination of the body with the feet; the pants were the same black gabardine ones Don Alejo always wore, with the button missing and the fly half-zipped. The stomach and chest, soaked with the animal's saliva, reflected the flickering light of the candles, giving the impression that his torso was trembling. The right nipple looked especially abused and emitted a trickle of blood that ran down his side without reaching the sawdust on the ground.

Rocket didn't dare move any closer to take his pulse or to check if he was breathing. Instead, he chose a method that, according to a relative of his who was a doctor, was used during the war when they had to immediately distinguish the living from the dead on the battlefields. He reached for the pole made from ocote wood that was used for hitting the elephants and pushed it down on Don Alejo's genitals, first gently and then more intensely, as if trying to stuff them inside his body. Finally, and with more confidence, he landed a forceful blow to them, which had the added benefit of allowing him to avenge some built-up resentment. Rocket was convinced, and he crossed himself as he looked with horror at the old man's vacant eyes, rolled back into his head.

"He's not only dead," he said, "but he looks like a dead blind man."

Mágala let out a slight groan and took off running. Rocket became furious and went after her as fast as he could.

In the darkness, he was able to see her running clumsily. She was wobbling too much and not planting her feet firmly. He knew it was only a matter of seconds before she would fall.

"Mágala," Rocket yelled, annoyed.

If only she would run toward the town, he thought, because then he would have an excuse to go back. But she was going in the opposite direction, toward the mine. Rocket sped up and quickly closed the distance until he caught up to her. He grabbed her hair and with one pull, stopped her in her tracks. He felt tricked. Judging by Mágala's reaction, she had obviously lied when she had said, "You can see he's dead from a mile away."

"I risked my neck because of you." His eyes revealed his extreme anger.

"Stop exaggerating," she said, catching her breath. "You chose a little slip of paper making you a soldier, and now you believe you're risking your life at every moment."

Rocket still had her by the hair and took advantage to give it another yank.

"Shut up," he said.

"You're a coward," Mágala said. "I was frightened when I realized Don Alejo was dead. You, however, were afraid when you thought he was alive." Then she feigned a laugh to make her words even more humiliating. "Afraid of a decrepit old man; shame on you," and she relaxed, preparing to receive more tugs on her hair.

Rocket let her go and pointed toward the big top with his chin. They were much closer than he had thought. They must have run very slowly, as if under water. Although they didn't talk about it, each one had his own version of how Don Alejo had died. For Mágala, it seemed quite natural that an old man, alone, without his circus, his brother, or any other dreams than those of the night, would release himself from life. For Rocket, who was already familiar with the pig's fierceness, there was no doubt: the pig, starving to death, had sucked the life out of him through his nipple.

"Let's go," he said. "We have things to do," and as they were returning to the big top, he wished with all his heart for another kiss from Mágala.

She seemed to read his mind, because she said, "In your dreams."

When they entered the big top, they saw the pig licking Don Alejo again. Rocket picked up a rope and tied the animal to the flagpole, mindful of its reaction and very attuned to where the ocote pole was, in case he needed it to defend himself from an attack.

"Damned animal," he said.

Mágala immediately headed for the large chest where the fruit was kept. She counted about fifty pieces of fruit, which included oranges, pears, sapodilla plums, and a papaya.

"Go look for a sack," she ordered Rocket.

He began to rummage through the magician's props. Inside the box for cutting the girl in half he found a blue sack with yellow stars. Mandrake used it to cover himself up, disappear, and then reappear in another location. Now they used it to stash their booty. Rocket threw it over his shoulder, and the weight caused him to bend over. He regretted not having brought Hercules with him to use as a beast of burden, since Mágala did not have the strength to carry the sack for even a minute.

"And now what?" she asked. "Are we going to leave him there?"

"Do you have a better idea?" Rocket asked.

"We have to bury him," she said. "Or at least cover him up with a sheet."

Rocket felt terribly lazy just thinking about digging a grave, and too disgusted to even think about the texture of Don Alejo's old, stiff flesh.

"Let the big top be his mausoleum."

Mágala untied the animal and glanced one last time at the body. Rocket bowed his head, as if saying good-bye, and then they headed toward the exit. They were about to leave the big top when they heard the unmistakable voice of Don Alejo.

"Don't take the pig," he said, as he rubbed his genitals in obvious pain.

Hercules barred the door of his house after advising everyone not to bother him or to even think about asking to use the toilet. Stretched out on the bed in the total darkness, he couldn't decide whether to close his eyes or leave them open. No sooner did the toilet allow him not to feel like a dog any more than the lack of light turned him into a chicken, forcing him to sleep with the moon and wake with the sun. We can't remain isolated from the world like this, he thought. We have to make contact with some other town. At the very least, we need candles, or a lamp, and if we don't want to look like animals, we need a lot of things: cutlery, towels, soap, clean clothes, toothpicks. Surely we can take Don Alejo's money. It's not much, but it's enough to get started. I hope Rocket thinks of coming back with some money.

He lay on his side, his face pressed up against the wall. His breath bounced back at him in the form of hot, smelly air, and just as he was getting used to the pleasure of so much silence, he heard a few light knocks on the door.

"Who is it?" he asked, wondering whether there really was someone outside or if the knocks had come from his imagination.

"It's Mandrake," a voice whispered. "Open up."

Hercules looked out the window as he finally accepted his new status, unable to command any respect. Just a few minutes ago, he had demanded not to be disturbed; now he hadn't even settled into bed and there was already some idiot knocking at the door.

"Don't even think about asking to use the toilet."

"Don't be stupid."

Hercules shrugged and decided to adopt a more friendly attitude. He removed the bar and stepped aside.

"I'm glad to see you," he said. "I can't sleep and I've been thinking about things."

Mandrake focused hard as the door closed behind him. He could barely make out the enormous silhouette moving awkwardly, dragging its feet and finally sitting down on the bed.

"Ah, yes," he said, disinterested.

"We can't go on like this, isolated from the world," Hercules declared. "There must be a town nearby. We should perform without the big top so we can make some money and buy things."

"That's fine, but we can talk about that later."

Hercules didn't seem to listen. Though lately his muscles did not make him feel so strong in front of Mandrake, being invisible emboldened him to continue his speech.

"Of course we would go to the towns to perform without letting anyone know where we came from. Santa María will always be our secret."

"Yes, of course, yes," Mandrake said as he dried the sweat on his forehead.

"But to begin with," Hercules went on, "we've got to get the old man's money," and as he didn't notice a positive reaction from the magician, he added, "as a loan. Then we would pay him back."

Mandrake was losing his patience, and he looked for a spot on the bed.

"I didn't come here to talk about that."

Hercules was silent, and he felt a warm hand on his leg. The hand was still for a moment and then, timidly, it began to caress his thigh. When Mandrake saw that there was no reaction from Hercules, his hand became seductive, skillful, prestidigitator.

"Better yet, tell me how you ended up like this," Mandrake said.

Hercules struggled to speak. He was repulsed by those fingers, like a plague of ants invading his body.

"You know," he spit out. "I picked the paper."

"Don't spoil the mood," Mandrake told him. "All your kind have an interesting story."

How long, Hercules wondered, am I going to keep up this farce? Is my toilet worth such a high price? He asked himself these rhetorical questions, without making the slightest effort to answer them. He wanted to think of their job draft as a game, but then he recalled Narcissa asking if anyone had knives to sharpen. He thought about kicking his visitor out, but he did not want to think about the consequences. What's more, hadn't he confessed to Harrieta how greatly he was tormented by seeing his body deteriorating and becoming less and less desirable? Wasn't Mandrake offering him vindication, a second wind? Do I need it? Despite my decline, there are still many women in the world who are willing to pay for me. He ended up confused, immersed in complete disinterest, and he lay down on the bed again. I'm not part of this world anymore.

"I was fifteen years old," he began, "and my dreams were like those of any boy—"

"Girl," Mandrake corrected him. "The darkness helps, but I already asked you not to spoil the mood."

"Like those of any girl," Hercules nodded. "With the added difficulty of being too beautiful, too desirable," and he smiled, discreetly, picturing himself fifteen years old and solid as a rock.

"Don't overdo it," Mandrake said, bolder now with his caresses, "even though Narcissa would take your tits any day."

The story went on, with a father who raffled her for bids during town festivals for two pesos a ticket, a raffle without losers, since the unlucky ones were permitted to spy on the winner through holes in the wall.

Mandrake lost himself completely in the fantasy and was only a stiff drink away from believing that he was in fact in the arms of an immensely desirable woman.

In the house next door, Harrieta heard a few peculiar snorts, and even with her ear pressed up against the wall, she could not figure out what was going on. Hercules must feel terribly lonely, she thought, with a hopeful smile on her face. That will make things easier for me.

H*arrieta thinks our* being here is my fault. She says that the Mantecón brothers fought over me, and Don Alejo was willing to hand over the best performers and all of the animals so that he could keep me. It would be very flattering if that were true, but the truth is quite different. It was just a plan the old guys made to get rid of us. You can be sure Don Alejo isn't in the big top right now. What's more, the big top isn't even there anymore. Don Ernesto came by to pick it up and they took everything, including the pig, the only performer among us worth anything. What a surprise Rocket and Mágala are going to get when they don't find anything. It was a good ruse. It's easier to leave eight circus performers in an abandoned town than to have to tell them, one by one, we're so sorry, we won't be needing your services any longer, it was a pleasure having you with us, good luck. And Harrieta, who said that I— She's blind. As if she hadn't figured out that we are the least-applauded performers in the circus. Haven't you wondered why Teary, Tufty, and Stretch went with Don Ernesto? Correction: I do get applause, but a pretty girl can get that anywhere. Even Don Ernesto told me that the audience preferred a bustier woman with a bigger bottom. I'm not surprised. It's not the most refined elements of society that go to the circus. It's a pity I wasn't born with a voice for the opera. Those genteel people would certainly appreciate my beauty over the massive bottoms of the sopranos. Even so, among those unschooled individuals with bad breath who wear their pants above their belly buttons, I have won great acclaim. On the other hand, look at the others: Mandrake has arthritis or something like that, and since he has now lost the agility in his hands, I have to wiggle my rear end to conceal the secrets of his tricks when he pulls flowers out of his hat or aces from his sleeve. Plus, he must have inherited that box for cutting the girl in half from his grandfather, since the Festival Orchestra has to play so loudly to drown out the creaking of the hatches and hinges. The midget might be miniscule compared to normal people, but he is tall compared to other midgets. Poor guy—they just hired him and he's already been kicked out. Harrieta has to see that. If there was a reason for the brothers' fighting, it was Nathaniel. 'You're incompetent,' Don Ernesto must have complained. 'So many nice small midgets and you get this scarecrow.' That's why nobody can come up with a name for him. What do you call such a useless thing? You simply get rid of him, just like they got rid of us. And what could they say to us? 'Thanks for everything, we're going to miss you, here's some money to tide you over until you find another job.' It's the Mantecón brothers' eternal problem: the good performers leave to join better-paying circuses, and the mediocre ones, at least until yesterday, stick around forever. Harrieta stayed with the Mantecón brothers for years despite never convincing the audience.

Some thought her hair was fake, others assumed she was a man. After every show, I was solicited by horny guys with money; Hercules would be hounded by women who were just as horny, but without money. As for Harrieta, she was the perfect solution for closet homosexuals. They could feel like they were in the arms of a man without having to completely compromise their reputation. Idiot that she was, she always refused. Yes, of course I refused too, but it's different with me because I aspire to be something. She has to make do with rotten fruit. That's why for a long time Don Ernesto wanted to kick her out; she was too hairy to pass for a bearded lady. 'We can present her as a *castrato*,' Don Alejo proposed in her defense, because he had become fond of her ever since he had taken her down from the cross. 'Are you crazy?' Don Ernesto objected. 'With that deep voice and that coat of hair, we could promote her as an *implantato*.' For a few days he was excited about the idea, until he realized that in order to present her as such, they would have to show the evidence of the grafted male member in her crotch. I don't know what you think about Rocket, but his act is so boring to me. Anyone jumping on a trampoline looks more spectacular flying in the air than the human cannonball; they even do flips and don't use a helmet, nor do they wrap themselves up in that ridiculous thick red suit with orange lightning bolts. Even Mágala, the most useless of us all, once did a flip in the air before falling into the net. After that, she walked around quite satisfied with herself thanks to that small feat, and she wanted to call herself the fourth Cabriolé. The Mantecón brothers must have grown tired of waiting for that last bit of dignity that would prompt us to offer our resignations, and since now every fool believes he has the right to demand compensation from his boss . . . I don't blame them; you must get rid of deadweight without a second thought, like garbage, like blacks on an overcrowded ship. Forgive me for that, but you know what I mean. Forgive me also for including you in those who are applauded the least. It was you, after all, who spoke to me about the audience's preference for seeing female contortionists. We have to be honest with ourselves: we aren't lucrative for the circus. Look at Hercules. He's more fat man than strong man. The Mantecón brothers know us too well, for Don Alejo was insisting that we follow him back to the big top. Was he so sure we would stay behind? Or maybe there is a traitor among us. Someone subtly seduced us into settling in this town with the promise of a better life, with a house that would always be in the same place and without the smell of animal feces. Did Hercules raise our hopes with the story of the toilet? Or Harrieta with the idea of having our own house? Or Nathaniel with the chance of having a life that measures up to ours? Was it so easy to predict that we would take the bait? I don't deny it. I would love to live under a solid roof, have an address, a place where people can send me letters, a floor that I can sweep. But I don't think it's possible. The idea of staying here in Santa María of the Circus is not feasible; I now see that very clearly, even though it was fun to pretend we were colonizers. I don't want to be the first to suggest that we leave. I can already picture them all accusing me of being a deserter, a coward, a sellout to Don Alejo, and things like that. If no one says anything, you and I can leave as soon as your leg is healed. It's important that we move fast, because at times I think about another possibility: we are part of a new act, and over there, hidden behind the hills, with canvas-covered seats and binoculars, there is an evil audience that paid for an exorbitantly priced ticket just to witness our downfall, watching what we are doing, if we are destroying each other, if we are dying of thirst or of hunger. They have placed bets on who will be the first to fall.

Surely they gave us a polite ovation when we found water. 'They aren't total morons,' they must have said, although perhaps it disappointed them a bit not to see us desperate, our mouths parched, drinking our own urine, and going mad like they say people dying of thirst do. It's extraordinary to witness the effects of thirst, because the soul comes undone, the brain becomes delirious, and the body twitches. Hunger, on the other hand, is quite boring. Not only does it wear out the spectator's patience, but it looks no different than intense fatigue or a casual sleep from which you never wake. For that reason, they are not going to be satisfied to see us survive. They are going to do something; they will poison our water or let loose one of Bengalo the tamer's tigers or send in a ravenous army to invade us, raping our women and setting fire to the town. If the ticket was expensive, no one will settle for seeing us happy in our little village, like ordinary people, sowing the land, going to church on Sundays and days of obligation, sharpening knives . . . a peaceful community filled with good mornings and how are you's. Look over toward the hill. Those shadows that look like bushes are probably people, and they are waiting. I can tell you with certainty that with the worst performers, the Mantecón brothers have staged the greatest show on earth."

"My leg is going from bad to worse," Flexor said, and he took hold of his knee, in severe pain.

It had been a long day for Don Alejo. At his age, he had run out of the strength, patience, and talent to train animals. He would jump from one lesson to another hastily, losing hope the third time, at the latest, that the animal failed to follow his orders. First he tried to teach the pig to roll over. He ordered it to turn and he lifted it up by the left feet to flip it over on its back. Then he himself did a few turns as he said, "Like this, like this." It was hopeless. Don Alejo felt powerless, defeated, since along with the animals, his brother had also taken the props that were known in the Mantecón Circus as "the gimmicks."

When the circus first got started, they trained the animals with a system of punishments and rewards, where the punishment never went beyond making the animals go hungry along with a scolding, and the reward was a piece of food, a pat, and a few affectionate words. This technique was slow, since sometimes the animal did not feel hungry for a long time. However, in those days, the circus animals were mostly dogs, which, according to Don Ernesto, learned faster than humans.

Then the circus grew, and they hired a few performers with animals, and these newcomers had their own methods and gimmicks, like whips, electrodes, hot irons, knitting needles, barbed wire, poles, acid, pliers, torches, spears, corkscrews, and other devices, all of which were much more persuasive than a scolding. And even though Don Alejo asked for moderation when using those methods—"I want them well-trained, not crippled"—the time came when he himself used them and ended up killing one of the animals.

While showing off when he was drunk, he bet that he could make the camel dance to the *March of Zacatecas* on two feet. Sobriety came too late, since the bet had spread too far to save his reputation by blaming it on alcohol. The camel in the Mantecón Circus was a mere zoological curiosity. It wasn't trained for anything, but it brought in a lot of money from the photographs of children sitting on it, and it was a celebrity in the circus parades, surpassed in popularity only by the elephant. Don Alejo soon learned that the camel, built to resist the torturous natural conditions of the desert, did not react satisfactorily to "the gimmicks." The hot iron was not effective on such a sturdy-hoofed animal, the whips made it break into a trot, and with the electrodes, it barely half-closed its eyes. "He's a masochist," Don Alejo would explain without admitting defeat. During another drunken moment, Don Ernesto made a fool of him in front of the managers of the Atayde Circus, who, laughing hysterically, began to hum the *March of Zacatecas*, and danced after stuffing cushions up the backs of their shirts to simulate a camel's hump. Don Alejo left and headed for the camel's pen, where he scolded the animal for its ungratefulness and beat its front legs as he yelled, "Now, you bastard, you are going to stand on two feet." The animal whimpered, and instead of crouching down as it usually did, it lay down on its side and did not get up again. They decided to kill it at once, before it lost weight and, therefore, meat for the carnivores.

At that time, they used to begin the shows and the parades with the *March of Zacatecas*, but Don Alejo took such a dislike to it that he crossed it off the repertoire, along with anything that had the rhythm of a march. Despite complaints from the Festival Orchestra, it was decided to use the waltz *Over the Waves* to begin every show.

"Stand up, animal," he said to the pig for the last time.

The only gimmick that had remained in Don Alejo's possession was the ocote pole, and the memory of what had happened with the camel, along with his lack of energy, spared the pig from also having its front legs broken.

"You're the privileged one," and Don Alejo lay down on the ground on his back. Disgusted, he deeply wished that everyone were still sleeping in the small tent, including his brother. Just as it began to grow dark, he realized that Don Ernesto had also taken the generator, but it didn't bother him; after all, the electricity was for the shows. Candles were good enough for him.

Whether by choice or out of inertia or instinct, the pig began to do laps around the ring, one after the other, with no signs of fatigue, even after an hour.

"You will do something for me," Don Alejo said.

Knowing that the animal had to be hungry and thirsty after so many laps, he took his shirt off and squeezed an orange on his chest, aiming near the right nipple. He let the juice dry and applied another coat, and he repeated this procedure until he had applied eight coats. Then he placed two lit candles in the ring and lay down between them. He cut the edge of his nipple and a little blood appeared, and he mustered his patience, prepared to wait as long as necessary.

Soon the pig became curious about the body lying on the ground. It went over to it and immediately sensed an odor of something edible, inviting it to lick the old man's chest. The bitterness of the orange caused it to excrete saliva, and more than a thirsty animal, it looked like a rabid one. When it finally found the nipple, Don Alejo let out a long, loud groan, and his entire body tensed up. The pig seemed to like the aftertaste of the blood because it was licking with the greatest passion it had ever experienced, for it had never known a female and wasn't very fond of its dive into the pool. When the taste began to wear off, the animal lost interest and left its task to resume walking around the ring. In the meantime, a little more blood dripped from Don Alejo's nipple, and the pig went back over to him and started licking him again with great delight.

Don Alejo entered into ecstasy, and he shouted and cursed Narcissa, and kicked his legs in the air. After a while, he fainted, and his eyes rolled back into his head, completely blank, and anyone who saw him would have thought he was dead.

. . .

Don *Alejo was right.* No one decides to be a circus performer. At least I didn't, and you probably didn't either, so don't look at me in such disbelief. I had plans just like everyone else, or dreams; maybe there is no difference, because they all go down the drain just the same. I used to live in a big old house on Plateros Street, you know, in the capital. We had a library with several thousand books, I'm not kidding. Nobody read them. They were passed down from an uncle or a great uncle, I'm not sure. Like anyone who does not know what to do to change his predestined fate, one day I decided to read a book. Have you heard that bunch of jerks talking about the virtues of reading? They don't know what they're saying. I prefer libraries that have books made of wood. They look prettier, they are easier to dust, in the event of a fire, they don't ignite as quickly, and best of all, they have no pages. They also have a greater resale value. When we were forced to sell off the library, we would have gotten more money from wood blocks. Anyway, there were all those books made of paper, and I had the virtues of reading on my mind. I looked over the titles one by one, and I glanced at the flaps and the back covers so that I could make a good choice. With so many classics of literature, medical synopses, law books, philosophical treatises, encyclopedias, and works on all sorts of subjects of different lengths and for different tastes, do you know which one I finally chose? Of course at that time, I really believed in a human being's ability to choose. You know, we are free, architects of our own— How naive. I went through the same thing that happens to all children that age. Did I already tell you when this was? No? I must have been ten or eleven years old. We are constantly asked what we want to be when we grow up. Why waste time on questions like that if there are never any real answers? Maybe they are useful for measuring people's failures. That's why it's a question asked to children and never to adults. Take a workman, any kind of work-man, let's say one of those poor chumps *who make bricks*. Ask him, 'What *did* you want to be when you grew up?' I wouldn't be able to listen to the answer without laughing in his face. What differ-ence does it make if you want to be a doctor, lawyer, engineer, or a miserable bricklayer? Don Alejo fell short. Nobody decides to be a circus performer, or anything else, for that matter. Yes, I'm killing time because I don't like to talk about those things. I chose a medium-sized book. It didn't look old, the pages weren't yellowed, the cover wasn't worn, and it had illustrations and large print. It was called *The Perfect Magician*, by a man called Fran-cisco Olegaroy. 'Master, step by step, the magic tricks that have fascinated mankind around the world throughout the ages! Become the life of the party! Win applause, friends, and admirers, and be the most popular man with women! Feel loved by them.' Could you resist promises like that? I couldn't. My second choice promised only: 'You will learn about the workings of the human brain and the truths hidden in every dream.' The meaning of dreams sounded interesting, but that is not much compared to being the life of the party and the object of women's admiration. *The Perfect Magician* dealt mainly with card tricks and the sleight of hand. I came to believe that the name Francisco Olegaroy was the pseudonym for a woman, because the tricks had prissy names like 'The Mischievous Seven,' 'The Crooked Kings,' 'The Queen of Lilies,' and queer things like that. The one we all know as 'Where's the Ball?' was called 'The Lost Little Ball,' which is, after all, the same thing. One by one, I mastered each of the thirty-seven tricks detailed in the book, and it wasn't long before word had spread that I was a magician. I began to perform at school assemblies, small get-togethers and parties. I would go to the Zócalo and the money would come pouring in from naive churchgoers on Sundays. The 'Where's the Ball?' was always the most successful because everyone, including you too, no doubt, concentrated only on not losing sight of the container where I had placed the ball. They weren't expecting a trick. When I showed them they were wrong, there were always plenty of disgruntled people wanting to punch me in the face and demanding their money back. People like that drove me to share my earnings with a big idiot who watched out for me. One unfortunate afternoon, I discovered a place called 'Downtown Tricks and Novelties' on Donceles Street. It mainly sold explosive cigarettes, chocolates with laxatives, flowers that squirted water, and stupid things like that for people in search of trouble. The owner recognized me as he had seen my tricks in the Zócalo, and he whispered to me, 'You're different, not like my other customers,' and after two or three more compliments, he invited me to step into the back room. There he spoke of the importance of hiding the trick behind every magic act, for the continuity, dignity, and benefit of our profession depended on it. At first it was exciting: being in the back room, hiding, whispering, I felt I was being welcomed into a secret lodge. The man picked up a black tube that had covers on each end. 'Watch carefully,' he said to me. 'You have to see when the ordinary eye is blind.' He removed the covers and showed me the inside of the tube, which was empty. Then he put the covers back on, shook it and took the covers off again. It seemed that my eye was ordinary, because I didn't pick up the trick. The man began to pull out thin scarves made of a very fine cloth of all different colors, green, red, yellow, and blue. To me, this was witchcraft, something marvelous, far superior to Olegaroy, and it must have shown on my face because the man offered to sell me the tube. I paid for it without a word, and only then did I wonder whether I could make those scarves appear. 'Don't worry,' the man said as he handed me my merchandise with the same vulgarity he used when he sold the exploding cigarettes. 'The instructions are in the box.' My secret lodge had existed for only a few minutes. I held in my hands a commercial product called the 'Magical Mystery Tube.' It was made by a company in Connecticut, and God only knows if they had made a thousand or a million tubes just like mine. That day I swore that I would give up magic. Instructions in the box, big deal. Had I wanted to follow instructions, I would have mass-produced bricks or bread, with no secrets: take mud, compress it, bake it, done; take flour, milk, eggs, yeast, mix 'em up, bake it, done; remove the covers, show the audience, put the covers back on, turn them halfway, release the hidden mechanism, remove the covers, pull out the scarves, done. I discarded the tube and tore out every page of Francisco Olegaroy's book, which had won me much applause and a few pesos, but not a single friend and certainly not the love of a woman."

"Does a whore's job entail listening to your garbage?" Hercules asked, falling asleep.

The mechanism that made the bell ring was completely rusted. Nathaniel had to climb up into the tower and use his feet to make the clapper swing until the bronze piece announced it was time to come to mass. The halo of the sun on the horizon was barely visible, and a few frightened birds flew out of the nearby trees. Harrieta was the first to stick her head out the window. With each ring of the bell, fragments of rusted metal came falling down, and the mechanism gradually loosened up. Nathaniel climbed down and tried again. He pulled the rope with all his might, and this time the bell swung, and as he rang the bronze bell louder and louder, he wondered happily how many more tolls of the bell would that frayed rope endure.

"Shut up, you weasel," Harrieta shouted. "I'm trying to sleep."

More because of the yelling than because of the bell-ringing, Hercules decided to go outside. He had slept well. Even though they were rotten, the slats on the bed were still flexible enough so as not to break, and they provided some comfort similar to the softness of a cot. He had also used his porcelain toilet for the first time, leaving far behind the need to act like an animal every time nature called. He went outside in his black tights, the red marks from the slats on his back. Like the big whore I am, he thought, as he waved to Harrieta.

"Did you see the puddle?" she asked.

The horse had spouted water all night long, and the street was now a swamp.

"How nice it is," Hercules said, "to get up in the morning and greet your neighbors."

Harrieta didn't respond. She wondered if Timoteo had a valve to stop the flow of water. If not, the town would be flooded with water and mosquitoes in a week at most. In that moment of silence, Hercules, for the first time, thought that maybe all the houses had toilets, and why not? They could be even more elegant and comfortable than his. He decided not to investigate so he could go on enjoying his privileged status.

"There must be a valve," Harrieta said at last, "or at least a gutter for the water to run through."

"That idiot, Rocket," he said. "And that good-for-nothing Mágala."

"We can't live in the middle of all this mud."

"They stayed with Don Alejo, no doubt. The old man must have offered them something."

The bell tolled once again, a single toll.

"I told you to shut up, midget." Harrieta's voice resounded over the the bell again.

"It was an accident," Nathaniel apologized.

"He's the priest," Hercules said. "Don't talk to him that way."

"My whole life I had respect for things like that, and look at me," she complained. "Do you think it's done me any good?" She shook her head and went back inside her house.

Hercules had a strong urge to splash in the mud and roll around in it, but he was embarrassed to behave like a child. Instead, he headed toward the equestrian statue and stood right beneath the stream of water, in an attempt to relive the pleasure of a shower. The sun put him in good spirits. He was hungry, and he craved prickly pears, lots of raw prickly pears, preferably with the thorns removed.

"Paradise," he said softly, "even though the water is freezing."

He scrubbed under his arms, rinsed off his back, and stretched out the waistband on his elastic tights to let the water in to clean his private parts. Harrieta watched him from the opening in the door, trying to think of some excuse to go over to him.

"What the hell," she said, and without any excuse, she walked to the square.

She hitched up her skirt just enough so as not to splatter the flounce with mud and not to show her hairy legs, and she crossed the street quickly. She stood next to Hercules for a while, motionless, with her arms crossed, hoping her passiveness would get his attention. He pretended not to notice her. He stuck his head under the stream of water, happy because of the water splashing like a crystal crown. Then he closed his eyes, ran his fingers through the stubble of hair beginning to grow on his head, and wondered if the running water would conceal the fact that he was urinating. Harrieta, however, was too perceptive.

"Why do you want a toilet, then?"

He continued to ignore her. For a moment, the water flowed irregularly, spitting out air bubbles, but almost immediately it began to flow uniformly again.

"Look, you idiot," she said. "And you were so sure they had stayed with Don Alejo."

Hercules turned toward Harrieta and saw what she was pointing to. Very still, tied to a tree at the entrance of the town, the diving pig was watching them with its ears turned up, its nose running, and its belly on the ground. The velveteen robe made it look almost human.

"I got up on the wrong side of the bed," Hercules said. "I have to start doing Sandow's exercises again."

Then a cry of alarm echoed through the square. They both spun around instinctively toward the bell tower.

"A doctor!" The cry was coherent now. "I need a doctor!"

"They're talking to you," Hercules said sarcastically.

Harrieta identified the shrill, untimely voice as Narcissa's.

"Coming," she said, annoyed.

Narcissa waved her arms in a signal for her to hurry. Harrieta hitched up her skirt a little more and walked slowly, like a bride heading for the altar.

"What's wrong?" she asked when she finally reached Narcissa.

She looked back. Hercules was still ignoring her. Damn. Not even a hundred years is going to make us equal.

"It's Flexor," Narcissa said. "He woke up with a fever and his knee the size of a melon."

Sandow. The photograph must be touched up. Would it do me any good to read that book, or is it just for men?

"Let's see," she said firmly.

Flexor was lying on the ground. His hair was soaked with sweat, and though he didn't make a sound, his movements were as hysterical as a shriek. His right knee was covered with a piece of cloth. Harrieta recognized it as a scrap of Narcissa's dress. She stood looking at the boy, wrapped as always in his yellow leotard, and it moved her that he didn't even take it off to sleep.

"I never knew if you had several of that leotard or if you always wore the same one," Harrieta said, not wanting to remove the piece of cloth. She imagined she would find a mishmash of flesh and worms.

Narcissa beat her to it and uncovered the wound, and just the sight of the inflamed, pus-filled knee reminded Harrieta of an odor that in her mind, she described as tuberculous vomit. Even more than the stench, she was struck by the size of the swelling, which was just as Narcissa had described—a well-developed, rotten melon. Not even bread in the oven, she thought, grows as fast as the monstrosity in this leg.

"Only yesterday he had a little stick of a knee," she said, and she covered it back up so she wouldn't be nauseated anymore.

"You're the doctor," Narcissa said. "You shouldn't make such stupid comments."

Harrieta adopted a pensive air. Her medical experience did not go beyond her own colds and menstrual disorders, and it was clear that Flexor needed a more effective remedy than a lime-blossom tea or a hot-water bottle on the womb.

"We have here a case of an inflamed knee," she said, trying to appear intelligent, but as Narcissa was watching her with piercing eyes and her arms crossed, she knew that she was being asked for a cure, not a diagnosis. "Take him to Timoteo's fountain," she said with complete conviction. "He is to submerge his leg in the water for an hour. Then leave him in the sun until it dries."

"For years, I took care of an old man and nothing ever happened to him," Narcissa said. "Now I have a little boy and he gets sick on me the very first day."

Flexor continued making wild gestures and, without a word, leaned on Narcissa's shoulder so she could lead him to the fountain.

"I'll stop by later to see how the patient is doing," Harrieta said.

She paid no attention to the protests of Hercules, who said that Flexor would poison the water if he stuck his leg in it, in part because it was infected, and in part because he was black. The leg looked bad, and Harrieta wasn't prepared to face the possibility of amputating it. She would give up her position as doctor first, and if necessary, she would leave town in search of another circus, since she got goose bumps just thinking about the screeching of a saw cutting through bone.

In the distance, and with no more energy to ring the bell, Nathaniel could be heard shouting, "Isn't anybody coming to mass?"

A*ny problems?"* Mandrake asked.

"None," Rocket responded. "Don Alejo was asleep and it couldn't have been easier to steal the loot."

Mágala looked at the ground without lowering her head. She wanted to tell the truth, but she wasn't sure to what point she had become Rocket's accomplice.

"I don't know if we should eat the pig," Mandrake said, "or if it would be better to kill it and leave it on the mountain to attract the buzzards," and when he saw the strange expression on their faces, he explained, "You can eat buzzards."

After thinking about it for a few seconds, Rocket said:

"We can eat the pig and leave the guts as bait."

"Count me out," Mágala said, repulsed. "What does an animal like that taste like, anyway?"

"A bird is a bird," Mandrake replied. "It might even taste like quail."

She was thinking not about the taste, but about how it would look. A quail was graceful and friendly while alive; fleshy, soft, and swollen when dead. She had never seen a plucked buzzard. Even so, she pictured it clearly, spread out on a table, a gigantic bat with a menacing face, fierce despite being cooked with potatoes, daring anyone to tear off a bit of that tough meat sticking to its bones.

"And we can always use the leftovers to catch the next one," Rocket pointed out encouragingly.

"Besides," Mandrake said, "it seems to be the only animal that's plentiful around here," and he pointed above his head.

Four buzzards were flying around the town square, high above Flexor. Rocket turned in the direction of where the big top was, behind the hill, and he looked closely. He thought he saw another bevy circling, in a famished flight, and he chalked it up to his imagination.

"It doesn't seem very appealing," Mágala said condescendingly, "even though we could use it as our traditional dish." Then she headed home.

She hadn't cleaned her house yet. The night before, when she had returned from the tent, she had dusted a section of the floor with her clothes so she wouldn't have to sleep in the dirt. Her house had no toilet, just a hole in the backyard. On the other hand, the previous owners had left an armoire, and a dining room complete with table, six chairs, and a sideboard, all made of a thick, heavy wood, heavy enough that they'd had to leave it behind. Mágala made up her mind to go back to the big top and get her cot. Houses should begin with the bed and end with the sideboard. Not until she spent a night sleeping on her cot would she feel like the house was hers, and only then would she feel like cleaning it.

She went over to the window and motioned to Rocket to come. He interrupted his conversation with Mandrake and went over to her at once.

"Did you say anything to him?" Mágala asked.

"No."

"I think you should—"

"Shut up. We soldiers have no obligation to tell anyone anything."

"I'm a journalist," Mágala said.

Rocket turned around to hide his rage. His mouth twisted, his forehead broke out in a sweat, his face took on a bluish tone, and he began to grind his teeth. Even though Mágala felt safe behind the bars in the window, she took a step back when she noticed that Rocket was tensing the muscles in his arms and clenching his fists, the same thing she had seen him do just before he hit Don Alejo.

Rocket was not a big man; he was short and thin enough to fit into the mouth of a cannon and be shot out with ease. However, when Don Alejo had appeared behind him, asking him not to take the pig, the scare had filled him with such energy that his punch had sent the old guy flying several feet backward. When the body hit the ground, Rocket heard the same sound that Funambula the tightrope walker had made when she broke her neck. Mágala hadn't witnessed that, which is why the cracking bones reminded her of stands giving way under the weight of too many spectators. Don Alejo sat up halfway, and Rocket and Mágala were again surprised to see him alive, waving his arms and trying to speak, but only a begging tone was comprehensible. Rocket picked up the rope that he had just untied from the pig and tied it around Don Alejo's wrists and ankles, like a maneuver in a rodeo.

"What are you doing?" Mágala asked.

He remained silent, choosing not to respond to something so obvious. Once Don Ajelo's feet and hands were immobilized, Rocket tied him to the flagpole, disappointed that there was no tiger's cage to throw him into. Instead, he picked up the ocote pole and gave him a couple of jabs in the ribs.

"Please," Mágala said. "There's no need for that."

Rocket quickly tightened the knots, wondering why he was so angry at that defenseless old man who continued to babble awkwardly, like a drunk. He'd found the answer on the way back.

"Why did you treat him like that?" Mágala had asked.

"He deserved it," Rocket responded, unconvinced.

"I think it was the scare he gave you," she said, making fun of him. "You should have gone to the academy for those with no balls."

Rocket shook his head, even though he knew she was right. The adrenaline released by the vision of Don Alejo was still surging through him. Before he realized that he had erred in his diagnosis of death, he had seen the old man as a walking cadaver. He was ashamed for having been so frightened, and even more so because he had let out a faint yell, pretty effeminate in his opinion, and he hoped that Mágala hadn't heard it. A minute later, everything changed. Now he was proud of himself for having crushed a man with a single punch, and he felt a strength that until then, he had never known, and he was tempted to use it again.

"I don't want you to think I'm a coward."

"What difference does it make?" she said to him. "I won't be kissing you anymore anyway."

His blood began to boil again, and he swore that if Mágala said another word, he would punch her.

Mágala said nothing more. It troubled her to leave the old guy tied up, waiting to die of starvation or hunger, or of old age. Rocket, in the meantime, was getting rid of his aggression by kicking the pig in the rear end to hurry it along.

Sure I regret what I did today in Timoteo's fountain. It's just that yesterday I cleaned my toilet bowl, and it looked so clean and shiny . . . I promise not to do it again. In Santa María of the Circus, we have to lay down and observe a few basic laws if we want to live together in peace. Especially you women. There will be days when you will be prohibited from going into the fountain. And we need to talk to Mandrake. Just a little while ago, he shouted, 'Look out below!' and he threw his sewage out as if he were living in one of those crowded cities with no drain other than the public thoroughfare. Fortunately, we have a lot of space, patios, a thousand places to choose from. If I wanted to live in a pigsty, I would go live in the capital. Don't look at me like that. This matter is more important than all the others put together. None of you realize it because you aren't as fortunate as I am. The feeling of porcelain is nicer than a woman's skin. It's always smooth, firm, white, and cool. No other piece of furniture or fixture marks such an emphatic boundary between civilization and barbarity. I don't know who invented the toilet bowl, but it seems like a much more privileged creation than those Flexor mentioned—the electric lightbulb, the leotard, and the others. How come nobody thinks of opening a store where they rent porcelain toilet bowls? Not even a brothel would be so successful. In the outlying areas, there are probably only rustic outhouses with wooden or cement seats, and that's if times are good; if they're not, there's probably no seat or outhouse at all. I would open my own business if I had two toilet bowls, but nobody will sit on mine, none of you. Listen to me. As the doctor, you are the last person who should want an unhealthy environment. You know how it is, an epidemic arrives and who is going to go around draining the pus? You'll be the first to get fed up with your job, there's no doubt. Doctor! You saw how Narcissa was shouting. Why do we all need to know about her sick little black boy? Did you like it? Of course not. What did he do to you? Did he sneeze in your face? I'm warning you: I don't want to see Flexor with his knee in the water again. Do you hear me? I used to think that the body could handle anything, and that a dose of sickness was good because it made me stronger against other illnesses. Sandow's book proved the opposite. I learned the importance of being clean, eating healthy, and breathing clean air. Maybe it's not good to read those things, because you feel sicker, and you feel an infection coming on with every bug and every cough. I have never let on that I feel this way. A strong man must never show his weaknesses, and if I'm telling you now, it's because of your job, not because I am confiding in you, so don't get excited or go telling everyone. You are obligated to keep professional secrets. Sandow talks about the symptoms of deterioration, and I have felt them for some time. My belly is swollen, my chest sags, and I gasp for breath. I feel every heartbeat in my temples and a tingling when I urinate, and the list goes on. When you are young, your body is as you see it. When you get older, that is just the shell, and your real body is inside, where things can break down. Don't get me wrong. I don't think, like the midget, that I might die tomorrow. However, my problem is dramatic because the process of deteriorating is sadder than the end. And the midget? What difference does it make if all of a sudden a little shapeless statue of clay breaks? Who cares? I am a Botticelli hopelessly devoured by termites, fading and crumbling. There is no brush for retouching. *That* is unfortunate. Maybe I would feel better if Sandow had not made me so aware of my situation. 'O Sandow, Sandow, sublime athlete, I have been sad for many years, I have been sick for many years, just for the book you sent to me!' What are you worried about? When you get bored playing doctor, you can join up with another circus. I have no way of turning back the clock. For me, there is no choice. This despicable town has to work; only here can I have any sort of life. In the circus, I was already living on borrowed time. Do you think I don't know that there are hundreds of strong men with much better and stronger bodies than mine? I am a member of a species in decline. Almost no circus nowadays will hire a strong man unless it's to raise the poles, tighten ropes, and unload equipment. It's about competition now, not exhibition. They gather in some arena and challenge each other with heavier and heavier weights, and there are even judges who impose rules and hand out trophies to the winners at the end. I heard about an Italian who lifted five hundred and seventeen kilos. Tell me how I stand a chance with guys like that. The worst part is that at those events, they separate the competitors by categories. *That* I can't accept. It's like prostituting the job of the strong man. Can you believe it? They hang a medal around a guy's neck for being the least weak of the weak. You, my friend, are the champion of those who weigh between forty and forty-two kilos. And they give the same medal to the guy who lifted fifty kilos and to the one who lifted five hundred and seventeen. Poor guy, the judges probably justify; he's skinny but his heart was in it. I don't get it. You are either the strongest or you're not. If we don't stop this, one of these days, Nathaniel could be presented as the Hercules of the midgets. Wonderful. Even that insect is threatening my job. That's why I don't want to talk about it anymore. Even if everyone leaves, I am staying here in Santa

María of the Circus. I've always gotten along just fine alone, so why not now? If everyone decides to take off, it would be better for me, alone, without anyone coveting my toilet, without nighttime visits, and without you. I can change houses every day, splash around in the fountain whenever I want, walk around the square on sunny Sundays without my tights on, and become the great walrus that is claiming my body. But if all of you decide to stay, you will do so without contaminating the water or throwing excrement into the street and by bathing every day. Everyone here must be clean. You owe me that privilege. After all, I was the one who discovered the water."

"Naturally," Harrieta said.

The contents of the sack of fruit were divided equally among the white people, and Flexor, despite Narcissa's protests, got only an orange and a pear, both of which were overripe. Mandrake ordered everyone to save the seeds, and he began to look for the best plot of land for the plantation. It was not hard to find, as he had only to follow the water. By that time, the puddle in the street had grown and found its way to a channel that emptied into a narrow and almost completely covered-up irrigation ditch, which in turn led to a flat piece of land behind the church. Mandrake did not seem at all worried by his lack of expertise in matters of the country-side. He took comfort in thinking that it did not require much knowledge; you just throw the seed on the ground and nature takes care of the rest.

"Are you crazy?" Narcissa complained when she saw the landowner in her house, urgently seeking workers. "My boy is sick."

"I am so sorry," Mandrake responded. "This is going to fail if at every sign of illness we don't fulfill our obligations."

Flexor, who was in a bad mood, nodded, and with great effort, got up. Something burst open on his knee and pus began to ooze out.

"It hurts," he said, "but I can move it," and while he was talking, he noticed that his jaw had become hardened and crunchy, like an old tortilla.

An outline of Flexor's emaciated body was left on the ground by his sweat. It began to evaporate when the wind started to blow. Mandrake gave him eight seeds from an orange that had just been eaten. The stench from Flexor's knee made him nauseous, and he decided to say something to explain the look of repulsion on his face.

"Contortions are for buddies," he muttered.

"Huh?" Flexor said, busy squeezing a glob of pus from his leg.

"Yeah," Mandrake went on. "In order to twist yourself up like you do, you need to have nothing there." He pointed to Flexor's loins, which were packed tightly into the leotard, and when he noticed the slight size of the bulge, he added, "They told me that Negroes were something else altogether."

"That's enough," Narcissa said, and she pushed Flexor toward the door. "Don't forget to air out your leg, and to go to church to pray for your health."

Mandrake explained to him how to get to the spot chosen for the garden, and, smiling, he said good-bye.

Up until that moment, Flexor hadn't worried about his health, since even though his knee was causing him tremendous pain, he thought that was normal for an infection, and the stiffness in his jaw seemed of little importance, given that he was in the hands of the best doctor in town. Nevertheless, Narcissa had ordered him to go to church, and God should be bothered only when an illness overtakes the medicine.

He entered the church, and his first impulse was to kneel

down, but the thought of his knee bursting open and spilling out all its contents in a sacred place made him decide to sit, with his arms crossed and his legs stretched out, in a pose that resembled a customer waiting for a drink more than a person praying.

"I'm over here," Nathaniel shouted from the confessional. "Come and tell me your sins."

"That's not what I came for," Flexor said.

The midget shrugged. After all, that little boy can't have very interesting sins, he thought.

"Then tell me how I can help you."

The boy looked at him with what energy he could muster, and he didn't have to respond, because just then they heard footsteps echoing throughout the church like blows from a hammer. It was Hercules, who from the vestibule said, "I have a great idea."

"Stop right there," Nathaniel shouted. "One thing is to welcome Negroes in my church, and another, quite different, is to open the doors to damsels like you."

Hercules took a deep breath to check his anger and answered him in a calm, affected voice.

"That's exactly what this is about, Father," and after he said that last word, he shook his head, was quiet for a few seconds, regained his patience and continued. "I am sorry about everything, Father. I've come to ask for your forgiveness so I can begin anew, without sin."

For the first time in his life, he was proud of having used his voice and not his arms to negotiate. In an attempt to be more dramatic, he bowed his head and knelt, so that his eyes were just slightly above Nathaniel's.

"I'm sorry my child—" the midget said the first thing that popped into his head "—but it is written in Ephonias, chapter twelve, verse fourteen, 'There shall be no mercy for those who offer their bodies as if they were pieces of bread.'"

Hercules didn't let him go further. Taking advantage of their even height, he grabbed Nathaniel by the hair and threw him facedown on the floor, rubbing his face into it as if he wanted to polish the tiles as he asked him, insistently, "So then, Father, are you going to forgive me?" And the midget, determined to beat him even if just that one time, responded, between squeals, that he was very sorry, really, but he couldn't do anything about it because so it had been written.

Sure enough, by the time Hercules finally gave up and left, three tiles were shining more brightly than the rest, and Nathaniel, though smiling, had a series of red marks on his face, eyebrows full of dirt, and his blind eye half-opened.

Flexor would have liked to see the priest invoking a god to free him from that punishment, but when he saw how completely powerless Nathaniel was, he was certain that there was no one there to help him with his knee.

"I'm going to die," he said.

"Me too," Nathaniel said, for the torturing had aggravated the pain in his joints and had reminded him of the matter of the horses.

"I know that," Flexor added, "but I'm first."

Mágala knew that the only way to avoid any responsibility for what had happened to Don Alejo was for the press to denounce the incident. She picked up Hercules' pen and some flyers, and just as she had planned, began writing: "The big top was nothing more than a great big bubble about to burst." She recounted, to the best of her ability, how they had arrived, how strange it seemed to find the cots empty and their nostalgia for the odors of the circus. She went on to describe Don Alejo, lying in the middle of the ring, apparently dead and "with a pig that seemed to be sucking the life out of him through his tit." Then she had some fun describing Rocket's surprise when Don Alejo came up behind him: "He let out a cry like a terrified old lady," and she finished off with, "In revenge for looking so ridiculous, he beat the poor, defenseless old man brutally, and then tied him to the flagpole, leaving him there for time, hunger, or thirst to kill him like a dog." She didn't want the first issue of the newspaper to seem like mere gossip, so she included a second article entitled "They Will Eat Buzzard," in which she wrote of the advantages of making that bird the traditional dish of Santa María of the Circus, and she included a recipe for preparing it with nuts and pear slices, pointing out that it tasted like quail. Her handwriting was very small, and even after these two articles, she had space left on the page. She had intended to make five copies of the newspaper, but having finished only one, her fingers were stiff and she thought she heard the joints cracking. Now I just need an advertisement. After all, I have to make a living. She filled the space with: "Amazing Mantecón Circus, Fun for Young and Old," along with a drawing of a happy elephant. Last, she had only to write the name at the top: *The Circus Gazette*, finishing it off with a subtitle taken from her hometown newspaper: "Organ of Free Thought."

She looked at it for a while, satisfied, and she wondered who deserved to be the first to read it. She couldn't come up with an answer, even though there was no doubt that Rocket should be the last, or better yet, he shouldn't even find out about it at all. She looked out the window and spotted Harrieta.

"Psst," she said, waving the paper in her right hand.

"I'm in a hurry." Harrieta made a signal with her hand. "I'm going to see a patient."

"The Negro can wait," Mágala said. "You have to read this."

Harrieta scanned the first article a couple of times, completely ignoring the one about the buzzards.

"Is this true?" she asked.

Mágala, trying to pique her interest, answered the question that was obviously not the right one. "Maybe," she said, "but I've never tasted quail."

Harrieta grabbed her by the arm and squeezed it as hard as she could. It was not very painful, but Mágala gave up anyway.

"Yes," she said. "When we left, he was still breathing, but who knows now?"

Harrieta ran her fingers through her beard as she reflected on the situation. She looked at the stone statue: the sword resembled a machete ready to cut sugarcane, and it struck her as odd that the arm was still raised in the air, untouched by vandalism, since just as they had broken the horse's muzzle, a blow from a stone would be enough to leave Don Timoteo armless.

"It seems strange that Rocket didn't steal the sword."

"We're not talking about that," Mágala said.

Harrieta stared at the puddle of water and mud in the street for a long while. Already there were hints of green in the town square, where just a day before, there had been only dried up weeds.

"If we don't make it run," she said, "we'll soon be invaded by mosquitoes, and then you'll see how busy I'll be with all of you sick with malaria."

"Maybe," Mágala agreed, "but we're not talking about that, either."

Harrieta shrugged. She didn't feel like making a decision, despite a sense of obligation she felt, remembering how Don Alejo had saved her from being crucified and the conviction that a doctor's obligation was, before all else, to save lives.

"All right," she said, and she bowed her head, as if ashamed. "Don Alejo might be the devil, but we can't just leave him there."

They quickly drew up a plan to rescue him, and since the two of them would not be able to carry the body, dead or alive, they decided that Hercules should pull the cart. They showed him the issue of The Circus Gazette and waited for his reaction. They had thought up a series of humanitarian arguments to convince him to join their mission; however, he immediately gave his approval. By bringing Don Alejo back, he saw the chance to begin that new life that the church had denied him.

"Of course," he said. "We need Don Alejo's strong hand to make us focus on worthwhile things and to forget about those stupid slips of paper."

"We'll see about that," Harrieta said. "But for now, you'll be a cart-pulling whore."

They decided to disguise the reason for their trip, for they suspected that there would be more than one dissenter.

"We're going to look for food," Harrieta explained. "With a little luck, we'll find a thriving garden, unlike Mandrake's patch of dirt." Before they left, they gave the newspaper to Narcissa, recommending she pass it on to the others in any order she pleased, just as long as Rocket was last. Narcissa began to read, disinterested, until she came to a sentence that made her heart skip a beat: ". . . with a pig that seemed to be sucking the life out of him through his tit." She read it over and over again, ignoring the rest of the article and the one about the buzzards. Her eyes began to fill with tears, but then she composed herself and her expression was one of harsh resentment. The cart vanished in the horizon, and Narcissa knew without a doubt that they were not going to look for food. She only hoped that they found Don Alejo dead, because she knew she didn't have the courage to kill him.

The newspaper continued to circulate. Nathaniel did not show much interest and said, "Why did she include the notice for the Mantecón Circus if on the back of the flyer there is already a full-page ad?"

Flexor did not feel much like reading, so he just read the shorter article. His mouth began to water with the recipe for the buzzard smothered in nuts and pears.

Narcissa could not find Mandrake, so she went to Rocket and read the article to him out loud. With each line, he got angrier and angrier. He felt betrayed and humiliated, especially when he heard the part where Mágala compared him to a terrified old lady.

"Lies," he interrupted her.

Narcissa paid no attention and read on until the end: ". . . for time, hunger, or thirst to kill him like a dog."

"And exaggerations, too," Rocket added. "Dogs don't die tied to flagpoles."

"He's worse than a dog," Narcissa said solemnly, with a cold, sinister smile.

They stared at each other for a while without saying a word. Narcissa tried to thank him, to tell him she hoped Don Alejo was dead, but the harsh, resentful expression disappeared when she tried to say the first word, and tears filled her eyes again.

"He left me for a pig," she finally said, sobbing.

Rocket raised his eyebrows in disbelief.

"That's nonsense," he said, annoyed. "Don Alejo took the worst of the circus in order to keep you, we all know that, and now you come up with the idea he left you for that animal," and he pointed at the pig, still tied to the tree, tired of pulling on the rope.

"He kept the big top," Narcissa explained.

"He couldn't care less about the big top. He kept you."

She shook her head in denial. The words in the newspaper that described the animal sucking the life out of Don Alejo through his tit were still resounding in her head. The right one, she thought; it had to be, and she began to back away from Rocket after insisting, "He kept the pig, not me."

Mandrake was the only one who didn't find out about the news, for satisfied with having left Flexor in charge of sowing the seeds, he had gone back inside his house to take a long nap, and he didn't wake up until well into the night, when he felt a yearning in his entire body and the need for quick relief. He went to Hercules' house and knocked patiently on the door for a long time, calling out affectionate words like "Come on, sweetie, we're going to have a good time," and offering to pay him first with an orange, then with two or three, until he was convinced that there was no one inside to open the door.

The return was quite arduous for Hercules. They made the most of their trip by throwing into the cart cots, planks, ropes, sheets, clothing, a washbasin, and the box for cutting the girl in half, which had been filled with utensils, frying pans, candles, a couple of useless rolls of tickets, the ocote pole, and as many useful and useless things that fit. Curled up on top of all that was Don Alejo, his wrists and ankles sore, his eyes teary, and babbling a litany of "Where did they take you? Don't leave me alone."

"He's talking to Narcissa," Harrieta said.

"I think he's talking to his brother," Hercules said as he struggled up a hill.

[134]

Mágala smiled silently, not wanting to share her thoughts.

When they found Don Alejo, he had wet his pants and was in the same position in which Rocket had left him the night before, or at least that's how Mágala remembered it—a dying calf lying on his left side, his head drooping, chin against his chest, the fingers of both hands finely interlaced, forming a pleading stump. She wondered if he had been in that position all day, or if he had moved around so much that he had fallen back down into the original position.

"We've come for you," Harrieta said with that affectionate tone used indiscriminately to address both young and old. Don Alejo glanced at her, confused, and the only sign of life in him was an occasional blink of an eye.

She untied him carefully, fearful of hurting him, and while Hercules and Mágala were taking care of loading the cart, she massaged his feet with great tenderness. Perhaps this revived the old man's senses, because it was then that he seemed to regain consciousness and for the first time, said "Where did they take you?"

Harrieta thought it was a question that required a response, so she said, "Nowhere, Don Alejo. I'm right here."

After listening to him repeat this question several times, along with, "Don't leave me alone," she was convinced that this was a delirious man.

"Quick," she said. "The poor guy is dehydrated. We have to take him into town at once."

Hercules carried Don Alejo in his arms as though he was a sack of potatoes, and so, like a sack of potatoes, he threw him on top of the cargo that was already in the cart. Don Alejo fell, sprawled out, on top of Mandrake's box without letting out a sound, and he curled up into a ball on impact.

"Careful," Mágala said. "We came to rescue him, remember."

"If he dies from that," Hercules said, "he would really have died of old age."

It was dawn when they got back to town, and there wasn't a soul in sight. By the final few meters of the journey, Hercules had already given up his fantasy of being a Jewish slave. For the first time, he was pulling a cart loaded to the top, and his muscles were tired, his bones about to break. The idea that he might really be turning into a whore troubled him, for he would then lose his strength even more rapidly. He looked at his legs in the darkness and thought they looked thinner and more shapely. He observed his chest and noticed it was bulging somewhat. He closed his eyes and attributed it all to his imagination.

Don Alejo had sunk back into a comatose state, and Harrieta was doing all she could to revive him. With Hercules' help, she placed him on a cot in one of the empty houses and brought him water in a pitcher they had taken from the big top. She trickled drops of water into his open mouth, and after a while, a movement in his neck indicated that he had swallowed. She emptied the pitcher over his body to get rid of the smell of urine. She also did it to see if the cold water would revive him. Hercules came into the room with a lit candle.

"Here," he said. "So you can see what you're doing."

"Since when are you so considerate?" Harrieta asked.

He answered only to himself. Something is happening to me, I feel different. In his usual tough-guy role, he would never have offered a candle, not to his own mother. I'm a whore, he thought.

Just then the pig squealed as it tried again to free itself from the rope that held it to the tree. Don Alejo showed signs of waking up, for he seemed more alert and began to look from side to side, recognizing where he was and the people who were there. The pig squealed again, and Don Alejo sat up. Sitting on the edge of the cot, he folded his arms to warm himself and said once again, "Don't leave me alone."

Harrieta turned the pitcher upside down over Don Alejo's head. This time, only a few drops trickled out.

"Bring me more," she ordered Hercules. "The water is reviving him."

Mandrake awoke to the joy of seeing his box on top of the cart. He quickly opened it and was even more pleased to find the saw for cutting Narcissa in half, the cards, and the colored scarves he used to pull from his sleeve, hat, pockets, and mouth.

This time, the midget was more cautious. He climbed up to the bell tower and shouted, "Should I ring the bell?"

Mandrake and Narcissa had gathered around the cart. She shook her head no to Nathaniel, who came back down, disappointed, and said to himself that sometime that afternoon, when everyone was wide awake, he would make the bell explode with noise without asking anyone's permission.

"Don't count on the Negro today," Narcissa said to Mandrake as she handed him some seeds.

"Since when did you become an abolitionist?" he asked.

She shrugged, not knowing how to respond. She looked off into the distance and spotted the pig, who in turn was looking nostalgically at the mud in the street.

"When will we eat it?"

Mandrake was putting on his cape and it took him a while to figure out what Narcissa was talking about.

"I don't know," he said as he tied a knot at the neck. "When the fruit is gone."

"Look how skinny it is. If we wait much longer, it won't even serve as an hors d'oeuvre."

"Do you want to eat it?" he asked, tilting his hat and making his black cape flutter. "Or do you merely want to kill it?"

Narcissa crossed her arms and, to herself, agreed. Killing the pig was enough, yes, but with a bit of torture, although at the same time, she thought about the pointlessness of punishing an animal that would die completely ignorant of why it had been dealt such a fate. And it would die kicking its legs about, with the same vulgarity as any fattened-up pig.

"Flexor is very sick," she said, wanting to change the subject. "He might not make it."

Mandrake seemed to have read Narcissa's mind and said, "What good did it do him to learn how to dress up in velveteen and dive?"

"Don Alejo is here," she said.

"I know, I heard them last night," Mandrake said, kicking a stone that bounced, landed in the water and sank. "We either force him to choose a slip of paper or this will all go up in smoke."

Narcissa shrugged, turned around and walked over toward the nearest house. She knocked on the door and waited patiently. After a minute, she heard some slow, shuffling footsteps, and the bolt slid open.

"What do you want?" Rocket asked, squinting.

"Knives to sharpen . . . scissors to repair . . ."

"Get out of here," he said and slammed the door.

She moved on to the house next door. There was no need to knock, because Mágala had poked her head out the window.

"Knives to sharpen—"

"Inside Mandrake's box," she said, "are Dagoberto's daggers."

Narcissa's eyes were smiling, and instinctively she touched her thigh in the spot where she had a small scar, near where she would stick the silver stars. Dagoberto's daggers punctured more than they actually cut. They had hollow handles that would be filled with oil and lit with a wick. Just a month before, Narcissa had had her back up against a wooden board, her body in the form of an X, completely motionless and her eyes closed as Dagoberto put his aim to the test. With great precision, he would drive the daggers into the board, beneath the armpits, along her sides, next to her ears, up and down the sides of her legs, and finally between her legs. Before that final throw, Dagoberto would approach the woman at his mercy and point to her crotch. The Festival Orchestra would begin a drumroll, and the announcer would call out to the audience: "Perhaps this fair maiden who has never known a man will now know the knife." Narcissa never lost confidence in Dagoberto, not even when one of the daggers slit her thigh. But the day came when she refused to take part in the act for two reasons: first, she complained that Dagoberto got all the applause, even though the only skin on the line was hers; second, it bothered her that the handles were set on fire. "They want to cook me," she said, "especially on that last throw." In the previous show, the removal of the final dagger was held up, and her pubic hair got singed. With no other volunteers to stand X-shaped against the board, Dagoberto had to go, leaving his equip-ment behind as payment for a debt he had incurred with the Mantecón brothers.

Narcissa opened Mandrake's box and did not have to rummage long before discovering the black-lacquer case. Inside were the eight daggers and a box of matches. She dusted off the daggers one by one and chose three. By the sloshing noise, she identified the handles that contained the most oil. She had never thrown a dagger, but she had seen them coming so many times that she was sure she had the ability and aim necessary to hit a target. She located the wick on each handle, and with a single match, lit them all. The pig smelled the intentions of that woman who was moving closer and closer to him with a cynical smile on her face, and it began to squeal and pull desperately on the rope. Don Alejo, in his slumber, managed to hear the squeals and he made his way over to the window as best he could to see what was happening.

"No!" he shouted, paralyzed, for it was clearly too late for him to act.

Narcissa picked up the first dagger by the blade and threw it with all her might in the direction of the frenetic animal. The throw wobbled and the dagger hit the ground, skittering away from the pig like a harmless torch. She had not gotten a good grip on the knife. The tips of her thumb and index finger had cuts, and blood began to spurt out. Mandrake, wearing his cape like a poncho, was watching, unwilling to intervene, and delighting in the powerlessness of Don Alejo, who was grasping the bars on his window like a prisoner.

The second throw would also have misfired had the pig not moved so much that it wound up getting in the dagger's path. The dagger sunk into its back with a hollow sound, which was immediately drowned out by the wailing of both the animal and Don Alejo. The velveteen caught fire at once, and the scare gave the pig the strength it needed to break free from the rope and take off running. Don Alejo saw his chance. He hurried to open the door as he shouted, "Come, bonito, come." The animal recognized its salvation and bolted toward him, and when the door closed behind it, all was quiet, and all that was left out on the street was the smell of singed hair and a trail of smoke and urine.

With one single jerk, Don Alejo pulled the lit dagger out of the pig. He was amazed to find it so deeply embedded and guessed that only resentment could have given Narcissa that kind of strength and aim. He stopped up the wound with his finger, and when he saw how shaken the pig was from the scare and the escape and, more important, how it was panting with its mouth open and tongue hanging out, he didn't want to waste the opportunity. He placed the pig astride him and moved his chest toward the pig's tongue.

"Come on, bonito."

The pig was not in the mood for fun, for it had a sharp, burning pain in its back. Its tongue moved sluggishly and monotonously, and its mouth smelled of stagnant water.

"Not like that," Don Alejo said, and he gave the animal a smack. The pig, so weak, spun over as it was hit and collapsed, almost dead.

The old man sat by its side, watching as the puddle of blood grew bigger and, with the dirt on the ground, formed a thick mud, and the only sign the pig was alive was the occasional movement of its legs. Every now and then it would stretch out its legs as if awakening, and Don Alejo cherished the hope of seeing it get up, regaining the strength in its body and its tongue.

Rocket knocked on Mágala's door. Almost immediately she opened it, sweaty, with a handkerchief tied around the top of her forehead. She had taken a cot from the cart, and at that moment she was busy cleaning the house.

"What do you want?"

After taking a piece of paper from his pocket, which Mágala recognized as The Circus Gazette, he forced a kind tone of voice and asked,

"Did you write this?"

She nodded, but Rocket didn't notice because he was immersed in the article, rereading it. She had to answer:

"Yes."

For a moment, he forgot what he planned to do. He had found the article on the traditional dish and was looking up to the sky in search of buzzards.

"Did you write the sentence that says," and he looked for the reference without finding it, so he quoted it from his poor memory: " 'He yelled like a frightened old lady'?"

" 'He let out a cry like a terrified old lady,' " Mágala corrected him. "Yes, I wrote it."

The kind expression still on his face, Rocket punched Mágala. She couldn't get out of the way, and her step backward wasn't enough to keep her from falling on her back and kicking up the dirt on a floor that was still far from clean. He thought about threatening her; he had thought up some things to say about the risks of a press that was unfriendly to the army. But in the end, he found that his punch was more persuasive than any speech. He closed the door and went back home to make up for the sleepless night caused by *The Circus Gazette*.

Later, seated on a bench in the town square next to Hercules as they both wondered whether Flexor was going to die, Rocket suddenly changed the subject.

"Do you like to beat up on the midget?"

"Yeah," Hercules said, without hesitation, "Flexor, too. Those poor devils have no way to defend themselves."

Then the bell began to toll loudly, with the droning sound of a hammer, over and over again, an angry, stubborn ring that was searching in vain for a believer.

"Well, I can tell you," Rocket concluded with a smile, sticking his chest out, "it doesn't compare to the satisfaction of punching a woman."

I'm going to tell you a story. Barnum had a soul mate. His name was James Bailey, and he too was a great circus impresario. Of course Barnum was smart enough to make him his partner and not his rival. A first-class guy, that Bailey. No doubt about it: we have to chose our partners by instinct and not by blood. At one time, the young Bailey toured around England. He was very successful, thanks for the most part to the star of his show—a giant elephant called Mandarin. This elephant did so many amusing things. He knew how to dance on two legs and had an expression of dour nobility. The people didn't hesitate to pay however many shillings it cost to get up on his back. However, on closing night there was a grave accident. They were celebrating the end of the season, and one of the unskilled circus hands drank more than he could handle, a real loser with his broom in hand and his blue kepi. Emboldened by the little consciousness he still had, he began to pester Mandarin. He pulled his tail, insulted him until he was blue in the face, landed blows to his trunk, and did other harmless but bothersome things like that, so bothersome, in fact, that the elephant, out of pure annoyance, decided to take him out. He charged at him like a bull, and once he had knocked him down, he trampled him several times, squashing the poor devil as if he were a watermelon. And that was that. All of a sudden, the animal was calm. He didn't hate the circus hand, nor was he angry; he merely wanted to get rid of a fly that was buzzing in his ear. When the young Bailey found out what had happened, his countenance did not change the slightest bit, nor did his plans to set off to sea the following day. They put Mandarin in his cage, the circus hand in a coffin, and set sail for New York. When they were well out at sea and to the surprise of all, Bailey ordered the elephant to be thrown overboard. It was a cold, calm order. The first one to react was Mandarin himself. There was no doubt he understood what awaited him, because he began charging the bars of his cage frenetically. Magicians, trapeze artists, and jugglers all together managed to push the cage overboard just as the animal broke the padlock and smelled freedom. He was unusually strong. Mandarin stayed afloat, trumpeting furiously, staring at Bailey with an unforgettable look of resentment, as his prison sank hopelessly into the abyss. They lost sight of him on the horizon, while the animal was still struggling desperately not to sink. They all waited needlessly for the countermand; maybe there was still time to save him. Bailey remained resolute; bon voyage, Mandarin. For the remainder of the trip, Bailey spent his mornings and afternoons looking out to sea nostalgically, they say, fearful that he would see Mandarin swimming after him. Nostalgia, I can believe that, but fear? No way. Bailey wasn't that kind of man. Today the sailors who sail that route say that Mandarin turned into a huge, gray iceberg with sharp tusks and that he sank a boat or two in search of revenge for that mob of acrobats who threw him overboard. Bailey loved his elephant. How could he not, if he was the star of his show, if he himself liked to ride on his back? But he had no tolerance for traitors. The circus could survive only with loyalty and discipline, and Barnum would have done the exact same thing. Travel by boat is the greatest test of a circus's success. It means that in some distant land they have already heard about you and are dying to see you at any cost, at a price high enough to defray the expense of erecting a new Noah's ark. Entire weeks are spent at sea, while the performers continue to earn money and the animals continue to overeat and, sometimes, when the sea makes them nervous, they have to put liquor in their water bowls. Who do you think earns the money for all that? Your fame, your greatness, your name in gold letters. That's why we continue to traipse from one place to another on foot with our mules, with all our stuff on our backs, like nomads, with our small tent where we live crammed together, miserable, and without any privacy. One time I had the chance to change my destiny. Success was sitting in front of me, asking me for a job, almost begging me, and I was a blind idiot. I said, 'No thank you, we don't need your act.' Without insisting, the man left, his head hanging down and his wrinkled felt hat in his hands. He went by the name of Urianguelo, and I have carried that name with me all my life like an illness. I lived with the constant feeling that someone was always one step ahead of me, like when I found out about Lucía Zárate, the smallest woman in the world. In a way, she had also been right under my nose. She was born in San Carlos, about thirty kilometers from where I used to live, and as far as I know, the Zárates were distant relatives of mine. Just as I was beginning the steps to hire her, I found out that she had frozen to death when the train she was traveling in got stuck in a snowstorm. The poor thing—twenty years old and only two kilos, she had no way to stay warm. But in the end, she and I never exchanged a word, and she earned eighteen dollars an hour. No other Mexican performer has ever fetched that much. She would have bankrupted me before her first appearance. The situation with Urianguelo was much more serious; I didn't call him, he came to me. 'I have telekinetic powers,' he said, and when he noticed the puzzled expression on my face, he explained that he exerted influence over objects by using only the power of his mind. He took a spoon out of his jacket and asked me to hold it. He stood arrogantly, with his arms crossed and an unyielding look on his face.

Then, slowly, the spoon began to bend at the narrowest point. It scared me a bit and I threw it down. 'That trick is in poor taste,' I said to him. 'How did you do it?' 'There is no trick,' he explained. 'Mental energy is converted into an invisible hand. I can exert physical force, slight as it may be, on remote objects.' I didn't believe him, and since I could not tolerate someone lying to my face, I threw him out. 'Get out of here,' I said. 'Nobody is interested in seeing a spoon bending.' I had no second thoughts about my decision, until one day, in a tavern, I overheard a conversation from another table. 'Yes, sir,' the guy was saying, 'It's as if by remote control, he could scratch the women there. I forbade my old lady to go to that show, even though you can't be certain, since they say his reach extends many kilometers.' I immediately questioned the guy. 'I'm not sure,' he stated. 'They're just rumors, even the name,' and he pronounced it as if he had no idea, as if he were making it up: 'A guy called Urianguelo or something like that, I don't know.' I was determined not to rest until I sat him down in the middle of my ring, arms crossed, with that stern look on his face. That would surely be the greatest show on earth. I looked for him, God knows I looked for him. Everywhere I went, the answer was the same. Either they didn't know him, or they spoke of him as a legend, and they scorned me for believing he was real, just as I had scorned him when he was standing in front of me. That was more than thirty years ago, and it still hurts to talk about it. I am certain that Urianguelo existed, even though people refused to admit it; the men because there was no defense against the adultery of their wives, and the women . . . well, it's obvious why. He would appear, secretly, like a rumor, in some obscure dive with no lights or marquee, because there was surely a price on his head, especially after a few girls accused him of getting them pregnant. I would have protected him; I would have hired a hundred strong men and lions and tigers to protect him so that I could show him off to all, so that I could travel by boat, even just one time, and to hell with all my faith if some parish priest in town tried to stop me. Barnum fetched more for a ticket to hear Jenny Lind than my entire box-office take on a Sunday, because Jenny Lind was like water laughing, with bubbles where the colored fish play. Seriously, I would have earned more with Urianguelo. I still have the spoon as a reminder to never cast aside another Urianguelo, but look what good it's done me. Fearful of making the same stupid mistake again, I hired a band of good-for-nothings. Look at them all, drenching themselves in the fountain, playing with the church bell, sprawled out in the square. They don't worry about a thing. To hell with the circus, for now they have their little town and their little houses, and with that, they have achieved the glory of being common, ordinary folk. For me, they are nothing more than a bunch of uncaged Mandarins, and although I may have to wait for years, I'll have my chance to throw them all overboard."

"Ggnt," the pig snorted, slobbering in pain.

W*hy do we feel* so important when we are applauded? As if we didn't recall that most of the time when we applaud, we are doing it merely out of courtesy. It's no different than a come in, good afternoon, thank you for coming, you're welcome, it was delicious. I had that feeling of being someone when I heard hands clapping, and pulling out the pages of Olegaroy's book wasn't enough to cure me. After a few days, I went back to DOWNTOWN TRICKS AND NOVELTIES and I got ahold of some tricks '*made in USA*,' and I even bought myself a black cape and my first top hat. And so, without any sense of shame, I became a handbook magician; I mastered do-it-yourself tricks with a one-year guarantee. And now, as never before, I needed the instructions. I was the last to put the slips of paper into the top hat. I had kept one in my sleeve, the one that said 'Mayor.' Now magic could certainly turn me into something great—the magician disappears and in his place appears the principal official of Santa María of the Circus. The bigwig. Hell, I believed my own words, and even now I am wondering if they are true. Chance is God. I let the slip of paper fall into the hat out of fear of committing a sacrilege. A lifetime spent pulling cards from my sleeve and it turns out that when something really important was at stake, I followed the rules and not the instructions. Maybe it doesn't matter. Being the bigwig in such a miserable place is as pointless as sharpening knives. No, it doesn't matter. Who am I kidding? Of course it matters. For the time being, we are going to stay put, a few months maybe, while my lands bear fruit. There is no need to manage such misery, but soon prosperity will come and elections will have to be called. Rocket is a soldier, and in this country, the government must fall into civilian hands. Flexor is disregarded because of his race. Nathaniel belongs to the clergy; he lost the right to vote and be voted for long ago. And you, pardon my saying so, but . . . with your reputation, I don't think you would make a good candidate. And the rest are women. It doesn't matter. Forget it. I swear it doesn't matter. You know . . . ? Don't you miss a drink? Right now I want one so badly that, look at me, it's like I'm drunk, I say one thing and then I say the opposite and . . . Really, forget the thing about the mayor. I don't know why I said that. I come from the City of Palaces and look at me now, aspiring to rule this waste-land of dirt and adobe. Have you been out for a walk lately? A town square without a bandstand, without poplars, with crum-bling monuments, benches that have names, Don Eduardo Parra,

Hugo Valdés y Verdad, the Bocanegra family, Rubén Soto and his heirs. What for? Did they want to leave us a reminder that this is not ours? Why haven't we seen anyone come through? Santa María of the Circus isn't even on the way to anywhere. Our main street isn't even on a trail for salesmen. Have you heard the whistle of a train, even off in the distance? Flexor wasn't so wrong after all. We need the knife-grinder's panpipes, the bells of the secondhand dealer, the whistle of the sweet-potato cart. There is no life here. I feel like a drink. A few drinks. There are some magueys over there, and if we weren't so incompetent, we would already have made pulque. Do you know how it's made? I have no idea. I don't know how to sow the land either. Did I mention that I am from the capital? People there are either lawyers or accountants or engineers or starving to death, because we know nothing about plants or fruit. Don't mind me, I want a drink. We have to find a way out. I don't mean running away, but in every home one needs to know where the door is. Supposedly we were heading toward Zacatecas when Don Ernesto left us. So where is Zacatecas? If not a circus, we could organize a vaudeville show. We would only need to rehearse a couple of dance steps, at least you, Narcissa, Harrieta, and the midget. I can do a bit of prestidigitation and 'Where's the Ball?', and we can present the act of the man who refused to be born. We will surely earn some money and, more important, we will stick around after the show to have a few drinks. What do you think? I need a drink."

"Me too," Hercules said. "It would make it easier to put up with you."

Sweaty, *disappointed,* and his hand aching from a whack from the clapper, Nathaniel left his church to preach the terrible fate that awaited all those who scorned the call of his bell. First he went in search of Flexor, who until then had been his only parishioner, since he knew that the sick are the easiest to intimidate with threats of the afterlife. He stuck his head through the bars in the window and began.

"Those who have not set foot in my church have ignorance as an excuse. But you, heathen Flexor, have already tasted the honey of faith . . ."

He stopped when he saw the boy writhing on the floor like a worm, shaking so much that it seemed too violent even for a contortionist. Narcissa was watching him, terrified and powerless, asking him what was happening and getting no response. She noticed Nathaniel and hurried over to the window to ask him for an incantation to free Flexor from his suffering. The midget was so spooked that he couldn't think of any prayers, and he justified his inability by saying that Flexor was a lost cause, that the devil had already entered that house and taken possession of his prey.

"Call Harrieta," he said. "When faith fails, there is always medicine," and he left to preach his word in the town square.

He changed his mind when he found Hercules and Rocket together. He didn't dare approach them both at the same time, especially after how badly Hercules had treated him in his own church. He stuck himself beneath the horse's mouth under the stream of water and later, dripping-wet and shivering, he lay down on a bench to take a nap, wondering if he was prepared to say a mass for the dead.

"What did you say your last name was?" he heard the voice of Harrieta just as he was about to lose consciousness.

"For the first time, I am happy to see you." He opened his eye and sat up. He patted the bench to his right, inviting Harrieta to sit down. "Lately I've had a pain in my chest."

"Olaguíbel, right?" she said, motionless, her hands clasped behind her back. "Or Bocanegra? Or Porcayo?"

"I still don't know how long horses live."

"By the way." She dropped her hands and folded her arms in a way that forced her breasts upward. "Don Alejo is here and you still don't have a name."

"Brother Nathaniel," he said, annoyed.

"I thought of a nicer one—" and she shut up when she saw the fierce expression on the midget's face.

"I stopped being a circus performer some time ago."

Harrieta burst out laughing. Nathaniel was captivated by the movement of her beard. He had seen other bearded women, but none quite like this one. The others were just that: women with beards who sometimes didn't even have a mustache. The one before him, however, had a thick, black coat of hair on her arms, legs, hands, armpits, and surely all over the rest of her body. What the devil is a bearded woman doing in the circus? he wondered. That was fine for a miserable little stand in a traveling carnival, but not for a big top that boasted of a great show.

"Do you really see a future in this?" Harrieta asked, pointing to the hamlet with a wave of her hand.

The midget lowered his head and thought that he was the only one with no future, or perhaps he had the future of an old horse, bowlegged and on the verge of dislocating something.

"I am going to spend the rest of my life here," he responded, his eye staring straight into hers.

"Have you read what's on the back of the bench?" Harrieta almost forgot why she had come looking for the midget in the first place.

He turned around and struggled to read the inscription faded by time: COURTESY OF THE BOCANEGRA FAMILY. He spit on his hands and used them as a moist rag so he could be certain of what he had read.

"That's not the only one," Harrieta said. "There are about six benches with the same inscription. The Bocanegras must have been important people around here."

Nathaniel went over to the next bench and learned that it was courtesy of Mr. Valdés. He moved on to the next, and indeed, there was his name again in gold letters, even though the B had completely disappeared.

"Six, you say?"

Harrieta responded indifferently, "Or five, I don't know."

"Do any say Olaguíbel or Rivera or Porcayo?"

She shook her head no. Instead of continuing to read each bench, Nathaniel went over to the fountain and stood next to the pedestal, pointing to the horseman.

"Do you know who this is?"

"Of course," Harrieta said. "Timoteo de Roncesvalles."

Nathaniel shook his head and smiled proudly.

"It must be my relative, the President," he said. "It's José María Bocanegra," and he knelt down, raising his arms high above his head.

"Listen to me, you little bastard," Harrieta said. "You, better than anyone, should know that it's not good to worship statues," and then she went over to Hercules and Rocket. "According to the midget, the man in the statue is a relative of his."

Rocket wasn't the slightest bit interested, and he gestured in disgust with his hand as he walked off. Hercules glimpsed another opportunity to humiliate Nathaniel, and he went over to him.

"It's Timoteo," Harrieta said, "but this idiot says it's a Bocanegra."

"Like the one who wrote the national anthem," Hercules said, not realizing that his comment would encourage the midget even more.

"Exactly," Nathaniel said as he sat up. "I didn't mentioned it before because it might seem like bragging."

Hercules kicked at the water. "Well, to hell with the national anthem and all that nonsense," he said and thought about grabbing the midget by the hair and submerging him in the fountain, but he remembered what Rocket had said and wondered if it wouldn't be better to punch Harrieta.

"If there's anything we should learn from Spain," he went on, "it's that hymns should have only music and not empty words."

"Don't pay any attention to the midget," she insisted. "The name is Timoteo de Roncesvalles, and he gave his life for the honor of a woman."

"He's Don José María Bocanegra," Nathaniel fought back, "the only unblemished President in the entire history of our country."

Upon hearing the word *history*, Hercules hung his head, for he knew nothing about that. Even so, he decided to stand his ground, believing that the midget couldn't possibly come from an illustrious family and, for lack of an argument, he muttered, "Someday I'm going to demolish that statue with stones."

Just as he was leaving, his fist still in the air, he bumped into Narcissa.

"Harrieta," she said, "something terrible is happening," and she took her by the hand to lead her to her house. Harrieta went along, but halfway there, she broke free and turned around.

"Your other relative," she addressed Nathaniel. "How many mine workers did he kill?"

"That doesn't matter," he said, but seeing that the penetrating look on Harrieta's face had not vanished, he answered, "A hundred and twenty-three."

"I thought so," she said and pointed to the 1, 2, and 3 that had been painted in red with a thick brush on the burnt-out house.

The air in Santa María of the Circus was heavy with the death throes of the diving pig, that who, once a constant presence, was now barely noticeable, like the whisper of the wind.

Mandrake *shuddered when,* peering through the window of Narcissa's house, he saw Flexor, in the candlelight, completely bent over backwards. Mágala, on the other hand, was amused.

"He's good," she said, her lip still swollen from Rocket's punch.

"Don't be stupid," Mandrake said, crumpling his top hat. "Something must be broken."

Inside, Narcissa was telling Harrieta that all of a sudden Flexor had had spasms, and that with each one, his back arched a little bit more until he was like as they now saw him.

"He only moaned a little," she said, finishing her story. "He's so brave."

"Those of his race," Harrieta explained, "are made to put up with pain."

"I had to put him on the ground," Narcissa said. "With all the spasms, I was afraid he would fall."

"Those of his race," Harrieta went on, "are made to sleep on the floor."

Flexor seemed to be resting. After an afternoon that Narcissa described as "interminable," the boy's face looked relaxed and peaceful. He seemed comfortable despite the grotesque position of his body, stretched out backwards on his side. Harrieta walked over to the window and with some waving and flapping of her arms, she scared away the onlookers. For lack of a better idea, she brought the candle over to the swollen leg and let a few drops of the hot wax fall onto the knee. Flexor opened his eyes when he felt the burning and, expressing a thought that was running through his mind, said:

"I want to be like Jules Léotard."

The women looked at each other in search of a pertinent response.

"That's nice," Harrieta said.

"All his life, he risked his neck on the trapeze," Flexor went on. "He was the first one to do a somersault, and sometimes he flew through the air without a net."

"You never told me you wanted to be a trapeze artist," Harrieta said.

"I don't," Flexor corrected her. "I'm going to invent some getup and name it after me."

Harrieta had always seen Flexor in his yellow leotard. To her, that garment was a contorsionist's skin, and she could never associate it with the trapeze artist from France, much less with the Cabriolé brothers, who also wore leotards, although theirs were more feminine and had different colors and sequins. Narcissa looked at the twisted body and was deeply saddened, wondering why those who were dying always seemed so full of plans.

"You have to save him," she pleaded with Harrieta.

"I've always needed a cover to keep my beard clean. Invent one and I'll let you name it after yourself, even though I gave you the idea," she said, more interested in what the boy had to say than in Narcissa's orders.

"What for?" Flexor asked. "There can't be more than ten women like you. I'll never become famous that way."

All of a sudden his body began to tremble violently and he broke out in a sweat. He closed his eyes as he heard Narcissa say, "Here comes another one."

The spasm made his back arch a little more, and there was a cracking sound, like dry branches breaking. To escape the horror of the moment, Harrieta recalled an article about another bearded lady who had been born into British royalty and who, on the same day, had received three offers of marriage. I have the beard, she thought, but not the royalty, and the only man capable of falling in love with me is a stone statue. And as she was thinking about Timoteo de Roncesvalles, the expression on her face changed from fear to pleasure.

Narcissa brought her back to reality with a slap.

"What's wrong with you? You have to save my little black boy."

"Science has its limitations," Harrieta said, her hand on her chin in a pose she thought conveyed intelligence. "If the railway passed through here—"

They heard footsteps outside and they both turned toward the window. There was Nathaniel, smiling and chanting like an idiot.

"By the hand of God, it was written—" He stopped his chanting when Narcissa threw the candle at him. The flame went out and the house was left in shadows.

"I hope your science works," she said to Harrieta, "because the midget is useless."

She picked up the candle and lit it again, wondering if anyone knew how to make fire with stones, since the matches wouldn't last forever.

"I'm going to try something," Harrieta said without thinking over what she was about to say. "I'm going to cut off his leg with Mandrake's saw."

As she said that, she imagined the screeching of a saw cutting through bone. I've made up my mind, she thought, I won't deal with amputations or births or contagious diseases. I'll leave town before I do that. She shook her head: I need a train.

"Are you crazy?" Narcissa looked at her, horrified.

Harrieta let her mind wander again, and she thought that even if she lost Timoteo, there was Hercules, also a man of stone, and with enough persistence, he might end up giving his life for a woman's honor, too. She ran her hands over her rear end, wondering when Hercules would feel desperate enough to appreciate it.

"I don't know what kind of bugs are inside him," Narcissa said, going over to Flexor and wrapping her arms around him without touching him, "but they are not just in his leg anymore."

"I've got a plan," Harrieta declared, making a sign to indicate she would be back later, and she left the house, without the slightest idea of what she was going to do. When the door closed behind her, Flexor opened his eyes.

"I just figured out how I got this way," he said.

Narcissa went over to him, happy to hear him speak with a steady voice and taking it as a sign that he was getting better.

"Try to rest," she said as she covered his leg with a piece of cloth.

"It was you, you wretch." Flexor's eyes turned dark, fiery, and bloodshot. "You poisoned me with your slobber when you spit on the wound," and he tried uselessly to sit up so he could satisfy the violent spirit that possessed him. His muscles were stiff and motionless, meat in a slaughterhouse.

Y*ou might wonder* why I am not called Olaguíbel y Ruiz or Porcayo or the ordinary, modest, made-up Rivera, and you see this as reason enough to roundly dismiss the notion of my origins being of good blood and deep pockets. It's not that simple. Remember that every two or three generations, due to various circumstances, we changed our name. The years passed and I became part of the Bocanegra dynasty, and I must now see that this momentum doesn't stop. The era of the Fernandos is over, and that of the Nathaniels has begun, Nathaniel the First, Second, Third, and so on, as destiny mandates. If you must know the truth, I have already chosen the woman who will bear Nathaniel the Second. Curious? Anxious? Hopeful? Don't tell me you're not interested. Should I tell you? No? I'll continue with that a little later. With my height, my eye, and my ugliness, no one is indifferent to me. People feel sorry for me, hate me, make fun of me, hit me, avoid me, or they might love me, admire me or respect me, and who knows, even use those words reserved for illustrious men. As for me, I have nothing against myself. I have never wanted to be tall, and quite honestly, I wish everyone were a midget. The world would be a nicer place if we were all small. I don't hate myself, nor I am repulsed by myself; in fact, I love myself and worry about my health, about this pain in my joints, and about not knowing the average life span of a midget or a horse, if they live the same length of time or if one lives longer than the other. And consider this: on that list of emotions that I inspire, I did not mention shame, since shame can only apply to the things that belong to us. Only three people could feel ashamed of my being a midget: me, and I am actually proud of myself; my mother, who if she felt that way, knew how to hide it very well; and my father, with whom the story of why I am a Bocanegra and not something else begins and ends. He was deeply ashamed of me. He wanted to keep me locked up in my room so that no one on the street would say, 'There goes the son of Fernando Porcayo.' I didn't care if he didn't like me. In the end, our relationship was nothing more than scoldings, thrashings, and smacks with a ladle. Some time after my mother died, a strolling player came to town. Among his repertoire of anecdotes, he recounted that he had a son who was very tall, more than two meters, 'because I don't know if I told you,' the guy went on, 'that the height of one's children is proportionate to the length of the prick.' Everyone laughed except my father, and the strolling player did not understand why his comment was so amusing. Naturally, the following morning, my father already had a nickname—Shortdick. He never forgave me, as if I had been the one who said it. He began to look at me with more and more ill will. Go look for a job, go off and see the world, get out of the city, go join the puny little bullfighters, a thousand ideas to get rid of me. It didn't bother him to overlook the memory of his dead wife, and he made up a story about her having had an affair with a traveling salesman, so that he could disown me as his own son. After that, he no longer suggested I leave; he simply threw me out of the house. We looked at each other for several minutes without blinking, me from the middle of the street, he from behind the window, the curtains drawn open, and both of us without a tear. With no roof over my head, no job or way to earn a living, and with no one better to hold responsible for the fix I was in, I blamed the traveling player who had delivered the fateful joke. I insisted that he hire me for his show. He accepted reluctantly. 'I need an assistant,' he said, 'even though I hadn't pictured someone like you.' That day I took my mother's last name, Bocanegra, and also on that day the traveling player named me Midge the Midget. How unoriginal. Not even Don Alejo had such lack of imagination. With that silly name, I was sure to be part of the show. However, the player's idea of an assistant was someone who would go ahead of him to the next town on the itinerary, put up a few posters, and reserve a place to spend the night. He never invited me to share the stage. My only participation had to do with his ability to make fun of himself. Just as he was explaining the relationship between a son's height and the length of the member, I would shout, 'Papa, someone's here to see you.' That was it. I must have said it a thousand times. The people already knew the joke, but they laughed anyway. He even had the posters printed with my name: MIDGE THE MIDGET. How tiresome. That's why as soon as I found the circus, I didn't hesitate to ask for the big boss. And it turned out that Don Alejo wanted to name me something just as silly, or worse: General Tom Thumb, Microman, Dwarfonio, the Cyclops of Lilliput, Midgetowski. That is why I have a first name and a last name that I use with more pride than I ever felt for Olaguíbel y Ruiz. That man may have been about to become a viceroy, but he didn't reach the level—holiness, I would say—of Don José María Bocanegra. Do you know which is the most productive mine in this country? Obviously, it's not the one we left back there near the big top or the one my relative blew up. There is one that continuously spews out gold, and that's the presidential office. It is there that the most vile acts of robbery are carried out, and no hand is able to resist. Not even you or I or anyone would have the resoluteness not to take a few pesos if we are 'honorable' people, or half the budget if we are of the sort of satrapy to which our governors here always have belonged. I know, that doesn't matter much. In this damned country, stealing isn't a crime. But we have to be grateful that amidst such garbage, there existed a President, only one, without a blemish. Just as there was only one man without sin, there was only one President without a blemish. The immaculate one of our political history. It was many years ago, and there is no one still living to testify to how he started his rule with his hands clean, and how when he finally left his seat, having properly fulfilled his duties, his hands were even more chaste of money, injustice, and blood. People loved him and celebrated him in the streets, even more than they did the bishop. My mother told me so, and it is true. And he traveled through these parts, I know; he had family and followers in this state. You yourself showed me the benches from the Bocanegras—that's why I'm sure that that statue is not of some Timoteo de Roncesvalles. We have to make note of that, you and I, to change the name, to have a commemorative plaque made, and to pay him homage every December fourth, the day of his accession. Tomorrow we will explain that, and then later we can discuss your conditions for bearing Nathaniel the Second."

"Over my dead body," Harrieta responded, and Nathaniel didn't know if she was referring to the matter of Timoteo or the next Bocanegra.

D on Alejo left his house and immediately ran into Mandrake. He was not sure of how to speak to him, for while he still regarded himself as the boss, lately he had received only signs of rebellion and arrogance from his subordinates. He decided to implore.

"Help me," and to show, weak as it was, some authority, he pulled on Mandrake's shirt. "The pig is dying."

"That's nice," Mandrake said. "It's about time for us to eat that beast."

Don Alejo gave him a shove, but it was he who was pushed back.

"Not as long as he can be saved."

Mandrake shrugged. "That's not my job," he said indifferently. "I'm just the landowner. She's the doctor," and he pointed to Harrieta, who at that moment was leaving Narcissa's house.

Even though Don Alejo had no idea of what Mandrake was talking about, he went over to Harrieta to ask her to save the pig. She was still, and her face revealed nothing.

"Please."

"I can't," Harrieta said. "Flexor is dying. It would be irresponsible of me to abandon him to take care of an animal that we are just going to cook anyway."

"Please," Don Alejo repeated.

"All right." She couldn't refuse. "Let's go."

For a moment, Harrieta missed her circus days, when her only responsibility was to stand in the center of the ring and wait for the announcer to speak, depending on the script of the day, about a pair of twins, a man and a woman fusioned in the same body, and as a consequence, a creature that displayed both sexes; or about the bearded lady's mother, who had been raped by a mandrill—"And if it weren't because good taste prohibits it, we would show you that, in fact, the woman before you has the rear end of a mandrill, pink and bald"—or about the risks of women not accepting their condition and trying to be like men. And there, waiting for the applause, she had no annoyance greater than putting up with the silly, stupid kids while they pulled on her beard to make sure it was real. She resigned herself to her fate, thinking that she had not become a doctor by pure chance, but by an unavoidable destiny, because it was completely natural for a doctor to have a beard.

They took a couple of candles off the cart and went inside to see the pig. After the repugnance she had felt over Flexor's pestilent knee and his arched body, Harrieta expected the pig to make an even worse impression on her, but such was not the case. Seeing the wounded animal only evoked the atmosphere of a butcher's shop. Not only was she not repulsed, but she savored the thought of a big dish of cracklings with sauce. She grabbed the animal by the robe and pulled it out of the pool of blood.

"I don't know why you're so concerned," Harrieta said. "Any pig can dive."

She pushed back the robe and held a candle up to see the wound more clearly. It didn't seem so bad, although the animal had evidently lost a lot of blood. It was blinking slowly and its eyes were following Don Alejo.

"Look at him. He's trying to tell me something," the old man said, and he sat down next to the animal to pet it.

Harrieta felt more pity for the old man than for the pig, and once again, for lack of a reliable cure, she let a few drops of hot wax fall onto the wound. This time, it seemed to work. The flow of blood now weakened; the wax formed a seal, stopping it completely.

"By the way," Harrieta said, "I have a good name for the midget."

"My brother," Don Alejo said. "Where could he be?"

"The Chubby *Charro*," Harrieta went on. "We can have him do rodeo tricks, mounted on a lamb and roping chickens."

Don Alejo opened his arms a bit and Harrieta took him by his armpits and put him on his feet.

"Could it be going as bad for him as it is for us? Could he already have his big top? Sometimes I think we never should have split up."

"Do you want a massage?" she offered.

He shook his head no and felt ashamed and angry just thinking that at that very moment, a crowd might be applauding his brother, and that he might carry out his plan of putting on a midnight show. "Nude flying-trapeze artists," Don Ernesto had explained his plan. "Obscene clowns, the lion tamer who sticks his genitals, not his head, into the lion's mouth, elephants making love—"

"Clap for me," Don Alejo said.

"Huh?" Harrieta dropped her shoulders and frowned.

"You heard me," he said impatiently. "Come on."

Again she pitied Don Alejo. Then she realized that there wasn't much difference between asking for applause as the old man had just done and asking for it with the language of the circus, just as every performer did after his act by raising his arms or lining up or, worse, using the announcer as an intermediary: "Yes, ladies and gentlemen, a warm round of applause for the bushy Harrieta, beautiful despite her ugliness." She applauded loudly for a few seconds.

"Thank you," Don Alejo smiled. "Thank you, beloved audience."

The pig began to kick its legs as if it were terrified and wanted to take off running, but with its weight all on one side, it barely grazed the floor with the back of its right feet, which caused it to slowly spin around in a circle.

"Something's going to happen," Harrieta said.

"Maybe," Don Alejo said, opening the door. "Now go."

"What are we going to do?" in the darkness of the street, Harrieta noticed an indecipherable omen that filled her with sadness.

"Any day now, we are going to leave," Don Alejo said. "In the meantime, try to come up with some good ideas. The Chubby *Charro* is the worst one I've heard in my entire life."

Nathaniel *could see* the sky through the nonexistent roof of the burnt-out house. He removed some charred planks and found several that still showed their original shape, an unmistakable sign that fire had also consumed the furniture. He crossed his arms and walked through the debris, trampling timidly on the planks and charred rubble, afraid of finding a burned skeleton. When he saw the house for the first time, he imagined that the damage had been caused by a lightning bolt or an oil lamp, but he did not dwell on the matter since that fire-scarred building had not impressed him much. Now Harrieta had put ideas in his head, though the more he swept through the debris with his feet, the more he was convinced that this was a case of pillage and not revenge, as he found no objects of value, nothing metal or clay that had survived the fire and, fortunately, no bones.

"What are you doing?" Mágala was looking for material for her second issue of *The Circus Gazette* and Harrieta had already alerted her to the possible connection of the 1, 2, 3 with the Bocanegras.

"You know," Nathaniel responded firmly.

"And you think he lived here?"

Nathaniel shrugged and continued to sweep debris aside with his feet.

"No," he answered. "That happened a long time ago."

"What difference does it make?" she asked. "In those kinds of massacres, revenge is passed on to the next generations."

"I already told you. Anyway, the Bocanegras lived here, not the Riveras, and I don't give a damn about telling that story anymore."

Despite his response, Mágala would decide to write the following as an exact quote in the newspaper: "There is no doubt about it; my relative, the murderer of all those mine workers, lived here." And, in passing, she would imply that this was the reason that Santa María of the Circus had been abandoned. "There were too many widows, too much pain, to keep living in this place that would inevitably make them remember, for no one was saved from having lost a son, a husband, or a father."

"The town is very small," Nathaniel said. "A hundred and twenty-three people couldn't have lived here."

That comment seemed quite logical to Mágala. She was disappointed for a few minutes, but in the end, she decided to add one more sentence to her report: "It was a time when everyone used to live in huts next to the mine, and these were moved when the survivors left."

"As far as I'm concerned," Nathaniel concluded, "that number indicates the address of the house, which at one time could well have been 123 Bocanegra Avenue."

"You're right about that," she said. "We have to name the streets, but not with the names of the same old heroes."

"Bocanegra was our only President without a blemish," the midget said proudly, "and he's not one of 'the same old heroes.' "

"Nobody knows who he is," she said. "I doubt very much that he even existed." She looked at the four streets in the town that formed the perimeter of the town square. "I was thinking of the real heroes: Barnum Road, Ringling Boulevard"—and with each name, she pointed to one of the uneven dirt streets—"Houdini Avenue and, why not, Mantecón Way."

Nathaniel let out a sarcastic laugh. "Now you want to raise the Mantecón brothers to the level of heroes?"

"Of course," Mágala said. "It's thanks to them that we're here."

"A pile of leftovers," he spit out. "That's what they are."

"I thought you would have a story, something interesting to tell."

"Are you with me or with Harrieta? Is that statue of a Bocanegra or of a Roncesvalles?"

"You tell me."

Mágala closed herself up in her house to edit the second issue of *The Circus Gazette*. She couldn't figure out why she was so willing to slander Nathaniel by writing sentences like: "He boasted of carrying the dynamiter's spirit in his blood, and he confessed that if he had a few cartridges, he would blow us all up regardless of race or creed." She simply meant to savor the pleasures that her new ability to lie with authority offered, especially by speaking for the midget, who would certainly not have the guts that Rocket had had to pay her back for the affront with punches. She touched her lips, still swollen, and decided to give Rocket another kiss to make peace. She wrote the headline: "Midget with Murderer's Blood," and hesitated for a moment, wondering if she should change the word "midget" to "priest." She decided that even in a cassock, Nathaniel was still, above all, a midget, and if it wasn't a good idea for a newspaper to pick on the army, it was even worse for it to pick on the church. Once again she needed another piece of news to complete the issue, and after thinking for quite a while and ruling out headlines like "Don Alejo Returns" and "The Pig Is Stabbed," she found the news of the moment in Flexor's imminent death. "I have seen two men exhibit the same symptoms, and both ended up dead after many days of suffering. The surprising thing is that everything happened so quickly with this boy. It may be because he belongs to another species, to a race that is so strong in work but so weak in illness." Just as she was about to finalize the issue, she decided to include a third article with the headline "Red Tide," in which she accused Harrieta of going into Timoteo's fountain "during her impure days." She made six copies—she wouldn't give one to Nathaniel, and one copy would be enough for Narcissa and Flexor. However, she changed the second article in the edition that she would slip under Narcissa's door. The headline read, "He Will Live," and she described Flexor's illness as a disease that was "painful and dramatic, but not life-threatening, since upon recovery, it made the body even stronger and the mind clearer."

· · ·

Mandrake *pushed the door* open and in one leap was inside Hercules' house. The slight squeaking of the hinges barely competed with the sound of the trickling water in the town square. Inside, the candlelight revealed the sagging humanity of what had once been the strong man. He was lying on the hard old bed in the corner, and his tights hung from a nail in the wall.

"Hi, honey," Mandrake said.

Hercules looked up, annoyed that the visitor had entered without knocking.

"None of that mushy stuff," he said. "I just do my job."

At that very moment, on the other side of the wall, Harrieta was getting dolled up. She felt overwhelmed by the health of her patients, especially that of Flexor, who was on the verge of becoming the midget's responsibility. She wished she had a mirror, her makeup case, her sweet-smelling soaps, and a brush for her hair and beard. She wiped her body with a wet rag, untangled her hair with her fingers and, for lack of rouge, smeared herself with a bit of red paste that she found in Mandrake's box, the kind used by Teary, Tufty, and Stretch to paint their faces. She tried it before putting it on her lips, and it tasted bitter, like medicine. No matter how attractive my red mouth looks, no one would give me a kiss without being disgusted afterward. She got dressed and, again wishing she had a mirror, ran the tips of her fingers along the corner of her eyes to eliminate any sleep that might detract from her beauty and add repugnance.

"Here I come," she said softly.

Her heart was beating quickly as she left her house, but it was filled with courage as soon as she saw the statue. "My life for your honor," she said to herself, but she corrected herself almost immediately: "My honor for your life." She walked with short, silent steps as she turned from side to side to make sure no one was watching her. When she got to Hercules' house, she opened the door decisively and went inside.

"What are you doing?" Harrieta asked, horrified by the scene before her.

Instead of responding, Hercules sat up and hurried to put on his tights.

"Doesn't anyone knock anymore?"

"I asked you what you're doing," Harrieta insisted.

Mandrake was on the bed, frozen. At first he thought the question was for him, but then he noticed that Harrieta was glaring sharply at Hercules. He wrapped himself up in his cape as best he could, put his hat on with dignity, and left without a word.

"What does it look like?" Hercules responded after an unbearable silence, for even the sound of Mandrake's strides had vanished. "You take care of your patients, the midget looks after his church, Narcissa goes around sharpening knives. Why shouldn't I do my job?"

"Finish with those," she shouted, exasperated, because in his haste, Hercules had not succeeded in putting on his tights and in just one second, she had seen more of a man than she had in her entire life. Then she added, "I don't know how to cure anyone, and my patients are sure to die; no one has so much as given Narcissa a knife; the poor midget has never even said mass. You are the only one who has willingly accepted this game."

"It's not a game," Hercules said, realizing that maybe it really was a game. "Anyway"—he began to feel embarrassed and wanted to say something to assure Harrieta that he had only done it with Mandrake—"you scared away my only customer."

"You have no idea of how long I've waited for this moment," she said, looking down at the ground, "and now I would rather give myself to the midget."

Hercules was not attracted to Harrieta's body in the slightest, but it pained him to lose out to Nathaniel.

"Mágala put out a newspaper," he said to defend himself.

Harrieta was tired, but she wasn't willing to sit on the bed, so she relaxed her legs until they gave way and she found herself sprawled on the floor.

"I should have picked that slip of paper."

"Thanks," Hercules said, for what he considered as a gesture of solidarity.

"I don't mean yours, you idiot," she clarified. "I meant Mágala's. I had an uncle who wrote for *El País*, and I might have journalism in my veins."

Hercules finally finished getting dressed, and still without having recovered his dignity, he said, "I didn't know my family very well, but I'm sure no aunt followed in my footsteps."

"Or maybe not," Harrieta went on without listening to him, "but it's easier to write than to save the dying. A blank sheet of paper is better than a pus-filled knee."

Despite the dim light of the candle, Harrieta could see a helpless expression in Hercules' eyes, and she now knew that it was he who needed her and not the other way around, as usual. At that moment, she could hug him and she would find not rejection, but a man in need of affection who would hold her for a long time, and they would even share their sweat and a few affectionate words. She glimpsed her long-awaited chance. He was at her mercy, helpless, a wounded walrus. All I need to do is move a little closer, take his hand and stop his downfall. But her body felt heavy, and she was unable to move toward him.

"I finally understand people," she said.

Hercules sat down on the bed. He looked at the floor and at his feet. His nails were long and dirty. He didn't have the courage to look at Harrieta.

"What do you mean?"

"It's not my defects that make me so horrible," she said non-chalantly. "The problem is everyone else's arrogance," and she got up slowly, using the wall to support herself, like a cripple. "That's what I was taught to think."

"You were taught wrong," Hercules said.

He was becoming irritated. Now he looked up. He was tired. Leave me alone, he thought. I want to sleep.

"We didn't have to wait until we grew old, did we?" Harrieta said. "Now circumstances have made us equal."

Hercules lost his patience. For lack of a response, he picked up a board from the bed and threw it at Harrieta, missing. The wood hit the wall and fell noisily to the floor.

"What was that?" she asked.

"What do you think?" he said, his anger in check as he bent down to pick up the board. "It was this."

"No," Harrieta said. "I heard something outside, something strange."

At once their expressions became calm and kind, as if they had just met and had only exchanged greetings, and Hercules had not thrown the board intending to do harm. Harrieta went over to him, put her hands on his chest and began to caress him awkwardly. Then she touched his cheeks and finally, she kissed him softly and quickly, barely feeling his lips.

"Boy, do I understand people," she said, taking a step back and searching Hercules with her eyes slowly, up and down, until she looked him straight in the eye. "Your rejections won't bother me anymore. In the end, I'm just like everyone else."

He walked over to the window and stared out into the emptiness.

"I don't hear a thing," he said.

"Me neither," she said from the door. "Good-bye."

And amidst a resounding silence, he realized that what Harrieta had heard was not a noise but just the opposite: the arrival of absolute silence, without even the gurgling of the fountain, for the water from Timoteo's horse had stopped flowing.

Pablo Fanque *was a great* circus impresario, and he was black. In fact, he was the first of my race to run a circus. It's not my color that worries me, it's time. It's clear that there's not much time, on the clock, that is, not on the calendar. At this point, only my last words could make someone remember me. But what can I say? More light? Now comes the mystery? Either that wallpaper goes or I do? I shall not completely die? Those are all stupid. Not even poets die with poetry. Help me, Narcissa, to think of something. Will you have my last words engraved on my tombstone? It's the least you can do after poisoning me. Don't even think about putting 'Encarnación Ruiz.' You know my name. For that, you wanted a son? That slobber of yours is killing me. What did you do with that mouth of yours? What do you eat, what do you suck on, what do you do to have the venom of a viper? Thank heavens I'm a good contortionist or I'd have broken my back a long time ago. This wouldn't have happened if I hadn't joined up with the Mantecón brothers. This wouldn't have happened if those brothers hadn't split up, if we hadn't hummed a waltz, if Don Alejo hadn't gotten confused by his map, if I hadn't taken off running like an idiot, if Hercules hadn't hurt me, if we hadn't decided to stay here, if you hadn't adopted me, if you hadn't licked my wound. . . . Does that seem fair to you? I am dying because the Mantecóns decided to split up. A waltz is killing me. I can't blame just you, for the final cause is no more to blame than the previous ones. Help me come up with my last words. Let's steal some. Do me a favor. Name the town square after me, or the statue, or a street. Am I going to die? No. Yes. I need to choose a slip of paper from the top hat to find out. Two to one, dead or alive, fifty-fifty. That's all I'm asking for, not ten to one, or a thousand to one. I'll settle for fifty-fifty. It was your damned slobber, but if they ask you, tell them it was Strauss . . . no, Juventino Rosas, even my mind is failing. I have a worthless hunch, like when I chose the paper that said 'Negro.' Did I tell you about Pablo Fanque? He was the first—hey! Where are you going?"

"I'll be right back," Narcissa said. "Keep talking if you want."

Doctor!" Narcissa's voice broke in like a noisy intruder. "It's an emergency."

Harrieta adjusted her skirt and then looked out the window with an annoyed expression that vanished in the darkness.

"Now what do you want?"

"It's Flexor, my Flexor. He's not going to make it."

Lucky him, Harrieta thought, as both of them headed to his deathbed. She wanted to go to Don Alejo and tell him, let's get out of here, you and me; alone we can put on a show, not as grand as a circus, but at least a booth at a carnival. Flexor's body, which reeked of death, lay completely still, surrounded by four candles. Harrieta thought he looked like a corpse at a wake. If you want, Don Alejo, we'll take the midget, but only him, not Hercules, please. The tension in the muscles arching the body mimicked the stiffening of dead flesh.

"He senses that the end is near," Narcissa said. "A little while ago, he was trying to come up with his last words, and he asked me to have them engraved on his tombstone."

" 'Sense' is a pretty mild word for something so obvious," Harrieta said, not bothering to lower her voice. Then she gave Narcissa a shove. "Hurry, go get the priest."

As soon as she was alone with her patient, she thought for a minute about how she might cure him. Narcissa was right, the disease was not just in his leg anymore, and it would now be necessary to lay the entire body across the railroad tracks. There was one position that would leave the body in nineteen pieces; it was a difficult position for normal people, but not for a contortionist. Mágala would surely accept that one as a macabre jigsaw puzzle. She picked up the candles and dripped the wax, forming three crosses around Flexor. Then she sat down to wait, wondering if it wouldn't be better to just stick one of Dagoberto's daggers into him and be done with the whole matter.

After a while, Nathaniel entered the house reluctantly, wearing no shirt and embarrassed, for he had no idea of what to do for a dying man.

"I've done all that's humanly possible," Harrieta said with feigned resignation. "Now it's your turn."

"If I'm as good a priest as you are a doctor, this boy will surely wake up in hell."

He asked them to leave him alone, but both women refused to go.

"Three prayers are better than one."

"Mine isn't worth much," Harrieta declared. "I lost all faith last night."

Nathaniel stretched out his arms and began to say a Hail Mary. He was just at the "Blessed art thou" when Flexor opened his eyes and stared at Narcissa with a look of hatred.

"It was your damned slobber," he said, and his body twisted with another contraction. He was clearly in great pain, but he closed his eyes and lost consciousness, not like someone who faints, but like someone sleeping peacefully.

Nathaniel stood watching, with an inquisitive look on his face, and Narcissa explained.

"I never kissed him. He means the spit I used to wash the wound."

"Open up," Don Alejo's voice came from the other side of the door.

"Beat it," Narcissa shouted. "Can't you see we are trying to save my boy?"

"I came for the same reason," he said, his voice choked with emotion.

"The pig is sick, and I'm afraid I'll lose him."

"You've got to be kidding," Narcissa said. "We're trying to save a human being here."

Harrieta saw her chance to wriggle out of her responsibility for the dying man. "I'm going to have a look at the pig," she said. "After all, it's my patient, too."

Narcissa watched resentfully as she left, but before the door closed behind her, Narcissa announced: "Now you shall see the midget's great powers. He's going to perform a miracle and bring Flexor back to me, safe and sound."

Nathaniel shrugged and began to recite a series of phrases in Latin that reminded him of being at mass with his mother and holding her hand, not knowing what the phrases meant, but repeated them now as a fervent believer nonetheless, for after what Narcissa had said, he felt certain that he held in his amorphous hands enough miraculous power to straighten out that body.

A sheet of paper appeared from underneath the door. Narcissa picked it up and began to read it eagerly.

"Thank God," she said raising her right hand to her chest. "Flexor is going to live. He has a painful and dramatic illness but it's not life-threatening, since upon recovery, it makes the body even stronger and the mind clearer."

"Great," Nathaniel said. "Then I shall go to bed happy to have performed my little miracle."

Narcissa raised her hand in a signal for him to stop.

"It also says here that you have the blood of an assassin in your veins, and that you would love to blow us all up regardless of race or creed."

The midget clenched his teeth and left.

Two houses down, Harrieta was kneeling in front of the pig. She was surprised by how quickly its chest was rising and falling and by how strongly it was exhaling the humid, warm, smelly air. Its tail was quivering like a spring, and mucus was dripping down from its snout, forming a slimy spot on the ground.

"Save him," Don Alejo begged.

His pathetic voice made Harrieta realize she had made a mistake; she should have stayed with Flexor. She used her finger to apply pressure on the swelling, and the animal bellowed with all its might, which at that moment was not much.

"It looks bad," she said.

"I know," Don Alejo snapped back. "That's why I called you."

She asked a series of questions that to her seemed appropriate for a doctor. Has it been eating? Does it have a temperature? How much has it slept? How has it been acting? Do its eyes look sad? Don Alejo just shrugged.

"Well," Harrieta said, with the intention to leave town for anyplace far from any and all arched or snot-nosed patients, "just shoo away the flies and throw hot water on him."

She stood up feeling overwhelmed and defeated, for in her role as doctor, her beard did not get her any applause. She thought back to life under the big top with such nostalgia that it seemed lost in the past, and even more so, unattainable in the future. Looking even farther back, it almost seemed preferable to have been crucified that Good Friday.

"Everyone dies," Harrieta said, staring furiously into the old man's eyes. "Neither you nor I nor anyone can change that."

Don Alejo was not in the mood for her philosophies. He was watching the pig's breathing, which was now a weak pant. Its tongue was no longer a young, provocative muscle and was beginning to look like a listless intestine, as if the animal were expelling its insides.

"You stay here." Don Alejo grabbed Harrieta's dress. "I'm a poor old man, and all I have left is this little animal and what it can give me."

She pushed him hard and, unable to maintain his balance, Don Alejo fell to the ground.

"Leave me alone," she said, and quickly left the house. Maybe she didn't need him after all. She could travel from town to town alone. I am the bearded lady, and I've come to sing you a song.

The old man dragged himself over to the animal and wrapped his arms around it just as he became aware that death was at hand. The pig began to kick its legs in the air and opened its eyes as if it wanted to pop them out of their sockets. It whimpered a couple of times and its entire body became so tense that someone could have stood it up like a piggy bank made of clay. Finally, as a posthumous offering for its master, its tongue went limp. Don Alejo hugged its body as hard as he could, and he wondered if all old people on the waiting list witnessed death in such a resounding way.

"You left me alone!" he shouted, and Harrieta stopped to gaze at him through the window, wondering whether she should comfort him or *get out of there*.

At the same time, just a short distance away, twisted up in a spectacular contortion that was making the back of his neck beat against the ground, and his wide-open eyes spilling out disjointed pleas, Flexor also ceased to live. Only Narcissa cried for him, and her only thought was that the boy had died like a dog, for in her mind, dogs died on the ground, in the silence, and in the dark.

The sun began to rise, and in Santa María of the Circus there was great pandemonium because someone had finally realized that Timoteo's horse had stopped spouting water. Mágala had finished delivering the papers and was already thinking about the next issue, in which she would talk about the deaths, the drought, and the different calamities, one after the other, all forming part of a curse that would probably wipe out every inhabitant in the town.

Only Don Alejo was unaware of the matter. He continued to stare at the ceiling, certain that inside that house, the affectionate spirit of his pig was still floating in the air.

The *funeral procession* moved forward slowly. Hercules, Rocket, Harrieta, and Mágala carried the coffin on their shoulders. The difference in their heights and the lack of coordination in their steps detracted from the piety of the sorrowful ceremony, as Flexor's body wobbled, and from time to time, you could hear his head banging against the wood. Hercules assumed that the dead must shrink, since he had had to squeeze Flexor into the box. Don Alejo stayed at home with the pig, and Mandrake refused to take part, first because he thought it was more important to force the horse to spout water again, and second because he'd become furious when Harrieta suggested that for the coffin, they use the box made for cutting the girl in half.

"You're crazy," he said, exasperated. "I make my living with that," and he explained that Flexor was a nobody, a Negro who should be buried naked in some ditch, without a cross, without a tombstone, and without flowers.

Narcissa immediately objected. "The first death," she said with authority, "is like the first child."

While nobody understood what she meant by that, they did perceive that the argument had disarmed Mandrake. Then they directed Hercules and Harrieta to throw the body into the coffin.

"Better yet, bury him in Rocket's cannon," Mandrake protested weakly, but no one heard him. Even though the box was wide enough for Narcissa to curl up into a ball while Mandrake sawed next to the soles of her feet, the arched position of the dead man made it difficult to secure him. He was unable to lie faceup without his belly forcing the lid off, nor could he lie facedown without his heels or the nape of his neck sticking out over the edge. Moving the body repulsed both Harrieta and Hercules so much that they tried to touch him as little as possible.

"We have to straighten him out," he said.

"You do it," she urged him. "You're the strong man."

He was no longer so sure he was, and he told himself that, either way, strong men had much more respectable tasks than straightening out the remains of a dead man.

"I've made up my mind," Harrieta said. "I'm going to offer myself to the midget."

Hercules shrugged and spit on the ground. His mouth was filled with the stench of death and the dirty, torn, and equally foul-smelling yellow leotard.

"Say, that little ape's got ideas about you."

"Jealous?"

"Me? I'll squash him like a bug."

The box was not very long, since it had to allow for a person to stick his head and feet out at each end. Hercules decided that instead of straightening the body out, he would twist it a little bit more. He leaned his left hand on the back of the facedown corpse and with his right, he pushed its ankles toward its rear end, applying more and more force, until he let all his weight fall down on top of the dead man. He closed his eyes, certain that something was going to crack, and he was relieved when Flexor responded to his pushing with dignified silence, just like a metal pole, resistant and malleable at the same time. Finally he let the body go and smiled, satisfied to see that the cold flesh did not behave like a spring searching for its original shape. At one end, the knees pushed up against the wood, letting some of the unhealthy odors escape, and at the other, the neck was bent in such a way that it looked like it was about to break.

"I read the newspaper," Hercules said, turning his back to Harrieta. "I warned you not to do that."

"Mágala is a liar."

After cutting the girl in half, Mandrake would open the box at the middle, thanks to trick hinges. Two boards hid the interior of each half, and you could only see the woman's head from one side, which, in the last performances, was Narcissa's, and from the other, some delicate feet, which were usually Mágala's. Mandrake used to say that the trick would be easier if he could use a female midget in the half where the feet appeared, but all the midgets had unrefined and shapeless extremities, not at all like Narcissa's lovely legs. One day it was decided that a horrendous bowlegged woman would be put in the box, and to more easily complete the trick, on the other half he put Barbarica the Midget, a freak who at that time acted with a French clown. Even though the trick was performed perfectly, it was a failure as an act, for the tension created in the audience by the mutilation of a beautiful woman vanished with an unattractive woman. The people not only accepted the fact that the ugly woman would be cut in half, they wanted it, to the point of booing when they saw her emerge from the box intact. For Mandrake, it was a tough blow to realize that Narcissa and not he was the real star of the act. Don Ernesto berated him over his lack of intelligence: "Since the circus has existed, it has been known that daring acts work only with beautiful women; the others are freaks or sitting in the stands."

"She's not a liar," Hercules said. "Just a little while ago, Rocket was beating the fountain with the ocote pole. He says that he saw your placenta floating like a jellyfish."

"You're kidding, right?"

Hercules adjusted the hinges so the coffin would not pop open along the way. He positioned the boards so that they covered the empty spaces where the head and feet usually popped out, and closed the lid firmly to seal in the stench of death.

"I am," Hercules responded, "but Rocket wasn't."

He checked the soundness of the coffin by knocking on it several times with his knuckles. He didn't know how the box's secret mechanisms worked, and he wanted to avoid the surprise of an escape act by the dead man.

"It's time," he said solemnly. "Let's go bury him."

They walked a long while with the coffin on their shoulders. The midget led the way, waving his arms as if bestowing blessings left and right on a crowd lined up along the road. Mágala complained of a sharp pain in her shoulder and asked Narcissa, who was following the procession from a few steps behind, to relieve her.

"I'm the mother," Narcissa responded. "I should only have to carry my grief."

Mágala convinced them to lower the coffin for a moment so she could rest, change sides, and shift the coffin to her other shoulder.

"I only hope Narcissa doesn't want to look at the deceased one last time," Hercules whispered to Rocket.

"Why?" he asked.

"All dead people are laid to rest in a coffin as if it were the most comfortable bed in the world," he responded, sensing he was talking too much.

They walked around the town square, then along the ditch, and then over to the garden where Flexor had sown the seeds, which to date showed not a single sprout. They returned along the side of the church, covering the same areas where a few days ago they had looked for water. Harrieta was waiting for the right moment to chide Rocket for the stupid comment about the jelly-fish. The sun was beginning to heat up, and the breeze was so light that it was unable to eliminate the odor coming from the box. Everyone respected the silence that death imposes until, at the foot of the hill on the outskirts of town, Hercules, annoyed from having walked for so long, said.

"Does anyone know where the hell we're going?"

"We're following the midget," Rocket said.

Then they lowered the coffin and all eyes fell impatiently on Nathaniel, who, in utter ignorance, asked, "Does anyone know where the graveyard is?"

They all looked at one another as if each thought they would find the answer on the face of someone else. Harrieta searched her memory in vain for a cross, a hillock, a tombstone, or a pit. Nothing.

"There must be catacombs in your church," Rocket addressed Nathaniel.

The midget shook his head no. "I know it well, and there's nothing like that there."

"Then we're going to bury him right here," Hercules said. "I'm sick of carrying this dead little guy around."

"Don't be ridiculous," Narcissa intervened. "He can be buried only in a place that has been blessed by the bishop or where there is already another dead person."

"I'm not a bishop yet," the midget said.

"This is the only dead person we have," Harrieta said, patting the box. "Someone has to inaugurate the cemetery."

"The soul of the first one buried in any place never rests," Narcissa protested. "Everyone knows that."

"As far as I'm concerned, we can open the box and leave him here for the buzzards," Hercules said, irritated.

It was quiet for a moment, while they all considered Hercules' idea, which did not seem at all bad.

"I know where there are some dead people," Mágala said suddenly. "One hundred and twenty-three of them, to be exact."

Nathaniel felt his stomach turn, and he wished he had the power to make her shut up.

"I already told you—"

"In the mine," Mágala interrupted, smiling.

"It's true," Rocket said. "I read it in the newspaper."

"Maybe," Nathaniel said, lacking the energy to swim against the current. "But I also had a relative who was President."

"*The Circus Gazette* lies," Narcissa said contemptuously. "It said that Flexor's illness wasn't fatal."

"That's funny," Rocket said. "I read just the opposite."

The women refused to carry the dead man all the way to the mine. Rocket said Mandrake was right and that it was more important to find a way to make the horse spout water. They went back to town, put the coffin on the cart and put Hercules in charge of taking it to the mine. Nathaniel, the one responsible for the blessings and the words of farewell, climbed up on the cart so he could get a ride. To the sound of squeaking wheels, they moved off, leaving the many hands waving good-bye behind them.

"Lay flowers on him," Narcissa said, well aware that there were no flowers for kilometers around. She had almost lost sight of

Hercules and Nathaniel when she remembered Flexor's wish to have his last words immortalized. She preferred to keep them to herself, since they did not seem appropriate for engraving on a tombstone. "It was your damned slobber," she said softly, making the sign of the cross.

The horse was standing on its hind legs, and Mandrake had only to decide which one to destroy first. He climbed up onto the pedestal and began to bang a stone against the right leg just above the hoof, where it looked the thinnest. He was fantasizing that the statue was a real animal and that he heard neighing each time a stone struck it.

"Stop!" Harrieta shouted. "What are you doing?"

"I'm going force this scoundrel to give us more water."

Narcissa and Mágala sat down on a bench to witness the scene, without much interest.

"There's no more," Harrieta cried out. "You're not going to get a single drop more out of him by hitting him."

"Water doesn't just stop all of a sudden like that." Mandrake hit the statue a couple more times and watched as the mortar turned to dust. "The pipe that leads to the mouth must be blocked, and there must be a spring still full of water right here under this pedestal."

"Then start digging," Harrieta said, "and leave Timoteo alone."

Mandrake paid no attention and went on with his work until he had exposed a metal bar. He hit it several times to make sure it wasn't hollow. The pipe, then, had to be in the other leg.

"As far as I'm concerned, you can knock down the horse and everything, including the horseman," Mágala said from the bench.

"Yeah," Narcissa added. "But we should collect some water before it all gets dirty." She went over to the fountain and picked up some water in her hands. She was thirsty but she didn't feel like drinking it, for it didn't look so clean; as he stood on the pedestal, Mandrake's feet were dripping, and she recalled that Flexor had submerged his knee in that water. She remembered *The Circus Gazette* and looked for the jellyfish, and she wondered if Hercules or the midget had urinated there. She was quiet for a while, splashing water on her face as she organized her thoughts. "We have to get out of here," she said soberly. "Flexor has already died, and now we have no water. What's next?"

They looked around at each other, waiting for someone to either refute or support what Narcissa had said.

"Let's go ask Don Alejo for forgiveness," Harrieta came up with a response. "Let's go back to the circus."

"I'm going home." Narcissa signaled good-bye. "I'm in mourning."

There was a long silence. The idea of returning to the circus wasn't bad, but asking forgiveness was unacceptable. Mandrake went back to banging away listlessly. The noise of each blow soothed his thoughts. He had already grown used to the idea of not returning to a nomadic existence under the big top, and leaving town would necessarily force him to join up with Don Alejo again. Who else would take a magician with no magic? He was overcome by a feeling of fragility so intense that he climbed down from the pedestal in search of a hug. He needed the contact of another body like never before, and given that Hercules was so far away, he headed for Harrieta. He stretched out his arms and when he was close to her, he changed his course and headed straight for Mágala, who was still sitting on the bench chewing an imaginary piece of gum. She did not object, nor was she surprised by the sudden hug. In fact, she had been waiting for that moment since the very first night they had decided to stay in Santa María of the Circus. She had expected this from Mandrake, and the other men, too; it wasn't normal to isolate yourself from the world without turning to a tempting young woman. On the other hand, she was surprised and even irritated when Mandrake, instead of getting carried away while touching her, stopped suddenly and began to speak.

"In the circus, everyone is as they appear to be: the midget is a midget, the bearded lady has a beard, the trapeze artists spin in the air—"

"Yeah, yeah," Mágala interrupted him, bored.

"But I am not as I appear. I am called a magician, but I am nothing more than a trickster. What would you think of a trapeze artist who pulled the curtain to hide the stage when it came time to jump, and when he opened it again, was safe and sound on the other side? Who would dare to applaud him?"

Now a bit more interested in the conversation, Mágala responded:

"Nobody, I suppose."

"Nobody, of course. Then why do they applaud for me if they know I'm tricking them, if they are all sure that behind every magic act is the scaffolding of the lie, if I don't even disguise it, hiding behind a curtain or a screen as I do, to do my cheating in peace?"

"I guess cheating has its merit."

Mandrake rejected this with a nod.

"They applaud for me out of pity, or at least out of that same condescension that is used with children. People praise them for every stupid little thing."

"All right," Mágala said. "You're right, but you should have told all that to Harrieta. I don't understand much about complexes."

Harrieta had remained detached from the conversation until she heard her name.

"What's going on?" she asked.

"This jerk would feel better if he knew your beard was fake," Mágala said.

Mandrake lowered his head. That night he would talk to Hercules about all of this. Surely the whore would understand him, and the two of them could share a long, sincere hug. But for the time being, he had to vindicate himself and perform the trick or the magic or whatever to make the stream of water appear and earn, for the first time, applause of admiration and appreciation. He made his way back over to the pedestal and picked up a stone. He was about to resume his work when he was distracted by a squeaking noise. It was Rocket approaching with his cannon.

"Wait for me," the human cannonball said. "You'll see how easy it is with this."

The ground was uneven, and the wheels of the cannon refused to turn smoothly.

"What crazy thing are you planning to do?" Harrieta exclaimed, without expecting an answer.

"This is a job for a soldier," Rocket declared, his chest swelling with pride. "You—" He pointed to Mandrake. "You should go look after your plot of land, now that your laborer has died."

Even though Rocket used to come flying out of his cannon thanks to a spring, a small charge of gunpowder was also set off simultaneously. The ritual of lighting the match, as well as the explosions, the blaze, and the subsequent burning odor, lent the show a larger dose of realism. His act always came before the trapeze artists, as they could both take advantage of the nets that were already spread. Furthermore, Rocket had to precede the Cabriolé brothers because the show proceeded *in crescendo*, and a man shot ten meters was nothing compared to three brothers doing a thousand pirouttes in the air. At first, Rocket only stuck himself inside the cannon, detonated the charge, flew toward the net, and that was the end of it. But Don Alejo complained that he was paying him too much to entertain the audience for only ten seconds. He told him about Mademoiselle Zazel, a beautiful woman who was fired out of a wooden cannon at a height of twelve meters, "and she did not fall without risk into a net; no sir, at the highest point of her trajectory, she was grabbed by a trapeze artist." For Rocket, there was no comparison: if she was fired out of a wooden device, she could be compared to a dart or an arrow, but a cannonball? Never. Don Alejo insisted that the issue was not what to call the projectile, but that that woman was giving a lesson in guts.

Rocket agreed to redesign his act, and he brought in the Festival Orchestra to announce it. The percussionist played a drumroll which, in the circus environment, indicated that something dangerous was about to happen, and in the judicial environment, accompanied a man to the scaffold, and whichever the situation, it ended with a beat of the drum and a clash of the cymbals. In the middle of the ring and between each drumroll, Rocket would bid farewell to a few coworkers, alluding to his possible death. Then, using pulleys, he would tilt the cannon, and three cannonballs would come rolling out. Hercules would pick them up and juggle them awkwardly a couple of times. Rocket would work the pulleys again and aim the cannon at an angle of exactly sixty degrees. He would climb up some stairs and stick half his body inside. His bright, reddish-orange outfit was the flashiest in the circus.

The announcer would talk about the hundreds of men who in the history of the circus had died attempting that reckless act and which, long ago, had been one of the most important tactics in

war, for the Visigoth warriors were catapulted in order to pene-
trate walled cities. "Never were there men more valiant than
those Visigoths, and now, only in Rocket have they found their
equal." He would take a torch that had a long handle and he himself would light the fuse and make the sign of the cross before disappearing into the mouth of the weapon. The old fuse took five
to ten seconds to burn itself out; the new one would take about a
minute, prolonging the tension on some occasions and causing
impatience on others. Then the Festival Orchestra would play
the final chords of the *1812 Overture*, and to the roar of the cannon, a cloud of smoke, and the complete anticipation of the audience, the human cannonball would be shot out in the direction
of the net. Don Alejo was happier with the act because they were
now entertaining the people for close to five minutes. However,
he continued to insist that what was missing was Rocket really
putting his life in danger, and he suggested he set fire to his
clothes or place some poisoned lances beneath the trajectory of
the cannonball. Rocket did not dare do either such thing.

"Don't even think about it." Harrieta planted herself between
the cannon and the pedestal. "Timoteo de Roncesvalles is part of
our history."

"Don't be ridiculous." Rocket shoved her aside. "We have no
idea of who that son of a bitch is."

"He gave his life for honor," she argued. "We need more men
like him."

Rocket opened a keg of gunpowder and mixed the ingredients
conscientiously, for the sulfur had surely sunk to the bottom. He
asked Mandrake to turn the wheel that wound the spring exactly
ten times. He stuck himself headfirst into the mouth of the cannon to empty out the keg and to compress the gunpowder with
his hands. In addition to its visual and odiferous effect, the pow-

der activated the trigger that released the spring. Only a few grams were needed for that. This time, Rocket had poured out a devastating quantity. Very carefully, he put into the cannon the three cannonballs Hercules used for juggling. He put the fuse in place and finished lining up the cannon so that it was pointing directly at the horse's rear.

"Give a little power to the soldiers," Harrieta mumbled, "and you get stupidity like this."

"Leave them alone." Mágala was smiling excitedly. "Rocket is going to give me the lead story."

For Rocket, this was more important than just demolishing a statue. It was his chance to show that all these years he had really been shot out of a cannon, a piece of artillery, a destructive, lethal weapon, and not just a steel pipe, which ejects a man the same way it carries filth in a sewer. He struck a match and lit the fuse at once. He missed the drumrolls of the Festival Orchestra, and only when he saw the crackling of the fuse enter the opening did it occur to him that the gunpowder might burst the fragile metal walls and send splinters flying all around, killing Harrieta, Mandrake, Mágala, and even himself, and amid bloody shouting and the smell of burning, there would be the damned horse, standing tall and proud, without so much as its ass burned. In the big top, when there wasn't even the slightest risk, he would bid farewell to his colleagues with brotherly hugs. Now, with his life on the line, he didn't even have time to wave good-bye.

The explosion filled the air, and it could be heard clearly at the mine, where Hercules and Nathaniel were disposing of the box.

"What was that?" Hercules asked.

"I'm not sure," Nathaniel responded, "but I guess they'll be sending us back here in a little while with another body."

. . .

Nathaniel had started to feel uncomfortable ever since they had crossed the first hill and left Santa María of the Circus behind. He remembered the last time he had been with Hercules and Flexor. That time in the church, he had behaved in an authoritarian way, and despite having been used as a rag to scrub the floor, he had been left with a feeling of victory. Nothing Hercules said could get him his own way, and Nathaniel had made it perfectly clear that a priest rules over a whore. On the other hand, now, in the middle of the open country, he thought it convenient to adopt a friendlier attitude.

Seated on top of the cart, Nathaniel was admiring the sweat running down Hercules' back when he said, "Son, let's see when you can come by the church and confess your sins to me."

"The last time you called me 'my child.'" The strong man remembered more than the midget would have liked. "And you refused to have mercy on me."

The view of that ample back did not allow Nathaniel to see if Hercules showed any sign of resentment.

"I was an inexperienced priest then," he said, excusing himself.

The cart stopped dead and Hercules dropped the ropes.

"Look," he said, breathing unevenly, "I don't care about what happened, but if you insist on making it more important than it was, I'm going to smash your face in." And he went back to his task of pulling the funeral coach.

Nathaniel looked for a quick way to change the subject.

"I've never seen a corpse," he said.

"It looks just like someone sleeping," Hercules explained, "but with less dignity."

"Sleeping people aren't very dignified," Nathaniel commented.

"They snore, drool, fart, their hair gets tangled, their breath stinks—"

"Dead ones are worse," Hercules interrupted him. "They are stripped naked by some stranger so they can be dressed up as if they were going to their first communion. Their hands are clasped together and there is a look of calm on their faces that makes them resemble cake decorations."

"Will you let me see this one?"

"Why not?" Hercules responded. "When we get to the mine."

They passed the big top. Hercules did not bat an eye. Nathaniel looked at it with a mixture of nostalgia and greed. The big top had to cost a lot, and it didn't seem right to leave it to its fate, for the wind to put holes in it, for it to become a den for any old animal. He saw the folding sign that he himself had placed at the entrance, collapsed now, and as for the inscription, MAGNIFICENT MANTECÓN BROTHERS CIRCUS, he thought that MAGNIFICENT was an exaggeration, CIRCUS was a lie, BROTHERS just a memory, and, the way things were going, MANTECÓN would be a corpse.

"Do you know how long horses live?"

"No," Hercules responded as he huffed and puffed, "but I know you can tell their age by looking at their teeth."

"They're lucky."

"Why?"

"You could be with a woman forever if her age only showed in her teeth."

"Maybe," Hercules said. "As long as she kept her mouth shut."

And midgets? Nathaniel wondered. How is age measured in midgets? He ran his fingers over his teeth. They were crooked and covered with tartar. He looked at his deformed legs and his disproportionate feet. He touched his thin head of hair and thought that without a doubt, he was well into his downhill journey.

"Santa María of the Circus is a good place to die," he said. "Flexor can't complain."

They stopped at the foot of the hill and Hercules hoisted the coffin onto his back. He went up the slope, cursing his fate, and placed it right in the entrance to the mine.

"Is it true that a relative of yours killed so many mine workers here?"

Nathaniel went over to the box. It was small. Once his mother had told him that there is nothing sadder than a small coffin. He had always wanted to be buried in a big one, even though it would have to be filled with sawdust.

"I want to see the body," he said.

By now, Hercules didn't know which end was the feet and which was the head.

"All right," he said. "I'll wait for you over there," and he pointed toward the cart. "I don't feel like smelling that."

Nathaniel didn't dare open it with his hands. He began to kick the lid, first timidly and then more courageously. Something flew off and the coffin opened wide. He agreed with Hercules: a chicken with its head cut off had more dignity than Flexor. His position was grotesque. He pictured Hercules and Harrieta sticking him into the box as the boy, still alive, struggled furiously. He saw nothing that reminded him of a first communion.

"Are you sure he was already dead?" he yelled.

Hercules looked over at the midget without responding and came back to the entrance of the mine.

Nathaniel closed the lid with a bang and then leaned over to secure it.

"Let's put him inside," he said.

Hercules had not hesitated to explore the mine when he thought it might be full of gold, but now he didn't feel like going inside. Now he saw it as a cave that held more than a hundred corpses. This time he didn't raise the coffin onto his back but instead, just shoved it a couple of meters with his feet.

"We don't need to push it in very far," he said. "Just so it's sheltered from the rain."

And that is what they were doing, pushing the coffin hard to clear some rocks that were preventing it from sliding smoothly, when they heard the boom of the explosion and they decided to return to town at once. For Nathaniel, it came at an opportune time, for no matter how hard he racked his brain, he couldn't come up with any words to bid farewell to the dead man.

The explosion jolted Don Alejo out of his lethargy. He didn't know what he was doing there, hugging a stiff pig in a pool of blood, with no notion of time and having great difficulty remembering even the most recent things that might answer the questions: Where am I? Why am I here? What happened to this animal?

"Ernesto," he called to his brother. "Ernesto."

His memories began to fall into place. First he felt hatred for Narcissa, and then he remembered how the pig had been stabbed to death, which led him to think about himself in the big top, lying in the center of the ring in front of the cynical, gluttonous tongue of the animal, an image that aroused an excited pain in his right nipple. The other memories were instantaneous; he didn't even have to put them in order to understand fully his situation and to feel deeply sad again because of the dead pig.

He took the pig by the front legs and pulled it out of the pool of blood. It was difficult, for the already-dried blood was like glue. The animal's skin was stiff, and Don Alejo wondered how long it had been dead.

"Ernesto," he said again, resting his head against the pig's back, and he stayed there for a long time, in a state halfway between sleep and consciousness. This time he did not say his brother's name as if calling him, like the first two times, but rather as if he were invoking an ethereal being, someone powerful who would come and take him away from that miserable town.

He smiled as he recalled the years past. Yes sir, he said to himself, there was no one like the Mantecón brothers, the greatest jugglers in the world. Known as the Manty Brothers when they appeared in Barnum & Bailey's circus, they could keep twelve objects in the air at the same time. Sometimes the objects were as simple as balls or pins, and other times as dangerous as knives or lit torches.

"We promised to stay together for the rest of our lives," he began, speaking to the pig's remains as he stroked its head. "But we didn't know life was so long."

He was certain the pig was smiling in agreement.

"We trusted each other so much that sometimes we juggled bottles of acid," and he stood up and awkwardly simulated the movement. "I would throw them, he would catch them and send them back to me, and at a given time, there might be several bottles flying over our heads. A single one thrown at a different speed or height would cause tragedy. Back then, the circus was a show for those with balls. Nowadays everyone wants a net or declawed tigers or sterile knives."

He turned toward the window to make sure no one was spying on him. He was relieved to see the door was barred.

"I'm not delirious," he said. "There's nothing wrong with a man who talks to his dead other half. It was you and me, if only for just a little while. We were very different from what Ernesto and I were, more like what Narcissa and I were, but a couple in the end."

With the excitement of someone undressing his sweetheart in bed, Don Alejo took the velveteen robe off the pig. His hands were patient one moment and impatient the next, sometimes tugging at the garment, and sometimes trying to remove it delicately to make sure it didn't tear.

"Okay," he said, and for a long time, he just stared at the animal, admiring its naked body.

He leaned over and kissed the pig softly on the mouth, and not without some disgust, for there were more and more flies fluttering around the animal. He had never been sentimental, and he reprimanded himself for being so now. Where did that kiss come from? What was the point of remembering the good times with his brother? He thought it over for a minute and opted for indulging his emotions. He forced himself to think a little more about Ernesto and Narcissa, and he felt like kissing the pig again, even though it would be reciprocated with only a cold stillness. He leaned over once more, wet his lips, and just as he felt the pig's mouth, he heard knocking on the door that jolted him from his fantasy.

"We want the pig," a voice from the other side of the door demanded.

Rocket closed his eyes when the explosion was imminent. He heard the thundering noise. The recoil of the cannon struck him in the stomach and threw him backwards. He felt neither pain nor fear, and later he would wonder why, at that crucial moment in his life, he recalled having punched Mágala. A few seconds later, he opened his eyes and saw a cloud of smoke, which was dissipating little by little in the wind. The statue, with its headless horseman, was leaning slowly forward as if the horse wanted to rest on its front legs. Despite its condition, the horseman was still holding his sword high with the same grace as always. Rocket turned to his left. He breathed deeply when he saw Harrieta, Mágala, and Mandrake. They looked frightened, but were without any scratches. After a moment, the tilting of the horse was enough to break the resistance of the back legs. With a slight cracking noise, the animal with its horseman fell flat on its face into the fountain, spattering water on those whom Rocket thought would be spattered with metal shards and blood.

The cannon looked inflated, and the blast had left it pointing toward the ground. It was still smoking and emitting a clicking noise as the metal cooled down. Rocket smiled proudly.

"You louse," Harrieta said. "You just destroyed the only thing that linked us to the past. Now we are a people without history, without honor."

"History is valuable," Mágala refuted, savoring her job as journalist, "though creating it is even more valuable."

"That's nonsense," Mandrake mumbled. "The worst thing is that no water came out, not one drop."

The only thing coming out of the pedestal were the two legs of the horse up to the pasterns, the left one with a twisted pole, the right one with a broken pipe.

Together they reconstructed what had happened. Although none of them had had their eyes open, there was no doubt that one of the cannonballs had decapitated the horseman, and they surmised that the other two had attacked the rear of the animal, which was lying on the ground, without a tail and its surface covered with nicks.

"Were there three or four?" Mágala asked.

"Three," Rocket answered, still looking satisfied.

"Only one hit the back of the horse, then" she went on, pointing toward the church. "Because the other one hit the bell tower."

Scattered in the church entrance were small slabs of stone, and in the tower, up near the bell, a crack had opened up.

Rocket started to jump up and down like an excited little boy, in part for having tested the great range of his cannon, and in part because he believed that the most convincing way to demonstrate the boldness of a weapon was by using it against the clergy. He was not saddened by the fact that it had been his first and last blast. Those ballooned walls would not endure another detonation, and the spring mechanism was probably shattered to bits. It was time to retire the monstrosity with honors, just as a galleon is sunk when it has no more missions to fulfill. He hugged the cannon and caressed it, withstanding the heat of the steel without complaint.

"Yes, sir," he said, his head held high. "I was always a real human cannonball, I only just now proved it."

I could have used the poisoned lances, he reproached himself, or flown much farther than ten meters with each shot. I could have been the star and not just an extra. At the very least, I could have presented my act *after* the Cabriolés.

"I guess now you find value in artillery and in trenches," Mágala said.

He stared at her with a sincere smile.

Mandrake understood Rocket's satisfaction: I would feel the same way if I had the means to prove that I were a real magician, if all I had to do was raise a hand or snap my fingers to get water from the pedestal or a rabbit from the top hat or trees from my plot of land.

"Believe me, I envy you," he said, going over to Rocket and stretching out his hand. As he walked toward him, however, his envy turned to resentment, and he exchanged his extended hand for a fist, his congratulations for a complaint. "Look at the mess you made. I could have told you there was no water, without you having to destroy everything."

A star—Rocket was still thinking. He looked around and wondered which of them would be the star. He discarded the three in front of him, figuring their talent wouldn't even keep an old-folks' home entertained. He reached the same conclusion about the other three, and he didn't even consider Flexor. What could Don Alejo have been thinking, planning to travel around the country with this group of losers? I should have taken my cannon and set out after Don Ernesto.

"Now you have your story," Harrieta addressed Mágala.

Mágala shook her head no.

"What I have is a hungry stomach," she said, "and I'm sick of that rotten fruit."

"Rocket." Harrieta spoke with an apparent calm. "This girl wants to know if your little cannon can shoot down buzzards."

Mágala ignored the bearded lady's comment completely, and she addressed Mandrake.

"Let's go eat the diving pig."

Just imagining the animal skewered from head to tail, rotating over a burning fire, made Rocket's stomach eager.

"Let's go," Mandrake said, and the water was no longer as important as the meat.

Rocket offered to collect the firewood and start a fire while the others took care of the animal. They assumed it was dead, since they had not heard it whine since the night before, and since Harrieta said that the last time she saw the pig, it had one foot in the grave.

"In case it's still alive," Rocket added, "one kick should finish it off."

"That's what Dagoberto's daggers are for," Mágala said.

They stopped outside Don Alejo's door and Mandrake banged on it furiously.

"We want the pig," he shouted.

A few seconds passed before they heard the old man's weary voice.

"In your dreams."

Mandrake charged the door. The bar moved a little, but it was far from giving way.

"Open the door or we'll bring it down with the cannon."

Rocket overheard this, annoyed. "Unless they use my cannon as a battering ram, it will be of very little help."

"All this time you've known the old man and you still don't know how to deal with him," Harrieta said softly, and she went over to the window. "Come on, Don Alejo. We're hungry, and even if the pig survives, it won't be able to dive anymore."

"The pig is absolutely dead," the old man responded sadly. "It's already rotting."

Mandrake charged the door again.

"What are you waiting for, then? In a little while we won't even be able to eat it," and he kicked the door halfheartedly.

"Wait," Don Alejo said. "Wait just a little while."

Rocket had already gathered the firewood, which was so dry it would catch fire in an instant. He had no experience in cooking animals and was worried about how they would cook this one, since they didn't have a grill or spit or pit or stove or anything. It didn't even occur to him to cut the pig up; he was thinking about the entire body, with all its innards, and even though it didn't seem wise, his mind kept picturing a scene in which everyone was nibbling on the animal at the same time, like starving hyenas. He was picturing this when he spotted Hercules and Nathaniel coming toward town. That's it, the carriage. We'll impale the animal on the axle and hang it at the height of the wheels, and then we'll make it spin so that it cooks evenly.

Mandrake was beginning to grow impatient outside Don Alejo's house. Harrieta thought about the old man's affection for the pig and imagined a farewell filled with memories of the first dive, of the day it first wore the velveteen outfit, and of the times it refused to jump.

"Either you give us that pig at once or I'll set this house on fire," Mandrake said.

"Those are just threats," Mágala told him. "You wouldn't dare."

They too spotted Hercules and Nathaniel. Both looked dejected without the coffin.

"Now not even he can knock the door down," Harrieta said.

There was no need for force. The door opened silently and Don Alejo appeared, holding the pig on his shoulders like Atlas. His arms were trembling with the effort, and his normally flaccid face looked tense and about to explode. He threw the animal into the street. The rigid body let out a whistling noise as it deflated on impact. It didn't bounce or roll, but rather fell like a flat lump, barely kicking up the dirt.

"Eat up, you bastards," Don Alejo cried out. "He's all yours."

Rocket proceeded to light the fire, and when he saw the others standing there not knowing what to do, he mentioned his idea about the axle and the wheels. Hercules immediately began to struggle with the cart, but Harrieta stopped him dead.

"Do you want to roast a pig or burn a witch?"

Someone suggested they knock down the iron gate of one of the houses and use that for the grill, and that they open the animal from top to bottom. They would have to cut its head off, since they would cook that separately in a pit, and they would save the viscera in the kitchenware they had taken from the big top.

Hercules and Mandrake got busy pulling down the gate of the burnt-out house, taking advantage of the structure's weak-looking walls.

Detached from the starving confusion, Nathaniel slowly walked toward the town square where José María Bocanegra lay, without a trace of his former arrogance, flat on his left side, half submerged in the water like a soldier mortally wounded in a swamp. Nathaniel had never doubted the family accounts of that man whom his mother used to call "the only President without a blemish" and whom his grandfather would refer to as "the Bocanegra who gave us a homeland." The sword was now just half a sword, and even this was threatening to sink into the fountain, for the horseman's wrist looked cracked and about to break off. Nathaniel stood before the ruins of the stone on which he had planned to build his own magnificent image in Santa María of the Circus. He could hear Hercules and Mandrake laughing behind him, and he turned around to find that the burnt-out house was being abused once again, now without violence or elation, as might have occurred if the murderer of so many mine workers or one of his descendants really lived there; that, at least, gave some dignity to the sacking. But now Hercules and Mandrake were behaving like contemptible vandals, and so, Nathaniel thought, even pillaging loses its decorum. Hercules climbed on top of the iron gate and, balancing himself, began to remove the four pegs that attached it to the façade. The framework finally fell, and they picked up the gate and dragged it toward the fire. Nathaniel noticed that Hercules' expression was just as cold when he was hauling iron as when he was hauling a corpse. It was beginning to grow dark, and the fire cast its spell over everyone who was nearby.

Narcissa looked out the window to see what the racket was about. She had thought of going into seclusion for at least a couple of days. Therefore, when she heard the blast, she didn't go out to see what was going on. However, the uproar got the best of her. She was happy to see that the pig was dead and about to be roasted. Now no one would come between her and Don Alejo. She wasn't looking to settle an amorous debt but rather, a debt of pride, for she had not accepted the fact that a vile pig could have defeated her in her work, and jumping on the trampoline would not equal the score.

She was bothered by the unconcerned way in which her coworkers were preparing the food, without asking about her or coming to look for her. They're happy, she thought angrily, as if no one had died today and the horse was still spouting water and all this land was an orchard—as if life *was* really wonderful.

After a while, she noticed that Nathaniel was not with the group either. It did not seem odd to her, since midgets don't have much to laugh about, and other people's happiness only adds weight to their misery. She searched the open country from the window again and again, until she detected the silhouette of the midget on the pedestal. He was illuminated by a multicolored mix of firelight and moonlight and he stood erect like a statue, with the half sword raised and pointing toward the bell tower.

Dagoberto's daggers were not very sharp, and the saw Mandrake used for cutting the girl in half was nothing more than a prop, so the task of slitting the pig open from top to bottom was not an easy one. Harrieta turned out to be the most experienced in matters of the kitchen, and she recommended that for lack of a cutting tool, they stab the carcass several times along the belly to form something like a dotted line that could then be torn open easily.

"The idea of impaling it was better," Rocket protested.

Hercules pecked away at the flesh forcefully and viciously, not caring if the dagger was thrust in too far or if the internal organs were torn and bones broken.

"Why isn't there any blood?" he asked.

"He left it all with Don Alejo," Harrieta responded.

In order to facilitate things, Mandrake and Rocket took the pig by the feet and pulled in opposite directions until the flesh was completely torn open and the entrails were exposed. Mágala found it odd that they were mostly a whitish color and not the bright colors she had seen in an anatomy book.

They set about skinning the animal at once. Again, for lack of tools and technique, they did not do things in the most effective way, and they wound up peeling the skin off in small sections, as if it were a mandarin.

"Now we have to cut its head off," Harrieta pronounced.

The fire was dying down, and Rocket used this as an excuse to go in search of more firewood.

"It's fine just like that," Mágala said. "Let's roast it whole."

Harrieta forbid it, insisting that the head needed to be cooked over a low flame in a pit for three days.

"If we cook it all today, it will all be spoiled by next week."

"Who's thinking about next week?" Mandrake asked.

A silence that lasted for several seconds confirmed that Harrieta was right. He got on top of the rigid animal and began to stab at the neck while Hercules twisted it. First the vertebrae cracked, then the head began to turn on its axis more easily; one, two, three turns; five, ten, twelve stabs, and the two came apart.

"There," Hercules said, holding the head with the pride of a gladiator.

They threw the meat on the grill and placed the grill on the fire. The spot where Narcissa had landed the fatal stab did not look very appetizing, and everyone made a mental note not to eat that part. The aroma in the air filled Hercules with nostalgia.

"I would trade my porcelain toilet bowl for the joy of this smell."

No one said a word. They encircled the fire, spellbound, impatiently watching the meat slowly change color, and excited each time the animal turned and they heard the sizzling of fat on the fire again, which gave off a cloud of smoke with the intense aroma of paradise. Harrieta thought of the pig as a performer in the circus, not as an animal to be fattened and slaughtered. She recalled how the children would applaud it and visit it after the show in its pigpen. One advertisement for the circus showed it on the trampoline standing on two legs, wearing a cape, undershorts, and a shower cap: "THE ONLY DIVING PIG IN THE WORLD." Maybe there are others, she thought, I don't know. But it was certainly the only one in the circus without a name. Bongo, Jumbo, Maya, she went over the names of the elephants; Lionides, Lionardo, Liondegario, the kings of the jungle, never of the circus. She lost interest when it came to the names of the tigers, llamas, and dogs. Even the trained rats had names. To hell with it, she thought when she heard the sizzling of the fat again, it doesn't matter. But her mind took control and she said, "The pig had no name."

"That doesn't matter," Mandrake said, and Harrieta got mixed up between what she thought, what she said, and what she had heard.

The meat was finally done, and they ripped it off in bits and pieces and ate it. Hercules missed salt, Rocket missed salsa,

Mágala the tortillas, but nobody missed Narcissa or Nathaniel; or if they noticed they were absent, they chose to keep quiet so the meat would go farther.

"I haven't tasted anything so delicious since the tacos from The Rampant Lion," Rocket said, and Harrieta's heart fell, for it was clear that they were eating a most tasteless meat.

They ate until they were full, and then they ate some more. The pig was still a mass, with plentiful meat and fat dripping down on the lukewarm ashes, and the head and offals were still waiting for another feast. Hercules would have liked to spend the entire night next to the fire, nibbling on the meat whenever he felt room in his stomach, but once again Harrieta's prudent voice made them save the food for the following days, and she suggested that they all agree not to eat any more meat until the next night. The displeased expressions on their faces revealed their disagreement, but no one said a word, and Harrieta's suggestion prevailed.

"I have a dining room in my house," Mágala said. "We can keep everything there."

Mandrake's full stomach had given him a sense of dignity and he complained, "If you have a dining room, why did you let us stay out here eating like dogs?"

They gathered everything together and headed for Mágala's house. They cleaned the table with their clothes and placed what was left of the animal on top. Hercules began to play with the pig's head, moving the mouth like a ventriloquist's doll and uttering a series of stupid things in an unsuccessful attempt to make the others laugh. He stretched out the pig's skin to give the face an expression, and this upset Mágala, for the stretching caused the animal's eyes to open and close in a most macabre way.

"Leave it alone," she ordered.

Hercules continued to have his fun, and while he was poking around in that head, trying to find a way to introduce his hand through the neck and make the mouth's movement look more natural, he discovered that the pig had no tongue.

Go on, my children, eat your pig, have your fill. Thou shalt take of the pig the fat, and the fat tail, and the fat that covereth the inwards, and the caul above the liver, and the two kidneys, and the fat upon them, and the right thigh, for it is a pig of consecration. Take its meat and cook it on your makeshift grill and thou shalt eat those things wherewith the atonement was made. But don't forget that it is written: 'And if ought of the flesh of the consecrations, or of the bread, remain unto the morning, then thou shalt burn the remainder with fire; it shall not be eaten, because it is a holy.' What do you think, Mr. Porcayo? Or do you prefer Shortdick? I am not a nobody, like you. Now I know how to preach. From my pedestal, grasping José María Bocanegra's sword of justice, I am experiencing a sense of nobility that I never knew before. I am watching my disciples devouring that pork with the manners of pagans. Nevertheless, I, who in several days have eaten nothing but nuts and prickly pears, maintain my spirit and avoid the diabolical temptation to go down and join the feast, for my position in the hierarchy demands distance between them and me. Now I am a living monument. I have taken José María Bocanegra's place in stone, and if it were possible to be two-dimensional, I would also take the place of Fernando de Olaguíbel y Ruiz in the Academy of San Carlos in a picture that would not be attributed to the greatest baroque painter in Mexico, but to the greatest baroque painter in the world, a picture that some asshole will name *The*

Meninos. Do you remember, Mr. Porcayo, the words you used to refer to me? I have them here, imprinted on the brain: 'He should assume his role of freak, beast, mistake of nature. He is and always will be the most unfortunate of the Porcayos.' How absurd. You didn't even consider that I might not use that surname forever. Things have changed since you threw me out. Did you ever see the posters of Midge the Midget? Maybe then you wouldn't be embarrassed about what an almost-forgotten son was doing, although I admit it, that silly name embarrassed even me a bit. I don't know if by now you have already been killed by alcohol, or one of your buddies, or an exterminating angel, or if you are still alive and drinking and tailoring jackets, shirts, and pants and listening to the usual comments: it's too loose, take up the hem, let it out a little more in the shoulders, these pants are high waters, while you, sir, take advantage of the measurement ritual to feel whoever is in front of you, man, woman, or child. I suppose that, stubborn as you are, you are still taking measurements in inches, like all those of your kind, throwbacks, clinging to the past. I don't know and I don't care. Enough babbling. I only wanted to introduce myself to you as King Nathaniel the First, sovereign ruler of all big tops, master of all trained beasts, and now the Bishop of Santa María of the Circus, too. Praise be to me. Just today I was unable to bless a cemetery, and just today I buried a man without even an Our Father. But right now I have just become a bishop, and I am informing you that tomorrow I will say my first mass, with bread and wine and an altar and indults and kneeling down and *Dominus vobiscum*, despite remembering well those short verses from Leviticus that you recited to me so often: 'No man who has any defect shall approach: a blind man, or a lame man, or he who has a disfigured face, or any deformed limb; or a man who has a broken foot or broken hand, or a hunchback or a dwarf, or one who has a defect in his eye or eczema or scabs or crushed testicles. No man among the descendants of Aaron the priest who has a defect is to come near to offer the Lord's offerings by fire; since he has a defect, he shall not come near to offer the food of his god. He may eat the food of his god, both of the most holy and of the holy, only he shall not go in to the veil or come near the altar, because he has a defect, so that he will not profane my sanctuaries.' Now I am a king and a bishop, and I propose the return of royalty to rule the world, since that was the golden age of my people. We were the favorites of kings and queens, czars and czarinas, illustrious members of the court, confidantes of palace sinners, lovers of princesses and duchesses, and we were even permitted to spend our wedding nights in the royal bed. Since nature provided fewer midgets than required, the now-forgotten technique of atrophying was practiced on two-year-old children. That is, I propose that everybody is to be atrophied, and then we will all be the same. After every golden age comes a fall, and when an attempt was made to hang the last king by the guts of the last priest, it was we whom they hung. In the blink of an eye, they sent us back to the dark, Levitical age to wait, for a long while, for someone to come and free us. It won't be long now, Mr. Porcayo; the redeemer has arrived with his sword held high and fire in his eyes. Are you listening to me? Did you hear me?"

"Loud and clear," he said, answering himself.

Narcissa fixed herself up as best she could and left for Don Alejo's house. She bit her lips, which were dry and cracked, and she felt a thick pastiness in her mouth. She wandered over to the fountain and took a little bit of water, telling herself that it was clean. She looked up at the pedestal. It was empty, and the midget was nowhere in sight. She made the most of her solitude and washed her face and under her arms.

At that hour, the town exuded a somber silence. Narcissa had waited impatiently for the embers to die out completely, and you could no longer hear the voices of those who had been eating the pig. Then she waited a little longer; it would take them a while to fall asleep with so much pig swill in their stomachs. The aroma of the roasted meat was still in the air, and despite her efforts not to think, a voice inside her was telling her that if defeating a pig had little merit, it was even less meritorious when the pig was dead, roasted, and half-eaten.

She walked quickly toward Don Alejo's house, wondering if she should approach him seductively or assertively. For the first time, she was looking for him. It had always been Don Alejo's cry coming from the small tent, calling urgently for her: "Hurry up, niña, I'm not going to live forever." This night would be different; yes, Don Alejo, a test just to arouse desire, to stir up nostalgia. Never again, Don Alejo, rot, squirm, but you won't have me, your precious lady pig, anymore. She stopped in front of the window, and what she saw horrified her. In the candlelight she saw the trembling, sweaty body of Don Alejo lying on the ground, naked from the waist up, pressing some object forcefully against his chest.

"It's useless," the old man said with deep sorrow in his voice. "This piece of shit is useless."

Narcissa's first thought was that of a man sacrificing himself with a jade knife. But this image vanished at once, for the object in Don Alejo's hands had neither the color, the consistency, nor the beauty of jade.

. . .

Furious *about what* they had done to José María Bocanegra, Nathaniel was determined to drive them all crazy with his bell. It's not fair, he said to himself; any other President would deserve it, but not him. I'll make them pick up that statue right now and place it back in its spot. I'm not the bishop of this diocese for nothing. He pulled the rope with all his might, but not a sound came from the bell, and the bronze piece did not move. He looked closely and noticed that the mechanism was damaged, and that it had a crack that had not been there before.

"More vandals," he said, his spirit crushed, and he went inside the confessional to wait for something, anything, to happen. He had made up his mind to say mass, and he wasn't ready for a new snub.

When he had first taken possession of the church, it had been hard to accept such austerity and such little faith. He spent his time beating on the walls and stomping his feet on the ground in search of a hollow space, a secret passageway, a vault containing the religious treasures that even the poorest of churches have. That task kept him entertained for a while, until he became convinced that Santa María of the Circus, or whatever it had been called before, was a pretty nonbelieving or miserly or thieving town, since he didn't even find rusty nails on the walls where the portraits of saints and virgins would have hung. Now, accepting his failure, he was left with no other entertainment than to settle into his confessional and wait hopelessly for a penitent.

In spite of all this, he was comfortable in the church. He had placed two benches together, making a bed that was more satisfying than the cot in the tent. He lacked only the generous and steadfast Sunday congregation that would slowly but surely fill that adobe house with crosses, idols, oil paintings, and choirs. He imagined all of Santa María of the Circus inside the church, and the vision was not very encouraging.

"A church with seven parishioners is sadder than an empty church," he said out loud, certain someone would hear him.

But no one was within earshot of his words, and he sat for a long time before deciding to do something. It was then that he realized his mistake: he should have arranged a mass over Flexor's body. Surely then no one would have refused to attend. It could have been the starting point for making them all aware of the risks of not attending church regularly. Now the corpse was too far away, and no one would be willing to bring it back. The anger he felt with himself began to arouse new feelings of indignation over the demolished statue and the battered bell tower.

He left as quickly as his feet would carry him. His defects made his moving body appear to be coming apart at the joints. Harrieta and Narcissa were in the town square and they watched him approach.

"Look how he walks," one of them said.

"I'd like to see him dance," said the other.

They were both sitting on the edge of the fountain with their bare feet in the water, moving their toes to clean between them without the slightest concern about getting the already murky and yellowish water dirtier. Nathaniel saw the scene, and it struck him as a peaceful, happy painting, at least the closest thing to happiness he had seen since he had arrived in Santa María of the Circus, and his indignation changed to a desire for company. The previous night he had seen how cheerful his fellow citizens were as they devoured the pig, but that had seemed more like a gathering of animals surrounding their prey than happiness.

"May I sit down?" he asked.

Narcissa pursed her lips and Harrieta said, "Of course," and she patted the ground to her left.

There was still time to correct his mistake. There would be no mass with Flexor's body laid out, but he could organize a triduum to pray for the soul of the deceased. Nathaniel took his shoes off and stuck his feet in the water, too. He began to kick his legs playfully, splashing the two women, who looked at him, annoyed.

"We should play a game," he said enthusiastically.

Narcissa pursed her lips again and stood up. Harrieta asked him not to be ridiculous, and just picturing the midget kicking around in the water and wanting to play made her terribly depressed. She imagined them all holding hands and skipping around the pedestal, singing the same chorus a thousand times and moving their bodies to the same rhythm, night and day. "Timoteo, Timoteo, let's all find your head," she thought.

"Play," Narcissa said cynically. "You make me sick."

Nathaniel nodded. She's jealous, he figured. I am somewhat amusing. If not, what are people laughing at when a midget trips in the middle of the ring and gets up spitting out sawdust, or when he gets paddled loudly on the rear end, or when he gets a bucket of water thrown on him or, simply, when he enters the ring wearing those knickers with suspenders and his face painted with a stupid expression?

"Look what they did to the statue," Nathaniel said, changing the subject.

"I'm leaving," Narcissa said. "I have to continue mourning."

"All for nothing," Harrieta said, leaning over toward the water, looking for her reflection.

"José María Bocanegra has fallen," Nathaniel said, affecting a pompous voice. "The only President—"

"Timoteo de Roncesvalles has fallen," Harrieta interrupted him with a proud but pained voice. "My last rock of faith."

The midget didn't want to talk anymore. José María Bocanegra would be a memory now and not a mass of demolished stone. The memory alone was enough to give his relative the endurance of raised rock, firm on its pedestal. The bell tower would be a mute tower, since when it finally had a voice, no one appreciated it, and the burnt-out house would be just that, a burnt-out house where some stranger had lived.

"Today at seven there will be a mass to pray for Flexor's soul."

Once again, Nathaniel thought, like the night we set up the big top, I will talk and they will listen, even though this time I won't be talking about relatives who were presidents or how I wound up blind in one eye or about the mine where one hundred and twenty-three miners died.

"Is it really possible to cut off a lover's head with a machete?" Harrieta asked.

He nodded without turning to look at her. "You always doubt everything," he said.

He had already stood up when she grabbed his arm with a tug that was forceful, yet affectionate.

"Today at seven," she whispered in his ear. "Just you and me." Then she raised her voice and said, "And don't piss me off with some mass for the dead."

It's time to close the theater. The announcer holds the third curtain call, but it's useless: the seats are empty, the ticket seller is napping, and the actors are Carusos with tuberculosis. Close the doors, ladies and gentlemen, and set fire to it all. Nothing worth anything will burn. O circus memories! You are growing faint in the recurring syncopation of offbeat brass, in the mournful somnolence of gas, in the fatuous prowess of the tamer teasing glutted lions, and in the widowed swing of the trapeze. It's already twelve-fifteen in my life, the best time to generate great ideas that could never be wrong; for that, they would have to be used. Today I could hire a director to move my performers around that round, curtainless stage that smells like manure and sweat. I need arguments more convincing than a pirouette, less trite than a somersault, as resounding as an elephant. Today I am able to accept the obvious: the time has come for the circus to die. Today I don't care about anything, and tomorrow will be the same. So many years spent extolling the courage of my performers, inventing deadly risks and arranging every bold act with drumbeats that intimidate, every clown trick with silly honks, and every movement of the elephant with the sound of a tuba blown by some fat guy. So many plans, so many attempts to be different, to offer what nobody else had. But in the end, nothing mattered, not the circus or the applause or the skins or the love or the pigs or riding a merry-go-round. In fact, the elephants aren't as important as we thought they were. Maybe somewhere out there things are different, beyond those hills. I'll never know that now, because we ran aground here, for better or for worse and for always, and in Santa María of the Circus, nothing is worth a goddamn thing, starting with my seven Mandarins. I congratulate them. They're putting on a good show, very dangerous and amusing, but a pity without an audience. By the way, do you know who has the most dangerous act in the circus? The trapeze artist? Come on, don't be so naive, they use nets that are safer than a baby's cradle. Of course, once in a while someone dies, but babies suffocate in their sheets, too. The tightrope walker? You're getting warmer, but you're still pretty cold. I've seen a couple of them fall off a pile of ten chairs; one died and the other broke a leg. The lion tamer? Everyone thinks that the lion tamers are the bravest. Let me tell you something: I can't stand them. They are arrogant, and they enjoy taking their shirts off to reveal their scratches and bites, most of which they make themselves with warm knives or mounted claws. Think about it. Have you ever heard of a lion tamer being devoured by his beasts in the middle of a show? Of course not. I've heard of some circus hands who have been shredded to pieces by the beasts, but never a tamer. He knows them inside and out. He has taught them well who the master is, he stuffs them with meat before going near them, and he knows to avoid them when they're in heat. One time in a French circus, the knife thrower killed his assistant with a stab to the chest. Then it came to light that it had been deliberate, a matter of jealousy or something, but neither the girl's death nor the subsequent execution of the knife thrower can be considered as job hazards. Do you give up? I've heard of sword swallowers who bleed to death because they cough at the most inopportune time; fire-eaters who die of internal combustion; tightrope walkers whose balls are crushed, or are deflowered when they are lucky and break their necks when they are not; escape artists who drown in fish tanks because of bolts not properly locked or because of poorly made knots; young people crushed in unsuccessful human pyramids, and women who break their necks because they slip off their horses. I have also seen the fat lady die for nothing, simply because the body got tired of supporting so much lard. I don't want to take anything away from them. They are good kids and they try hard, and some of them really feel like artists, and if the risk they run is exaggerated, it's not their fault but the fault of impresarios like me, who write scripts for the announcers describing real death-defying acts. Ever since the circus has been a wandering big top, eighty-eight performers have died during their acts. Escape artists are in first place, maybe because they are the most stubborn, maybe because you never really know at what moment the trick failed and the man needed help. Sometimes they drown, sometimes the rope holding up the iron block burns too quickly, sometimes they enter into a state of claustrophobic hysteria and they split their heads open against the walls of their prison. Even so, the escape artist's act carries little risk compared to another much more heroic one—that of standing in line at the box office, men, women, and children, and looking for a spot to sit and watch the show leisurely. During the time that those eighty-eight performers died, thousands of spectators have died. I'm not exaggerating, thousands. It's not unusual for the stands to collapse. If it's just one board that breaks, thank God, for only one or two die. But if the entire structure comes tumbling down, the number of broken bones is massive. The most common and deadly, however, is the ease with which the sawdust and the straw and the canvas in the big top catch fire. The people burn, are crushed, stepped on, and asphyxiated. More than a hundred have died at once in these circumstances. I have even known of entire prides of lions and tigers that escaped in the confusion, like what happened on the so-called 'Ferocious Sunday' in Klagenfurt in 1889. They counted more than two hundred bodies, a few in the fire, but most devoured. The wild animals entered the church in the middle of mass. There were half-eaten children in the town square, and women dressed in their Sunday best howling uncontrollably. Some sought refuge in the trees, but it was just a matter of time before an animal would climb up and eat them. Many ducked into the first house that would open the door for them and stayed there for days on end because no one was willing to leave until the soldiers came and wiped out the enemy. Not even in the jungles of Africa was there anything like this. People were hunted like antelopes. They say that once an animal tastes human meat, it loses its taste for everything else. That's why, Father, we should consider the spectators. They are poor devils, yes, idiots who don't know how to appreciate the endless repetition of the circus, but they are risking more than you and me and all of us put together. They are the real heroes of the show, and furthermore, they pay. Maybe I always knew it, but in order to recognize it, I needed to lose my circus and my pig. Forget about plans, just memories. What I would give to put on one more show, just one. Then I would ask the audience to step into the center of the ring and we, scattered in the stands, would give them the most grateful round of applause, even those snotty-nosed kids that annoy me so much. Just one show, Father, that's all I'm asking for."

"*Ego te absolvo*," Nathaniel said from behind the confessional screen.

A *strong wind began* to blow. In the distance, a cloud of dust rose from the spot where the big top was. It moved, swirling along the road and passing right by Santa María of the Circus like a runaway train.

Mágala closed her eyes as the gust of wind passed. Her hair, straggly and dirty, didn't fly about like it did when she used to wash it every day and brush it every morning. She thought of her house, without panes in the windows, just like the others, allowing the dust to enter, inviting it to settle on the table and on the pig meat crying out to be eaten before it became so foul-smelling and worm-eaten as Flexor had probably become. She had a terrible headache, and she felt dizzy, inebriated. She was surprised to see the sun so high in the sky. It must be past noon, she grumbled, and I'm just getting up.

She regretted having taken the animal into her home. At first she thought she could use it to her advantage. She could eat some more, hide a little, bolt the door and make everyone beg her, "Please, give us something to eat." She thought about many things that night, and after putting off sleep several times to wolf down another mouthful, she noticed the house filling with the intense odor of pork, an odor that at first she found simply bothersome, but as the hours passed, plunged her into an intense dizziness that threatened to make her sick. First she was disgusted by the memory of Hercules playing with the head, and then it became more than a memory. Out of the corner of her eye, she looked at the table, and it appeared as if the pig's eyes were opening and closing, vividly reflecting the moon, becoming two moons. The decaying carcass was moving its mouth quickly and saying something indecipherable and plaintive in Flexor's voice. She thought it might be a reprimand for letting him die, a warning to leave Santa María of the Circus before it was too late, a revelation of the afterlife worth filling the entire newspaper. The sight horrified her and she wanted to run, but her body was like resin stuck to the cot. Several times she made up her mind to leave the house, but each time she slipped back into a state of unconsciousness.

It was mid-afternoon when she woke again. The room was filled with flies and a buzzing noise that was becoming louder and more maddening. The flies proved to be experts in entering through the window, but once inside, they became clumsy and bumped into the walls time and again, unable to find a way out. The bright light revealed the head of the pig, its eyes tightly closed, and this gave Mágala the assurance that they had never been open and, of course, that the animal had never spoken. Even so, she wanted to flee. The smell of the pig and the buzzing of the flies were very real and unbearable. She tried to get rid of them by walking around the town square, but no matter how hard she tried to focus on something else, her mind kept picturing foul-smelling, fly-infested, worm-eaten corpses, because, all things considered, she no longer saw on her table pieces of food or so many kilos of meat, and she couldn't think anymore about those butcher-shop words like loin, maw, blood sausage, sweetbreads, chopped liver, or whatever. No, lying on that table was a corpse, decapitated, yes, and pulled to pieces and ripped apart, too, but a corpse nonetheless.

She opened her eyes. The cloud of dust vanished in the distance, and the only remaining traces of it were a few particles floating in the fountain. The street, which just the day before had been a great big puddle, was now completely dry. Mágala spotted Hercules behind the town square, digging a pit in which to cook the head, and, irritated, she mumbled something that not even she understood. She stopped what she was doing and headed over to Rocket. She found him polishing his cannon and complaining about all the dust.

"Why don't *you* keep the pig?"

He smiled ironically. It was the only sign that he had heard her. He continued to wipe the rag over the metal surface, and in the spots where he noticed cracks, he applied with his finger a little grease he got from the cart. She watched him patiently, waiting for him to show some sign of having finished his work.

"The pig," Mágala said. "You can have it." Rocket had taken a few steps back to get a better look at his cannon.

"What do you think?" he asked, and answering his own question, he responded, "Worthy of the most powerful army."

She pictured the cannon being shot and bodies raining down onto the battlefield.

"It's yours," she kept on. "Eat it, do whatever you want with it."

Rocket stepped back a little more and with sad eyes, stared at the object that for so many years had earned him his living and his applause. Finally, a touch of satisfaction shone in his eyes.

"What would I want it for?"

"It's Hercules' fault," she complained. "All night long I felt like the pig was opening and closing its eyes."

"Then take it to Hercules," he responded, forcing a laugh, "and leave me alone."

Mágala was annoyed with herself for having mentioned her fear. She had opened herself up and now it would be harder for her to get rid of the animal. She thought about moving to another house, for there were plenty of others, but she quickly dismissed that. She would not allow herself to show such weakness.

"It's not because Hercules scared me," she assured Rocket. "It's because my house is full of flies and the meat is going to spoil."

It was useless. The sarcastic expression on Rocket's face was still there. Mágala picked up a handful of dirt and played with it for a while, not daring to throw it at the cannon. She turned around and with firm footsteps, headed home, determined to put up with that foul smell rather than a second more of Rocket's glare. She turned her head slightly and said, "Someone better come for that pig or I'll throw it into the street."

She went inside. The flies and the stench and her headache were even worse. Time passed, and no one came for the remains, but Mágala did not throw them out. It made her too sad to imagine the wasted meat, wallowing in the dirt, filthy and inedible. What would be the use of such a sacrifice, she wondered, and she was frightened to confront her irate comrades asking why their only food, their delicious, lovely pig, was now a fucking clod of earth. She could take another one of Rocket's punches, but the town was too small to have everyone against her. She curled up into a ball in a corner of the house and covered her mouth and nose with her hands, waiting for the hungry mob to come for their food. She tried to stay impassive to the flies, like a cow that doesn't even shake its tail. At first the odor scratched at her nostrils, but as the hours passed, she didn't even notice that it was becoming stronger and even more abhorrent.

Don Alejo went outside shirtless and in his undershorts that fell just below the knee. He glanced around and everything looked different from what he had observed on the day of the circus parade. Then I had arrived in a deserted town, he thought, and now I find myself in a ruined one. He had the velveteen robe in his right hand and the pig's tongue in his left. He spotted Hercules and went over to him.

"Here," he said, throwing the tongue in the half-dug ditch. "Bury it."

Hercules said nothing. He waited for the old man to leave and then threw the tongue as far as he could. Don Alejo went over to the fountain and dipped the robe in to remove the blood. He scrubbed it a little, ignoring the clots that floated in the water, squeezed it out and hung it to dry on one of the COURTESY OF THE BOCANEGRA FAMILY benches. Then he began to walk quickly, the way he used to when he would do five laps around the big top. He said out loud to no one, "You have to stay young."

He walked around the square three times, his legs straight, his arms swinging stiffly, and his hips swaying in a shockingly feminine way. Even though he was a thin man, he had bulges of fat on his sides that jiggled with each step. There was a marked contrast between his two nipples: the left one was pink and robust, the right was swollen and purplish. His back became pale when he began to sweat and, breathless, Don Alejo went back to the bench where he had left the velveteen robe and did a couple of squats, believing that the cracking in his joints was a clear sign of his vitality. He took a deep breath, picked up the damp robe, and headed for the church.

It was not yet nightfall, but Nathaniel had remained in the confessional, waiting for Harrieta to arrive. After a while, he fell asleep with the door open, barefoot, and his zipper open to his navel. He opened his eye and waited for his cloudy vision to sharpen. He saw Don Alejo and stood up.

"Back again, señor?"

"I've been waiting for you to come up with a name," the old man said. "Do you have one yet?"

Nathaniel's first thought was to attack Don Alejo, who looked weak and was trembling, and could surely be taken with ease: just shove him to the ground and then give him a beating. The old man was welcome to attend church as often as he wanted, but not as a boss or a circus leader, only as a parishioner or penitent. Forget names and acts and men who refused to be born. Despite Nathaniel's anger, something was preventing him from moving. He wondered if it was the commanding voice of Don Alejo or the unexpectedness of the question. Yes, that had to be it. If he brought up the matter of the name, it was probably because last night, when everyone was happily sharing the pig, they had cooked up a plan. They were probably going to return to the big top and their nomadic circus life. They didn't want to be doctors or knife-grinders or soldiers or anything else anymore.

"Traitors," Nathaniel said.

"I asked you if you had a name yet."

The midget shook his head.

"Then I'm going to call you General Tom Thumb, or if you prefer, I can respect your new investiture. Friar Tom Thumb."

Nathaniel corrected his thinking. No, it was impossible that that old man could suddenly convince them all to return to the circus.

"Look," Don Alejo said. "I brought you your cassock."

Even after being rinsed in the fountain, the robe was still scorched and stained with blood.

"No one wears a light-blue cassock," Nathaniel said.

"You do," Don Alejo declared. "If you want to keep playing priest."

Nathaniel agreed to try it on. After all, it wasn't such a bad idea to dress like a priest. The robe fit him tightly around the belly and was uncomfortably damp, but other than that, he liked it, and it seemed almost custom-made for him.

"What do you think?" the midget asked.

Don Alejo looked at him, asked him to turn around, then walked around the midget. He nodded his head in approval.

"Now stick out your tongue," he ordered.

The midget obeyed. His tongue was wide and reddish and rather short. He began to feel ridiculous and restless, and he flapped his arms to calm his nerves.

"Perfect," Don Alejo said, a baleful look in his eyes. "Just perfect."

The knocks on the door sounded like distant explosions to Mágala. She woke up dazed, with no idea of where she was, until little by little, the stench reminded her of her predicament.

"What do you want?"

It had grown dark, and her hands were still covering her face. She felt sick, as if she had been poisoned.

"Dinnertime," Mandrake said in a joyful tone that struck Mágala as irreverent.

"Come in," she said. "It's open."

No sooner had he opened the door than he was hit with the stench. He moved back and, all at once, like a hero going into a fire, he ran inside in search of Mágala, reached out to help her up, and took her out of the house, holding his breath in the process.

"It smells like someone died," he said.

"What do you think I have in there?" she snapped.

A cloud of flies took advantage of the open door and came flying out of the house like bats out of a cave. Mandrake hurried to close the door.

"They have the window," Mágala said. "I don't know why they don't use it."

Off to the side of the fountain, Rocket was engrossed in his work, placing firewood under the grill. Mandrake thought for a second about what Mágala had said: "What do you think I have in there?" Of course, he thought, thinking of the pig, but it's too soon for it to smell so bad.

"Did you bring Flexor?" he asked timidly, suspecting he was saying something foolish.

Mágala did not need to respond—her arms crossed and her mocking smile, an attempt to imitate the one Rocket had directed at her that afternoon, were enough.

Harrieta came up to them, intending to take over the kitchen duties again. She greeted them and asked for the pig.

"It's over there, inside," Mandrake said, wanting to take out his humiliation on someone. "Go get it."

Harrieta pushed the door open nonchalantly and went inside. A few seconds went by, many more than Mandrake had expected, before a shriek was heard.

"What happened here?" Harrieta cried, clearly upset, and she came running out of the house clumsily.

Mágala burst out laughing, even though the situation was not very amusing. Mandrake realized that his joke had not been nice, and he went over to Harrieta, sorry for what he had done.

"We have no food left," he said.

"Or water," she added.

Mágala, still sulking from having spent all afternoon in the midst of that stench said, "Look at Rocket gathering firewood. How stupid."

"Strange things are happening here," Harrieta pronounced. Another swarm of flies came out through the door, and Mandrake hurried to close it again. Harrieta went on: "It's not normal for it to spoil so quickly, just as it wasn't normal for Flexor to arch his back and die so suddenly."

"Now the doctor is talking," Mágala continued in a quarrelsome way. Her head didn't hurt anymore, but the memory of the pain did.

"I'm not surprised that the previous inhabitants abandoned this place," Harrieta said.

They calmed down when they saw Don Alejo staggering along, bent over, his arms in a knot. He stopped for a moment to cough; his body arched more with each bout and his legs were trembling like a puppeteer's strings. Mandrake was sure he was going to topple over, and he watched him with morbid pleasure, anticipating the sight of that shirtless man lying on the ground pleading for help, and he was disappointed knowing that Harrieta would probably go to him. The old man coughed once more, and this time, blood trickled down from his mouth.

"Go home and do those gross things," Mágala said.

Mandrake wasn't wrong.

"Come on, Don Alejo," Harrieta muttered, taking his arm. "Let me take you home."

With the little energy and dignity he had left, Don Alejo jerked himself free and stepped up his pace until he disappeared behind the door.

"That isn't normal either," Harrieta pronounced. "Look at how fast he's aging."

"We have to burn the spot where he spit up the blood," Mágala said. "Maybe Harrieta is right and this town is going to make us all sick."

She ran off, picked up a piece of burning firewood from Rocket's bonfire, and placed it right where the old man had spit.

"Maybe we should set fire to your house," Mandrake said. "Who's offering to go get the pig?"

There was a long silence. Harrieta felt impertinent, inquisitive eyes on her, as if she were the one who should decide whether to burn down the house or not. She was unwilling to accept that responsibility. How things change, she thought. When they set up the big top, nobody lifted a finger without the go ahead from Don Alejo, and then, in the town, it was Hercules who convinced us to stay here; later, it was Mandrake who got us caught up in the game of choosing jobs. Now they want me to decide if we burn the house down or if we burn down the whole town.

"Do what you want," she said. "You can count me out," and she left with her arms crossed and her mind on Don Alejo, Hercules, and Nathaniel.

"It's a pity Flexor's not here," Mandrake said. "You need a Negro for this kind of work."

Mágala shrugged, looking disappointed.

"Our fate is clear," she said, and she sat down on the ground in the middle of the street.

Rocket went over to her, his hands covered with soot and his right eyebrow curled from having gotten too close to the fire.

"The fire is ready," he said, "and I'm so hungry I could eat the entire pig."

There was such a resounding silence that Don Alejo's labored breathing could be heard clearly, as if the old man were still there, coughing in their ears.

Harrieta *took a long* time to make up her mind, so long, in fact, that the outline of daybreak became visible in the hills. Nathaniel had grown tired of waiting for her and was now sound asleep, a disappointed expression on his face. Before setting out for the church, Harrieta stopped in front of Hercules' window and looked closely. The interior was a dark, unfathomable cave.

"Are you there?" she asked softly, so only she could hear, just to make herself believe that she had tried everything.

She headed for the church, her mind made up and her eyes about to pop out from crying, pulling on her beard angrily, wishing like never before that she could pluck the hairs out and fling them at that being who gave them to her, who punished her for sins committed before she was born, a being whom she no longer knew what to call but whom she was going to confront inside that church.

"Midget," she said as soon as she pushed open the large door. "I'm here."

And as she felt her way through a darkness that her eyes slowly transformed into shadows, she pulled her clothes off, revealing, now without shame, that grotesque, grimy, hairy body with only a few traces of femininity.

"Midget," she insisted. "Where are you?"

Nathaniel peeked his head out over the benches he was using as his bed.

"Come," he said. "You are the chosen one."

Harrieta looked around her in horror. She did not see any crosses or statues or idols or any sign of anything sacred.

"There can be no sacrilege here," she said. "This is not a church," and she picked up her clothes to cover herself.

Nathaniel assured her that it was, for there was a bell tower, an altar, a confessional and, most important, a priest.

"This is holy land," he concluded.

She agreed, pointed to the altar, dropped her clothes and lay down there, ready and willing.

"Let's go," she said to the heavens. "My life for your dishonor, for mine, for whatever, for nothing; serve yourself."

Nathaniel, completely naked, climbed on top of her with great effort, and Harrieta, remembering Hercules' attributes, was grateful that not every part of the midget was small. She opened her arms, forming the only cross in that church, and as she was penetrated, she wondered if that was what she had been wanting for so long, a soreness between her legs, the sharp, pinching pain of hairs being pulled, and a monster mounted on top of her, a panting, slobbering monster the size of a chimpanzee and with the behavior of one, too. She felt no pleasure, but she did enjoy the feeling of descending into a hell, crucified on that pathetic altar the way they should have crucified her before. Fortunately, there was no way to repent now, nor was there anyone to save her. It was her moment of triumph, of corrupting a soul in a body that was already corrupt, of settling accounts with the one who had betrayed her, with the one who had given her that beard and that thick coat of hair that had ruined her from beginning to end, while he had treated Hercules and Narcissa so kindly. The feeling of revenge was immensely pleasing, a warmth running through her entire body, liberating her from all the unpleasant memories.

If they were going to pay her back for an original sin with that beard, let it be for something. I am one of your beasts, and here I am copulating with another one, and if you created me so no man would desire me, you will see that I can arouse the desire of another monster like me, worse than me, and right here in your house, because on this altar where they worshiped you, I am worshiped now. The idols came tumbling down, you have fallen, Don Alejo has fallen, Timoteo de Roncesvalles has fallen, Hercules has fallen, and now the priest of this shitty little town has tumbled down, too. You were my salvation, but when I tried to worship you, I was humiliated by a mob. Don Alejo was my salvation when he rescued me, but he rescued not the woman but the freak that he could show for a few pesos a month. Hercules was my salvation, my only handgrip, and Mandrake sacrificed him with his lewdness. Timoteo was my salvation and he collapsed in the most absurd way, like a crumb, with a single shot of Rocket's toy. Now I wanted to trick myself into thinking that Nathaniel was my salvation, and he turned into an ape between my legs, clumsy, eager, smelly, disgusting, a panting, slobbering ape. No more, she thought. Now there would be no other for her, only herself, and she forced herself to laugh because even though she felt vindicated, she was not happy. I am going to win this one and there's no way around it, make note of my victory, and do not forget that one day, someone defeated you. She felt that her blasphemy had the desired effect, that it had touched a sensitive chord of whoever was listening, because the world began to whine plaintively. Then the whining became deeper and more intense, and then Harrieta recognized it as the trumpets of the apocalypse. Yes, she thought, furious, the end. No sooner do I become defiant and raise my voice to you for the first time after so many years of lowering my head and accepting my fate as you dealt it to me, than you send me the end. Don't you know how to compete? Don't you know how to lose? The trumpets were becoming louder and their sound blended with the panting of the midget on the verge of ecstasy, and Harrieta was even more convinced that an ape was on top of her, for it wasn't possible for a human being to groan in such a bestial way, and she felt as if she were drowning in groans and trumpets from the midget and from the world. She faintly saw doors opening all at once, letting a bright, painful light come in, and she heard Hercules' voice shouting, "Here comes the circus!" with that screeching little voice the sloppy, snotty-nosed kids used to yell when the circus parade was coming. Harrieta woke up from her dreamlike state and the apocalyptic trumpets began to turn into a memory, something familiar, and it terrified her to recognize them as the Festival Orchestra, and the deformation of the sweaty, panting fetus between her legs became clearer, and, overcome with disgust, she started to kick her legs. Nathaniel clung to her like a bloodsucker with those horrible, small, womanish hands of his. He grabbed her by the hair and held on tightly, resisting until he drained himself inside her in hideous spasms. Then he looked up with a mischievous, relaxed, foolish smile, and it took only a push to knock him to the ground, just like a useless blob, and in Harrieta's eyes, that's exactly what he was, a useless blob. She stared at him, sickened, and if he looked so unpleasant to her dressed, he was even more repulsive naked. The man who refused to be born, Harrieta thought, kicking him again while he was still on the ground, watching him contract like a mollusk. Harrieta gave him one more kick and didn't hear a moan or anything. She loathed that body with its flat buttocks and bloated belly and short legs and disgusting head and small hands like a fat lady's, and she wanted to run to Hercules to curse him for driving her to do that, but Hercules was no longer anywhere in sight, and she crouched down on the ground, defeated, forlorn, scratching her crotch, listening to the Festival Orchestra trumpeting that sounded like the whistle of a speeding locomotive coming closer and closer, more and more omnipresent, deafening and ravishing.

W*ith the fascination* of someone seeing a circus for the first time, Narcissa and Mágala lined up on the side of the road to watch the procession and to wave to the performers and the animals. First came the elephant, the most revered animal in the circus, with its usual awkward movements and its trunk swinging, master and lord of the circus despite ranking among the stupidest of beasts. Dodging the excrement that Jumbo was dropping without restraint, the Festival Orchestra followed, playing the *March of Zacatecas*. Then came the cage of tigers, the Mi Alegría sisters, Ping and Pong, the llamas of Machu Picchu, and the dancing dog, walking on two legs and pitching its head nervously in an attempt to pull off Merlin the magician's hat.

"We're saved," Mágala said.

Narcissa shook her head and smiled at Bengalo the tiger tamer.

"Don't be so sure," she responded. "That depends on how much we are willing to humiliate ourselves."

Mágala looked down at the ground. "As much as we have to, or more."

They were distracted by a tall, corpulent man who was young and good-looking, wearing a white tunic that came to the middle of his thighs, sandals with straps, and leather wristbands. He had long hair and a three-day-old beard.

"Did you see that?" Mágala asked.

Narcissa, mesmerized by that man and thinking that she also was prepared to humiliate herself as much as she had to, did not respond. The remaining performers paraded by: Little Miss Bell,

Balancín and Balanzón, Timmy the Temarious, and Teary, Tufty, and Stretch, but Narcissa did not return their greetings.

On the other side of the street, Rocket and Mandrake were watching the parade with great nostalgia.

"We'd be idiots not to make the most of this and clear out of here," Mandrake said.

"I thought we wanted to live here," Rocket said. "To have a house, a family, to be like ordinary, common folk."

"Don't be ridiculous," Mandrake muttered as he adjusted his top hat and his black cape.

Rocket agreed and bit his lip, wanting to hurt himself. He was thinking about his useless cannon and he cursed the moment he decided to fire it.

"My cannon is useless," he said in a sudden spurt of confidence, and at once, after sizing up Mandrake's sinister expression, he clenched his fists and added, *"I'm going to kill you."*

"We're in the same boat," Mandrake explained, in an attempt to empathize. "I lost the box I used for cutting the girl in half."

Rocket was startled to see that Mágala, on the opposite end of the street, was smiling mischievously at him. It's impossible, he thought, she couldn't have heard.

The Cabriolé brothers went by, wearing their skintight, red-sequined leotards and holding hands. Then came Papillon the escape artist, tied up in chains and dressed in a straitjacket, followed by Computencio, carrying a folding sign like a sarape that said:

THE AMAZING MANTECÓN
BROTHERS CIRCUS
Box seats $2.00
Stands 50¢
All children must have a ticket.

[233]

Finally came the circus hands, and the carts pulled by mules. Don Ernesto was riding in the last cart, giving orders to the people and smacking the mules with the whip from time to time just to make it known who was boss. The mules would open their eyes wide and move forward, burdened by the weight of the big top. Amidst all the disturbance, only the shouts of the announcer could compete with the noise of the trumpets.

"Ladies and gentlemen, boys and girls, the joy of the Mantecón Brothers Circus has arrived, yes it has!"

Don Alejo had remained at his window, waiting and watching, not sure if he wanted to join in, but when he saw the big top, he took off running after the cart, still coughing and spitting up blood. He caught up to it, climbed on top and lay down on the neatly folded big top, saying that it was just as pretty as the day it had arrived from Italy, and he hugged it as if it were a giant muffin with red, white, and blue stripes, the Magnani Fabrics label right on top.

"What are you doing here?" Don Ernesto asked, annoyed.

Don Alejo did not respond. It took him a while to catch his breath, and the pain in his ribs had grown stronger. He coughed weakly, and he felt the warmth of the blood that gushed out like drool.

"Damned midget," he muttered.

The previous afternoon, he had relished the sight of Nathaniel dressed in the velveteen robe with his tongue sticking out. He was pleased to see that not only was he short, but the poor midget was so ugly that his facial features resembled an animal's, a pig's. Don Alejo lay down on the floor of the church next to the confessional and pointed to his right nipple.

"Enjoy me," he said.

The midget did not react as Don Alejo would have liked, but

he did not disobey, for he did enjoy giving the old man a kick in the ribs, and then he jumped as high as he could and landed on Don Alejo's stomach.

"Make no mistake," the midget said. "This is the church, not Hercules' brothel."

Don Alejo went home, and a few hours went by before he could move again. It hurt to breathe, it hurt to live, the dryness of his bruised nipple hurt, and the loneliness at night in the darkness without pigs or tongues or midgets or Narcissas hurt. Now, clinging to his big top, those four things were still hurting him, and he was tormented even more knowing that as soon as he caught his breath, he would have to ask his brother for forgiveness and beg him to take him back.

Don Ernesto signaled for the procession to stop, and the animals hurried to the fountain to quench their thirst.

"What's this?" he asked gruffly.

The Festival Orchestra was quiet, as was the announcer. Narcissa, ready to begin the humiliation process, went over to him with a friendly smile.

"Welcome to Santa María of the Circus."

"Don't be so cynical," Don Ernesto said. "No one can be welcome in a shithole like this."

Narcissa looked around. The dancing dog snuck between a llama's legs to drink water and then wagged its tail, forgetting for the moment about Merlin's hat.

"The animals look happy," she said.

Don Ernesto's attention was now elsewhere. "What happened to you?" he asked, surprised. "You don't look like a woman two brothers would fight over."

Narcissa was embarrassed and tried to arrange her hair as best she could. She looked at her dirty red dress and her thighs without stars, and she realized that any attempt to fix herself up would be useless.

"I'm exactly the same," she explained. "Even prettier, if only I could dust myself off and take a bath," and she pushed her breasts forward and took a step back, realizing that after so many days without washing, her mouth might stink like a sewer.

"All right," Don Ernesto said. "Go with the Mi Alegría sisters. They'll give you something." As soon as he saw her leave, overjoyed, he spoke to the mass of humanity behind him. "You're pathetic, Don Alejo. I leave you for a few days and instead of circus performers, I find a bunch of beggars."

Mágala, Rocket, and Mandrake went over to him, all with the same tattered appearance and pestering behavior as Narcissa. Mágala was the first to approach him, and she greeted him sweetly, with submissive eyes and a discrete wiggle of her backside.

"Hi, Don Ernesto," she said, moving closer and closer to the old man's face. "I'm at your service."

The Mantecón brother inspected her from head to toe, and Mágala facilitated his work by turning around. He saw promise. She needed more color, another layer of polish, to give her a fuller, softer, less bony appearance. It was a matter of time.

"And what do you know how to do?"

Mágala shrugged. Rocket wanted to respond for her, to say that she knew how to give kisses like a chameleon and that was it, and that was useless in the circus.

"Can you now tell the difference between a trapeze and a swing?" Don Ernesto asked, wanting to help her.

"No," Mágala replied, "but at least I have more balls than those three sissies," and she pointed toward the Cabriolé brothers.

"Okay," he said, satisfied. "You're hired."

Rocket waited his turn and then, fearful, asked, "Do you need a human cannonball?"

Mágala burst out laughing, and Rocket headed straight for her. He grabbed her arm and pulled her close so he could whisper some threatening words to her without Don Ernesto hearing.

"One word about my cannon," he said, "and you're dead."

Mágala could tell from his burning eyes that he wasn't exaggerating. This time he wasn't talking about a punch, like before, a punch that in the end she was grateful for, not because of the pain in her jaw, but because it made her assume a submissive role. Right now she was enjoying the pressure on her arm. All right, she thought, I'll give him the chance to return to the circus. She brought her index finger to her lips, making a pact to be quiet, and Rocket went back over to Don Ernesto.

"Do you need a human cannonball?" he repeated.

"Yes," Don Ernesto responded, "but I need a brave guy, someone who will set fire to his clothes and fly over poisoned lances."

"I'll be happy to do that," Rocket said, and he reluctantly endured the brief welcome speech that his once-again boss was giving, which included the possibilities of flying through the air for at least fifty meters without nets and being shot toward the trapeze.

"Either you grab hold of the trapeze," Don Ernesto concluded, "or I can't guarantee your life."

"Okay," Rocket said, thinking that either he grabbed hold of the circus or he himself couldn't guarantee his life. "I'll be Monsieur Zazel," and he left, his head hanging.

Mandrake was uncomfortable being the last in line. He wondered if Don Ernesto might be losing his patience and his ability to take pity on a group of ragged circus performers.

"I am Mandrake the Magnificent Magician," he said.

"Yeah, yeah, I know who you are."

"I want to go with you."

"I hired a magician in Zacatecas," Don Ernesto said, "but I fired him after the first show. All he knew were card tricks, and those were no good unless you were sitting at the same table with him. From the stands, a king of hearts looks just like a two of clubs." Mandrake agreed excitedly and the old man went on: "I need a magician who can do the usual tricks, like pulling rabbits out of a top hat or hundreds of scarves from his pocket, and most important, one who can cut a girl in half."

Mandrake was mortified when he heard those last words. He thought about running off to where Hercules and Nathaniel had buried Flexor.

"I'll be right back," he said.

He was just about to leave when Don Ernesto ordered him to stop.

"Look, you idiot," and he pointed to the cart that held his box.

Mandrake looked at it with a mixture of embarrassment and joy, and a doubt plagued his conscience.

"Is it empty?" he asked.

Don Ernesto grimaced.

"It's a pity," he said. "I needed a contortionist."

Mandrake went over to his box and caressed it, not daring to open it or to ask any further questions about its contents.

Don Ernesto gave the order to start moving. He looked from side to side, and the sight of that town in ruins sent chills through his body.

"I came here intending to put on a few shows," he said. "On my map, it says very clearly that this place is called Sierra Vieja, and it's marked with a star. Only important places have stars."

"That's what I thought," Don Alejo said, his voice faltering.

"Now it's called Santa María of the Circus, and we were the only ones who lived here."

"Don't speak of it in the past. I still haven't decided whether or not to take you with me."

Don Alejo struggled to sit like a lotus flower on the big top, and he fought back the urge to insult his brother.

"I found this big top abandoned and I took it," Don Ernesto said, "just like you took this little village."

"Please," Don Alejo insisted, his voice more distressed now. "The people here don't respect me anymore. Even the midget hits me."

Don Ernesto burst out laughing, pleased at his brother's lack of arrogance. "All right," he said, and after a while, he added, "It's incredible how much you've changed in just a few days."

As they passed before the church, he ordered them to stop again. Sitting in the entrance, looking totally helpless, were Harrieta, Hercules, and Nathaniel.

"That jerk is wearing the velveteen robe," Don Ernesto said, pointing at the midget. "Don't tell me—" and he stopped. By the look on Don Alejo's face, the fate of the diving pig was clear. "Thank heavens I didn't give you the elephant," he concluded.

The three went over to greet him. They took it for granted that they would just climb on top of any cart and rejoin the circus.

"Wait for me," Hercules said. "I'll be right back."

Don Ernesto stared at Nathaniel and Harrieta. He didn't like to show so much compassion. Maybe he had already filled his quota with his brother and the other four. Taking them all back would show a weakness of character, and would open the door so that, as with his brother, even the midget wouldn't respect him.

"Get out of here," he said shaking his arm. "This is a circus, not a freak show."

Harrieta and the midget looked at each other, not knowing what to say. It was she who came up with the first argument.

"We have a fantastic act," she said with imploring eyes. "The Man Who Refused to be Born," and as Don Ernesto didn't even turn to look at her, she stepped in front of the cart and lifted up her dress a bit. "Look," she explained. "Nathaniel will stick himself in here, facedown—"

"Shut up," the old man said, horrified by her hairy legs. "I'm not interested in your flesh."

With a signal from Don Ernesto, the wheels on the cart began to turn. Nathaniel saved his best for Don Alejo. He stood in front of him and shot out his tongue spasmodically as he smoothed down the velveteen.

"You jerk," Don Alejo said, and he pointed to some mules that, out of pure exhaustion, were swaying their tongues like clappers.

Nathaniel bent down to pick up a rock and threw it without aiming. The projectile rolled along the ground just a few meters away.

"Worthless midget," Don Alejo said. "Worthless Tom Thumb."

"Wait for me!" Hercules cried out as he ran after them, his porcelain toilet bowl in his arms.

Once again Don Ernesto ordered them to stop.

"What kind of act can you do with a toilet?" he asked, bemused.

The base was broken and had sharp, jagged edges that made it impossible for the toilet to stand upright on its own. Hercules stuck his hand inside his tights to put away his photographs.

"The same thing any other person does," he responded, bothered.

Don Ernesto shook his head in disappointment. He was quiet

for a moment, and then he noticed Little Miss Bell at the end of the procession singing, "I Am a Dove on the Wing."

"A good answer and you would have come with us. For a moment, I was intrigued by the idea of presenting an evacuation act. Did you ever hear of *Le Pétomane*? It was like he had a mouth on his bottom. He played the bugle—"

"Don't you need a strong man?" Hercules interrupted him. "You know it's not just my show of strength and juggling of cannonballs that I have to offer. There are also the females that I draw to the box office."

"Of course I need a strong man," Don Ernesto said, and forming a horn with his hands, he shouted, "Samson, come here."

The man wearing the white tunic approached them. Hercules was astonished that such powerful arms and solid legs could exist in a body without fat, without a big belly or flesh full of rolls, and with a firm, taut chest that looked nothing like a woman's breasts. Sandow, he howled to himself, Sandow.

"I used to be like you," Hercules said, aware that he had never, not in the least bit, been like him.

"If you want," Don Ernesto said, "you can have a competition, and I'll take the winner."

Hercules shook his head. It was useless. He felt like the most miserable man alive when he realized the absurdity of the scene: defeated, and hugging the toilet bowl like an old woman hugging her grandchild. To assuage his ruin, he told himself that Don Ernesto's rejection didn't matter; he was sad now because he wouldn't be able to fit back together the pieces of his toilet bowl, because he would revert to being an animal doing its business in the open country.

Nathaniel was also amazed by Samson and concluded that

there was no justice on earth. Harrieta looked from Samson to the midget, and felt disgusted.

"If you don't want to take me as a strong man," Hercules said, his voice cracking, "take me as a whore."

Don Ernesto laughed at what he thought was a joke, but the amusement did not change his mind.

"See you soon," he said, although he was thinking never, and he gave the signal to move on.

Don Alejo sat up and whispered to his brother, "We're going to throw them all overboard, right?"

The procession moved forward in silence. Only the squeaking of the wheels and the muffled steps of the animals could be heard.

Once the circus had disappeared beyond a hill, the three left behind heard the trumpets of the Festival Orchestra playing the *March of Zacatecas* again. Nathaniel thought that a march was too festive for a farewell, and he thought of a tango instead.

"Slow, sad, clumsy, as if grudgingly, the carts of the caravan move off . . ."

And Hercules, out of tune, added, "There is nothing sadder than the sadness the circus leaves behind when it's gone."

Harrieta was immersed in her emotions, which changed from anger to distress like the tick-tock of a pendulum. She clenched her fists, looked upward and, breathless, said, "I thought I could beat you at least once."

She began to run very slowly, following the same route the Amazing Mantecón Brothers Circus had taken.

"At least now she knows the history of my ancestors," Nathaniel said.

Hercules and Nathaniel watched her with some pity, knowing that the circus was too far ahead, but they didn't try to catch up to her or dissuade her. They just crossed their arms.

"The whore and the priest," Hercules said. "Nice town."

With no idea of what to do or what to say, Nathaniel hugged him, and he realized at once that their difference in height added something perverse to that display of brotherhood. Hercules pointed to the clock on the church. He saw the orphaned hand and the face stained with rust.

"It's the same time it was when we arrived," he said. "The same time it'll always be."

He dropped his toilet bowl and heard it break. He didn't care anymore.

Nathaniel felt compassion for that immense mass of flesh, so powerful, yet so helpless. He took the hand of the strong man, the whore, the walrus.

"Come with me."

Hercules was indifferent and let himself be led. They walked toward the church, the church without a bell, without crosses, without faith, without hope, without anything, and they climbed the stairs to the entrance. Before they went inside, they turned around. Santa María of the Circus looked like a scene from a lost war. Timoteo de Roncesvalles or José María Bocanegra, half-submerged in water that was dirty with animal slobber and pig blood, was a symbol of the devastation; as was the burnt-out house with the 1, 2, 3, destroyed then and destroyed now; the flies swarming around Mágala's house and taking it over; a useless barbecue pit, a tongue flung wherever, a grill with ashes that didn't cook anything anymore; the porcelain toilet bowl, broken and useless, lying on its side, like forbidden, rotten, half-eaten fruit. A fine dust moved down the road, pushed by the wind, covering up little by little the tracks of the circus, of the life that disappeared down that road headed for who knew where with the solemnity of a funeral procession.

The midget squeezed Hercules' hand because he felt him letting go, and he pulled him toward the entrance of the church, a black mouth regurgitating the desolation of the empty pews, of the confessional without sins, and of an altar as a sacrificial table.

"Where are you taking me?" Hercules asked, fearful of the present and even more so of the future.

But in the end, he let himself be taken by that small fat lady's hand that was leading him inside.

"Come on, little whore," the midget said as he closed the large door, as that great big hungry mouth shut, swallowing them forever in its tomblike darkness. "Come on, little whore," he repeated. "Let's go to hell."